D1109676

# SPEAKEASY

# SPEAKEASY

## ALISA SMITH

Thomas Dunne Books
St. Martin's Press
New York

JESSAMINE COUNTY PUBLIC LIBRARY
600 South Main Street
Nicholasville, KY 40356

This is a work of fiction. All of the characters, organizations, and events portrayed in this novel are either products of the author's imagination or are used fictitiously.

THOMAS DUNNE BOOKS.
An imprint of St. Martin's Press.

SPEAKEASY. Copyright © 2017 by Alisa Smith. All rights reserved. Printed in the United States of America. For information, address St. Martin's Press, 175 Fifth Avenue, New York, N.Y. 10010.

www.thomasdunnebooks.com
www.stmartins.com

Designed by Mary White

The Library of Congress Cataloging-in-Publication Data is available upon request.

ISBN 978-1-250-07955-8 (hardcover)
ISBN 978-1-4668-9220-0 (ebook)

Our books may be purchased in bulk for promotional, educational, or business use. Please contact your local bookseller or the Macmillan Corporate and Premium Sales Department at 1-800-221-7945, extension 5442, or by email at MacmillanSpecialMarkets@macmillan.com.

First published in Canada by Douglas & McIntyre

First U.S. Edition: April 2018

10  9  8  7  6  5  4  3  2  1

*But cruel are the times, when we are traitors*
*And do not know ourselves.*

—William Shakespeare, *Macbeth*

# SPEAKEASY

## CHAPTER ONE

# THE MINISTRY OF WAR

EVEN AFTER SIX months, I still had to locate the bunker by first spotting the nearby radio tower. Otherwise you couldn't see it until you were nearly on top of it: the back walls were built into a cliff facing the sea so that it was almost flush with the horizon. The bunker reminded me of a Greek amphitheatre, white concentric circles nestled in a grassy depression, but instead of opening to the sun each level was enclosed, secretive and seeking no audience but the participants themselves. The contentious November wind snarled my hair as I stood at the edge, and then all was calm in the hollow where I descended the stairs to the lowest door. Once inside there were rooms and rooms further below, which was where the codebreakers worked.

The metal door clanged shut behind me. The air inside was always dank no matter the weather outside. If I arrived with a wet umbrella, it would not have dried by the end of my shift. As I walked down the hall, I shivered and buttoned up my regulation Navy jacket. It was terribly drab, but at least the Captain overlooked the unauthorized tailoring I did on the skirt to make it shorter. Captain Bromley-Sinclair was not exactly regulation himself—he wore a paisley smoking jacket while on duty. Eccentrics flourished in the Examination Unit. Though Germany was at war with Britain, here on the Pacific coast we tracked the Japanese, who were allies of Hitler but not our sworn foes. It sometimes felt like our unit existed in a strange limbo. Thousands of miles from the front lines, we were mostly forgotten about by the federal government and High Command; but it suited me to stay unobserved.

Pulling my oak chair forward on its squeaky wheels—every morning I remembered they needed oiling and immediately forgot to do it as I got absorbed in my work—I opened the blue folder to read the day's Magic Summary. "Magic" was the American term, which the Captain had adopted, for the communiqués the Japanese ambassadors sent back to Tokyo. The Yankees had a lovely gift for naming that appealed to the Captain's poetic nature and he refused to call it JN-25, as the diplomatic code was technically known. It was highly valued for the briefings on German strategy.

I spread my papers out in front of me, and at first they all looked the same: a random mix of roman letters divided always into five characters with a space between each set, so no word lengths were revealed. I was searching for any repetitions. Even the simple word "and," *oyobi*, could be an entry into the messages. Each day the Japanese changed the starting point for the keys on their Purple machine. They believed their code was unbreakable because of its millions of enciphering possibilities. However, in their very effort to expand the number of possibilities, they had divided the keys into two sets—one of twenty and one of six—and this was a serious weakness. We always looked for the greater frequency of letters relating to the "sixes." The other flaw, even more basic, was hubris. The Japanese believed that their language and its phonetic symbols were so challenging to the Western mind that we would never grasp a code based on it. We had seen them mention this in their cables, which amused us as we decrypted them. Repetition is the codebreakers' manna, and the Japanese language—because it expressed the formality of their culture—was rife with it. Every diplomatic message began with the same tribute to the Emperor:

"I have the honour to report to Your Excellency . . ." People never could see their own weaknesses.

Flipping through my stack of papers, I searched for any group that might share the right pattern of vowels and consonants—they often cut their messages so that the preamble was in the middle instead. It took me a few hours, but I finally got what I needed. A good cipher was my greatest pleasure. I liked it best when there was an enemy message that nobody else could figure out, and I was the one to crack it.

"Hey Marguerite, do you know who has the JN-25 master?" I said as I walked over to her desk by the "window," which she had painted in watercolours on a large sheet of Arches paper that she'd taped to the wall.

"The new guy," she said, stabbing her pencil in the air at him. I looked to the opposite side of the room, where he was sprawled with his long legs propped on his metal desk. "I saw him adding words already."

"Maybe I'll get it later." I was annoyed that he was making progress with the code so soon.

"You don't want to meet Lieutenant Hughes? I think he's rather handsome."

Hughes had wavy brown hair pushed back from his forehead, much longer than military length. His features were regular, nothing terribly distinctive, the eyes blue, the nose perhaps a bit too broad, the lips admittedly well shaped, like those of Michelangelo's *David* statue, which I'd seen in texts when I took an art history class in university, and it made me wish to go to Italy. When I caught his eye yesterday I felt a kind of life force that I didn't discover in people often. In my experience, that meant he was best avoided.

"I wonder why they bothered to bring in someone else right now," Marguerite said. "It's been awfully slow."

I lowered my voice. "Have you been getting the Russian cables too?"

"It's frustrating. Why are we wasting our time on Allied messages? But ours is not to wonder why . . . "

"Stop right there. I don't like the rest of that expression."

"You want to grab lunch?"

"Sure."

I waited while Marguerite cleared her desk. She was my best friend in the unit, and we were both the same age, twenty-nine years old. Thirty, I corrected myself unhappily. It had been my birthday last month. Most of the other girls were just that, girls, of eighteen or twenty, and they worked as filing clerks. She put on her homburg—being French, she could pull off the ridiculous hat we had to wear with our uniforms—and I linked my arm through hers. We followed the labyrinthine hall past the cubbyholes stuffed with undecoded messages, past the tippety-tap of the room where the *kana* Morse operators grabbed Japanese telegraphs from the air for us to decipher, and past the huge file room where most of the women toiled, endlessly opening and closing cabinet drawers at the codebreakers' requests.

We reached the top of the stairs and buzzed the door, which an unseen person opened with a mechanism from afar. Fresh air surged against our faces and the light glared so we were blinded. We staggered into each other and giggled. "We're like moles, living underground," Marguerite said.

"It's not even really sunny out." My eyes soon adjusted to the grey film across the sky, the sun a feeble light bulb behind it. The wind blew cold off the Pacific, but at least it wasn't raining. November was the monsoon month, though by the time the storms reached us they were leached of any tropical warmth by their Arctic detour. There was a British luxury cruiser, the ss *Argonne Star*, in dry dock right now, welders scampering over her to transform her for war. The base had been busy the last few months with such jobs. We knew the Japanese were massing troops in French Indochina with the support of Vichy France. Not that the specific place names in the cables meant anything to me, whether Hainan Island, Lang Son or Dong Tac, but I feared they would soon.

The mess hall was a decrepit building, once a brick factory, but it had the virtue of large windows. We always sat near the windows, as did everyone from the bunker except for a reclusive fellow named Olson, who preferred a dim corner. We rarely mixed with the other units because it was easier that way—we were not allowed to speak of our work to anyone else, not even military personnel. Most of them didn't know there were codebreakers on the base at all; they just had a hazy sense that the bunker and its metal tower were for transmissions to the Allied Fleet. Marguerite and I stood in line to get a coffee and sat down at a table already claimed by some of our unit.

"You seen the headline in the *Colonist*?" Petty Officer Montague asked. She lived in the women's dorm and was much below me in clearance, so we'd never had cause to mix, though she often tried to be friendly. I suspected she hoped to get ahead through me, since she had neither the prettiness nor the wiles to succeed with men.

"I don't get the paper at home," I said. Unlike the other single women, I lived in my own house in town, and I had an aversion to receiving any deliveries, letters or subscriptions in my name. Even by the standards of the Examination Unit, I knew I was considered unusually private.

Montague pulled the day's paper toward her across the varnished mess table and began to read, her finger smearing along the headline.

## BORN TO HANG
## BILL BAGLEY'S REIGN OF CRIME OVER AT LAST

*Daring holdups, cunning jailbreaks, blood-thirsty murders in Canada and USA united police efforts to nab unrepentant crook*

*To be executed at New Westminster Prison
Made his infamous name with $100,000 bank robbery in Nanaimo*

"I'm from Nanaimo, and it's the biggest thing that ever happened there," Montague said, looking up from the paper. I stared into my coffee and blew on it. I took a gulp too soon, unwise, and scalded my tongue. I suppressed a gasp of pain.

I was surprised by how angry I felt. Angry at myself for burning my tongue, and at Montague for reading the gloating news aloud. Most of all, I was angry at Bill. I reminded myself that actresses were capable of laughing, crying or shouting, equally convincing each time, every single day on demand if need be. The absence of emotion, which I needed to call up now, should be easiest of all.

The paper had printed an old mug shot. With his dark hair slicked to one side, Bill was as handsome as I remembered. The only man I ever loved. I'd gotten used to seeing his name in the newspapers from time to time: a robbery, a chase, an arrest, a trial. At first I had been devastated on his behalf, as well as petrified, never knowing what Bill might say if he needed to save his own skin, or even out of sheer orneriness. Instead, I would soon read that he had escaped again. His latest escapade had begun with a jailbreak in Oregon three years ago; he laid low, crossed the border, robbed a bank and shot a police officer, was caught again and put on trial in New Westminster. It had seemed like his usual pattern, until now.

The death penalty.

"He got the whole payroll for the Dunsmuir mine," Montague rambled on. "Imagine! The biggest coal mine in the British Empire. What would you do with a fortune like that?"

"If it was not the war, perhaps buy a yacht and sail around the world," said Marguerite. "I would have men to wait on me, that much I know. I'm so tired of men expecting me to do little things for them. As if I have not important work to do!"

"I only asked you where the pencils were."

I hadn't noticed the new fellow come in and sit with us.

"No, you asked me to get them," Marguerite said. "I hadn't myself needed any."

I forced myself to smile at Marguerite, trying to be part of their petty conversation.

I did not believe the courts should have the right to take a life. What was the moral authority of an act equally atrocious as that being punished? In fact, what was the evidence of the system's superiority in any way? The reason Bill was caught was not because the law was so much more clever than he.

Bill Bagley was being punished because he had failed at something for which he once possessed genius.

## CHAPTER TWO

# DECEMBER 1931

THE FIRST TIME I saw Bill Bagley he was holding a wild-eyed infant that looked like it had seen horrors since the day it was born. He was on the landing of the Dowding Building in Seattle, where my accounting office was located. I had just come up the marble stairs and was straightening my tie, which was unsettled every morning by the wind that rushed up the hill from the sea. He seemed very out of place somehow in this business environment, though he wore an expensive-looking suit.

"This un ain't mine and don't tell me again that it is," he said, thrusting the baby back to a lady with burning red cheeks. She gave him a sharp look before bursting into tears and running down the stairs. I watched with concern, as the stairs were slippery and she wore high heels, but she made it safely out the revolving door with the infant.

Once she was gone, the man, Bill Bagley, and I were left staring at each other awkwardly, or at least awkwardly on my part.

"That woman is a whore and a liar," he growled to me.

I was taken aback at such words from a stranger's mouth and felt I should defend womanhood in general from such slurs—if not the woman herself, whose character I could not attest to—even though I rarely concerned myself with the private business of strangers beyond the numbers in the ledgers they brought me. Of course, these always revealed more than people knew.

"Sir? That is a harsh thing to say."

"I'll say it again and a thousand times. You blind? Didn't you see her painted bitch face?"

I was an accounting clerk from a line of genteel numbers men; I can safely say that such coarse words had never echoed through that quiet hall, nor hardly my innocent brain. I did not know what to answer this fellow. Meanwhile he stared at me, so wild-eyed and horror-stricken I could not help thinking he was lying about the baby, the resemblance was so acute. I felt sorry for him and wondered what he'd been through. Yet at the same time he had a defiant look that drew me. I imagined my own gaze to be glassy and uninteresting, reflecting shallow experience in life.

"Her cheek did have an artificial hue," I surprised myself by saying.

A grin like Clark Gable's flared on his face and then he asked me if I knew where the office of Byron Godfrey was. Strangely pleased to be known to him, I said I was that man and to follow me.

Once inside I sat at my desk and looked at him expectantly.

"I need an accountant. The IRS wants to audit me. Can you believe it? Merry fucking Christmas."

I told him that as an accounting clerk, unfortunately I heard of such a thing all the time. I had prepared many people for audits and said that I'd gladly look at his books, but I cautioned him I didn't have the full designation. He said he didn't give a damn about designations but the merit of a man only. This warmed me to him. He pulled a ragged-edged folio out of his briefcase and thumped it onto my desk. Twenty minutes poring over it gave me a funny feeling, and not just for having him there staring at me from across the room with his feet propped up on my coffee table. There were hardly any receipts, just a notebook with unlikely expenses scrawled in a shaky hand, and his address was constantly changing. Last year he was in Oakland, California. Now that he'd moved to Seattle, the district he had chosen was not known for respectable business. I finally looked up at him and, with a line of sweat uncomfortable on my forehead, said that his books had holes like Swiss cheese and he was bound to have trouble with the IRS.

"Whyn't you look through those holes and find something solid on the other side? I'll pay you good money for it."

I knew instantly he meant for me to fabricate. This was completely outside anything I'd ever done. But I felt oddly drawn to him; plus, I said to myself, one must eat. I was two months behind on my rent and I did not believe the landlady would give me credit any longer. Only one other man had walked through my office door with custom these last few months, and it ended in his bankruptcy, so I wouldn't be seeing him again. I said I would see what I could do.

To my surprise, I found the exercise quite interesting. Suddenly there was imagination in the numbers profession. I advised him to lease a warehouse stocked with inexpensive goods so he'd have something to show the auditors, and I made detailed ledgers of sales dating back a few years. Those mom-and-pop retailers would be out of business now, but he could find people to affirm their past existence. The profits were slim, but it was the Depression, was it not? Most boldly of all, in retrospect, I suggested he should pay a little tax to placate the government. The work was addictive because I'd only ever thought of myself as the most mediocre person—but this I excelled at.

Three months later he returned to my office while I was dusting my agave plant, carefully wiping each leaf. I'd had no more business since he'd paid me promptly on the completion of my work for him, and I had assumed I would never see him again. Grinning, he put a bottle of Canadian Club whiskey on my desk—illegal, I thought, wondering how he had got it—and a hundred-dollar bill. He said he passed his audit with flying colours and that he could use a good numbers man in his organization. Could he hire me on permanently? I said yes.

That was how I began my career as a bank robber.

"I DO BELIEVE I found myself a chicken to be plucked," Bill said expansively, waving his hand with the cigar still in it so the smoke trailed like the flourishes of a stunt aeroplane. We were sitting at his reserved table at the So Different speakeasy. I'd never been to a speakeasy before I joined his gang, but I had become a regular with Bill. I liked being an insider, and I liked the coat-check girl. She had a pretty smile and a knockout figure. She looked me boldly in the eye a couple of times and it got my hopes up for her, though I never knew how to catch a girl. Not like Bill. I feared he would catch her first, but he was the boss so that was his right.

"Let's go to Canada. They have hardly been robbed before, at least not by the likes of us. You in, By God?" That's what he called me now. I was pleased, for who wouldn't care to be godlike? My real name I'd always thought puny and mewling, but Bill had transformed me.

The first few months with him I was uncomfortable when he said the word "robbery," for I told myself I was operating within the law. I set up companies for Bill and it was his business where he got the money from to fill them up. But quickly I got drawn into helping him plan his jobs, and again, I was good at it. Still it felt like an intellectual exercise only, because I never had any part in the carrying out. That was for rough men like Moe and Sho-nuff and Ramon My One-Armed Friend. For everyone else Bill shortened their names, but he introduced Ramon with this additional description appended to him, perhaps to make up for the very lack of his arm below the elbow. But Ramon never seemed to notice it was missing since it was his left and he carried his gun in his right. Once I even saw him beat a man senseless with his wooden arm. Ramon maintained a vicious smile the whole time and I was afraid to intervene.

"Sure. I've never been to Canada," I said. I had in fact never left Seattle. Its geography of strangling peninsulas and awkward lakes restricted travel. Perhaps that was why my father left my mother and me here when he moved to New York when I was a boy. My mother had been a nervous and unhappy woman since that time, though she had pretended otherwise. Even as a boy I could detect her unease. She would wake in the middle of the night and scrub the house from top to bottom. A state of messiness became my comfort because it meant that she had slept through the night.

Bill proposed that we make our ways separately to Bellingham and meet at the marina on Tuesday where a large powerboat, the *El Toro*, waited for us. I had hoped he would find new thugs in Canada to replace Ramon and the others, but when I tried to hint about it Bill gave me a look that chilled my blood and said good men did not grow on trees and the gang would never separate until we were dead. Anyhow, there would be no one in Canada so well qualified, he said, grinning now; they were just a bunch of infants. This was why we would bowl them over.

As we zipped across Puget Sound in the *El Toro*, the cold ocean wind raising gooseflesh on my arms, Bill detailed our prize. There were some large coal mines on Vancouver Island and we would target their payroll at the bank before it was distributed. We would spend a month or so scoping them out. Bill asked me to set up a business account to get a look at the bank's vault and discover the man who knew the combination. I must have looked nervous because he thumped my back and said I was the only man in the gang who could look and talk like an executive. I was glad to be of such use to him, I said, hoping to recover his faith in me.

He gestured to Moe to take the wheel and he poured us whiskey in tumblers. A new man appeared on deck from below and I was startled but didn't say anything because Bill handed him a glass too, as though he was one of us.

"I do believe there will be a hundred grand in clean bills. They'll be ours, boys, sure as I'm Bill Bagley."

Bill downed his drink, his faced flushed and grinning, and his excitement was reflected in the faces of the others as they toasted him. I don't know that it was so much the amount of money that swayed me, but rather the boldness of the scheme. Bill did nothing in half measures, and this inspired people. I joined the toast and silently vowed I would go into this one up to the neck.

On a map splayed under a glass tabletop, Bill pointed to the islands as we passed them and said the names with tender benediction. He took special pleasure, I believe, in Deception Pass. We wove through the San Juans, avoiding the larger town of Friday Harbor, and slipped past the mouth of Blind Bay until we reached a short strait of open water. Soon we were enclosed within a crazy patchwork of small landfalls like God had grown angry with islands and crushed them in his hands before scattering the fragments to the winds. Yet Bill seemed to know them all.

"Gooch Island. We're in Canada now, boys." Bill had started out in rumrunning some years before and he'd lived everywhere from British Columbia down to California. He was a real bootstrapper who made himself who he was, and I admired his gumption.

"Gooch," I echoed. "Strange word. What's that mean?"

"It means 'Why the fuck we talk so crazy?' in Indian," Bill said, and the others laughed.

"Rhymes with 'hooch,'" said the new man. "Maybe you've still got some stored there, hey Bill? The stuff I let you bring into Puget Sound so nice and easy."

"Nah. Drunk or sold long ago. I have a steel-trap memory for that shit."

I was curious about what the new man meant, so before we got to shore I pieced together his story. He had been a crooked police officer in Seattle, helping Bill with his rumrunning in exchange for regular payoffs. He had recently switched 100 percent to this side, after being fired under a cloud of suspicions to do with our Bon Marché job. I supposed he had got a bunch of the loot then, and I was annoyed that I hadn't known it before since I had redistributed the money into various accounts, which made me feel proprietary over it. Cruickshank must have used his share to buy this boat. I had to admit it was something pretty with its trim lines and gleaming wood with chrome everywhere. He had installed a wireless apparatus surely as good as anything the FBI had. My brain worked to discover its possible uses for us in the future, now that I was supposed to be actively involved in Bill's schemes.

We landed at Yellow Point, a thickly forested peninsula some distance south of Nanaimo, and we concealed the boat in a shed there. The marina seemed deserted, with old fishing boats bobbing unattended, and the only sound was squawking seagulls. Our contact was waiting for us in a delivery truck and we piled into the back. As I smelled the onion breaths and workmen's sweat in the confined space, for a moment I doubted that this lot had the brains to bamboozle a foreign nation. But Bill always seemed to know what I was thinking and his next words reassured me.

"Can you believe this town ain't *never* been robbed in its history?"

"So we can bust her cherry like a sweet virgin," said Moe, drawing out the word "sweet." Moe was always sucking up to Bill.

I pressed my palm against the metal sidewall to steady myself as we rattled over a large pothole. I was glad it was dim inside the truck so no one would see my embarrassment. Though I was twenty-five I had yet to be with a woman. But I felt this job could forge me, and I'd emerge tough and swaggering and every last thing I feared would have burned away.

I WAS DISAPPOINTED when Bill decided we should first do some practice jobs across the strait in the larger city of Vancouver, where there were more banks and we could hide ourselves in the crowds until we got the feel of the people and customs here. However, I soon saw the wisdom of it. Canadians spoke in different accents, much more British I supposed, and probably we stood out to them. I took pains to mimic their speech. Maybe I shouldn't have bothered because none of the others tried to blend in; all but Bill were too thick, and Bill, he didn't care about anyone else or what they thought and he talked so one-of-a-kind crazy anyway you'd never pin down where he was from. He'd never told me and I couldn't guess.

The streets of Vancouver were only paved on the major arteries, even downtown, and there were fewer imposing stone buildings than in Seattle. Still, the place had a feeling of self-importance, as though it believed it would do great things one day. Of course the people failed to realize that America was so far ahead of them. But their optimism was bracing and I felt the possibility of launching adventures here. The city was prettier than Seattle, set on a peninsula round as a christening spoon as it dipped into a basin of water, and the mountains were in an orderly line in the background. The West End rooming house Bill had us holed up in was a letdown, though, being cramped and dark. He said we'd have a big old party soon to make up for it. "With luxuries," he said. The word had always sounded upper-class until Bill got hold of it, and he added a leer suggesting forbidden pleasures. The men grinned. Bill always knew how to raise morale.

They'd robbed a couple small banks on the edge of the city and now were ready for something bigger. For the first time I was going along so that Bill could test me in action. I hoped I was ready. The Bank of Montreal at Granville and Hastings, in the heart of downtown, was a pale grey granite and so newly chiselled I sensed the stone's longing for its ancient resting place. It was fashioned to simulate a Greek temple, and while Bill was no appreciator of historical style, he knew it advertised riches. "Banks are like women: they tart themselves up as much as they can afford," he told us when we drove around the block last week. Each marble column suggested another ten thousand dollars inside, he said. This one had four.

I heard the boys breathing heavy behind me in the sedan, a maroon Pierce-Arrow Bill had bought from a pal the day before; it was stolen, of course, but the plates were switched. The boys would never admit to fears but I told myself they weren't so calm inside, and my own nerves were natural. I pulled gently to the curb so as not to splash any bystanders with mud and draw their ireful attention. It had rained fiercely over the last week, though today the clouds were split to show blue underneath. Bill whistled under his breath, more relaxed than at any time since we arrived in the city. He always had the opposite feelings to everyone else: he was anxious when nothing at all was happening, and carefree in these moments of pressure.

The boys spilled out of the car, and my eyes were drawn to the bulges of sawed-off shotguns and pistols under their dark overcoats. I prayed that no one else was looking, or they wouldn't even make it through the doors. But it was eleven o'clock and the streets were quiet in the lull between businessmen coming and going from the office blocks. At least I was free of that tedium now. I drove round the block once as Bill told me to do. That would take six minutes in the muddy conditions, including putting down the top when I was around the corner; Bill had timed it. Then I waited in front of the bank with the engine idling, though idling was not the word for it—I was tense as a racecar driver on the starting line. I revved the gas when a man in a trenchcoat opened the brass doors of the bank, but I laid off the pedal when I realized it was not anyone from the gang. "Stupid," I said aloud, shaking my head. "Bill said two minutes more." I knew from the boys' excited banter after each job that Bill would appear exactly when he said. Cruickshank had said that Bill must have worked for the railroad once, he was that perfect. I watched the second hand, and the time grated like a saw blade sticking in wood. Two minutes later, I released the clutch. As the gang ran out of the bank I had a surreal feeling of wonder that I belonged with these masked thugs. Then I noticed something else, even more strange—there was a girl with Bill. That was the only way to describe it: you knew despite the chaos that Bill was the one she was with. He grabbed her hand and helped her onto the running board and then she pulled herself gracefully and naturally as a hurdles racer over the door and into the back seat with Bill. The rest of the boys piled in and I pulled away from the curb. It was so distracting to see her every time I checked the rearview mirror to discover if anyone was giving chase. No one was, but I kept looking.

She was the most beautiful girl I had ever seen. Her eyes were grey like the deep coastal skies on a day when rain threatens but refuses to fall, and her skin was pale and luminous. All the men were silent in the car at the peculiarity of her presence but she finally broke the spell by laughing a fresh, innocent laugh, so that I marvelled what on earth she was doing with us.

She had been a teller in the bank we'd just robbed. Bill found another room for her, and the men stayed up late with the awkwardness of wanting to confront Bill about getting rid of her but not having the nerve to do it. We sat around playing poker, with only one bare light bulb illuminating our cards. It was five-card stud, and I started to sweat as we reached the second round of betting. I only had a five of clubs and a seven of diamonds in my face cards, and no royalty in my hand.

"See you, and raise by five," Moe said, throwing in a chip.

"I'm out," I said, shoving my cards away from me. Ramon smirked. He had a jack and a king showing.

The rest of them stayed in until the final hand, and while Ramon had the best cards visible he kept glancing anxiously at Bill, who looked content as he clicked his chips together. That was the only sound in the room, until Ramon My One-Armed Friend exploded.

"What the hell is with the *chica*?" he said as he threw down his cards, losing the hand to Bill's royal flush.

"She's part of the gang now. You got a problem with that?" Bill's grin was more murderous than friendly and I was glad it wasn't directed at me. As always, I failed to match the others' mood. I wanted the girl to stay. In fact, I wished that I wanted it rather less.

## CHAPTER THREE

# MISTAKEN IDENTITY

I STARED OUT the window of the trolley as it left the Navy base and the metal wheels shrieked on the rails so that I shuddered. I felt a peculiar melancholy passing decrepit Victorian gingerbread manors, let go to ruin now that their day was done. The neighbourhood had fine aspirations once, but the Depression followed by a war knocked the inhabitants low. Dark clouds hung over the Sooke Hills to the northwest, threatening rain, but I hoped they would contain this threat as they usually did, leaving one to carry an umbrella about, eternally useless.

It had taken me a long time to find what suited me best, but I discovered early that I liked possessing unusual skills. The celebrated linguist Dr. Phipps had recommended me for the Examination Unit when I was his doctoral student. He had long hoped to do fieldwork with me in the Soviet Union to discover, he believed, the ancient origins of the Tlinkit language of Alaska in a Russian tribe, but he had been stymied as Stalin tightened his borders during the 1930s. That was disappointing because it prevented me being part of a breakthrough that could earn even a woman a professorship. I had learned Russian in anticipation of going, and then it seemed wasted. But the war proved it was not so. I can hope that no experience in life is ever truly wasted, since I have made so many mistakes.

I have always needed a mentor I could admire. First there was Dr. Phipps. He was a small, birdlike man with an unfortunate taste for large suits, like a professorial Charlie Chaplin, but his mind was as unusual as his appearance and that was the important part. The thoughts he hatched were different from everybody else's and he published leading papers. Captain Bromley-Sinclair, with his gift for ciphers and willingness to advance female recruits, had turned out to be a worthy successor. The interview for the Examination Unit—though of course I was kept ignorant of the meeting's purpose until later—was held in a grey block of an office building fronting narrowly onto a side street. Dr. Phipps had made me memorize the directions rather than write them down. The two men inside the spare room were the sort my eye would have passed over at a party at the Lieutenant Governor's mansion as not worthy of attention, a species of minor bureaucrat. One was in a brown suit, the other grey. The men asked whether I was good with crossword puzzles and chess, and probed my proficiency in math and music. I found these non sequiturs unsettling. I answered honestly that I had not played much chess but had a passion for crosswords that I had inherited from my father. I had played the viola as a girl, advancing to the provincial championships, and I had a high school math scholarship, but I had not pursued these inclinations since. Of course they asked me about my language skills, but they already knew about those from Dr. Phipps. French, Russian and Tlinkit, though I smiled and said I knew the latter had only limited application with the indigenes of Alaska. However, my abilities went beyond merely speaking—I knew how to untangle the structure of language so as to infer the meanings of words lost to the modern day, or to trace its bones to ancient lineages elsewhere in the world. In fact, the keys to ways of thought could be found in language, and this was something that could never be hidden. They stared at me unblinkingly and I told myself to be quiet.

Did I like reading romances, and was love and family a woman's most important aim, they asked. This is a strange job interview, I thought, and decided that they weren't expecting the usual answers. Such daydreaming was not for me, I said. All my family was dead now and I had no one I loved and I liked to be solitary.

Did I believe the good of the many outweighed the good of the few, they asked. Of course, I said. I was not so sure about that last, but I felt it was what they wanted to hear, and that rationalization had served me well in the past. I considered myself one of the many.

I got the job and a uniform with a braid across my sleeve. I was an officer with the Wrens, the women's Navy. I believed myself safe from my past—I had almost completed a PhD, which stamped me as a harmless academic. At the time, Bill had long been quietly ensconced in an American jail, and I had stopped expecting that every knock on my door could be the police. The sentries scarcely glanced at my ID as I came and went from the base. As long as you were good at your job, the higher-ups seemed not to pay attention to who you were—I had learned that a number of our clerks were carded Communists.

After crossing the blue bridge over the Inner Harbour, I changed trolleys downtown to get to my house in Rockland, only a few blocks from the Lieutenant Governor's mansion. My house was handsome, in the Tudor style, and inside it was rich with mahogany and rosewood. Though old, this neighbourhood had not yet gone to seed due to its proximity to government power. This was the same reason for my attraction to Constantine Middlebury, who was older, nearing fifty, and not handsome. He was generous with those who did not deserve it, as I have found many rich people to be. I myself was not in want of money but took great pleasure in extracting the unreasonable gift of a house from him. Since I wanted to remain off the public record, the title deed of the house wasn't in my name, but was assigned to a fictitious niece. Constantine never even asked to meet her, which was exactly as I'd expected. He had a surprising lack of curiosity for a Minister of War, but before the hostilities broke out his portfolio was agriculture. I'd met him when he came to inspect the Examination Unit, and he had studied us as if we were cattle at auction. His eye lingered on me longer than the others.

As time passed I was amused to detect he was kept much in the dark about the Examination Unit. He was, after all, only a provincial functionary. There were secret levers of power that he had nothing to do with—and I was closer to them than he was.

I unlocked the iron latticework gate around my yard, took the pale granite stairs two by two, and stopped at the mailbox, which was made of brass that I kept well polished. I checked it reflexively though there was rarely anything inside—perhaps a power or water bill, addressed simply to "Tenant." I was punctual in my payments, which I made at the bank in cash. I liked to leave no trace on the world, like a drop of rain that evaporates in the sunshine after a storm. Today there was a single brown envelope with nothing written on the front. I unsealed it to see a shaky handwriting.

You got connections now. Get me a pardon.

It was not signed but it didn't need to be. I gripped the brass handrail and made my other hand steady as I unlocked the door and went inside, not bothering to remove my shoes. I went into the parlour and lighted a fire, into which I tossed the note the moment there was a spark. The paper flared to nothing, but of course its threat was not really gone. Bill could ruin me.

There was little time for brooding. I was expecting Constantine in one hour, after he'd dined at the Union Club. His wife never expected him home early on those nights. I went upstairs to my bedroom and rifled through my closet, looking for a clinging dress. I had no clear plan yet, but it never hurt to look seductive, because it gets things done. I held a blue flowered dress to my face in front of the mirror, but threw it on the floor. Why did I have to be thirty now? It made me feel it was more difficult to be beautiful than it used to be. Bill had me when I was at my best, but he had squandered it. He had filled me with every extremity of elation and sorrow, pride and fear, love and hate, for almost two years, and left me empty afterwards. But sometimes that emptiness made life easier. I could do what I needed to do now.

When Constantine came through the door—he never rang or knocked, feeling proprietary—I took his camelhair coat from his shoulders, running my hand along his arm and smiling up at him. "Amor, I'm so glad to see you." It was Constantine's fancy to be called after Amor de Cosmos, a famous politician of vigour and originality from the province's history. Why he fancied this I didn't know, except he might have wished for a little more of both qualities. I could be objective about his character because I was no silly girl wasting away for love; we each used the other for our own purposes.

I pulled his armchair closer to the fire and urged him to rest himself. I placed the stool at just the correct distance to warm his feet. "Did you get everything done at the Union Club?"

"That is a business that never ends," he said.

"I know it's wearing." I smiled and leaned over, offering a glimpse of my cleavage. I wondered if that was how ladies of the night acted if they wished to get paid handsomely, and hated myself. But I continued, mixing his favourite aperitif, a Campari and soda, and worked round to my subject.

"But you're so good with your constituents. You helped that widow who wrote to you last month, when her son was killed in France. You got her a pension."

"The Premier was most agreeable in that case." He steepled his fingers in front of him.

"He listens to you. He respects your judgement." I sat on his lap and caressed his cheek. He grinned and gave me an inelegant squeeze. "I know of another case where you could be equally influential."

I hadn't had time to carefully consider my fabrication, but I plowed on. I explained that a dear friend of my father's was wrongly accused, and in prison for crimes he did not commit. It was a terrible case of mistaken identity. Yet he was under the death penalty, a miscarriage of justice that Amor de Cosmos would never have stood for in his day. I found as I told my story I was no longer comfortable on Constantine's lap, and busied myself with stirring up the logs on the fire with a poker.

"That's dreadful. What's the chap's name?"

"Bill Bagley."

"Bill Bagley!" Constantine slammed his glass onto the side table and the liquid sloshed over the sides.

"But this man is not the real Bill Bagley."

"Can you bring me the real Bill Bagley?"

I pulled a linen napkin from a drawer in the mahogany sideboard and patted dry his hand. "Of course not."

"I'm sorry, my love, but that name is notorious. I can't be seen to be letting free a man with a record like that. The press would eat me alive."

In that moment I felt frantic, not just for myself, but for Bill too. I grew very angry and, I am ashamed to say, hysterical. "Do you want to be party to a murder?" I screamed. "Have you no spine?" Somewhere in the midst of my rant, I threw his glass against the wall and it smashed to bits.

He stood from his chair and stared at me coldly. "I don't keep a mistress to be treated worse than at home."

He left the living room and slammed the front door, leaving me shocked. I should be the one to walk away, not that old milquetoast. I sat in front of the fireplace and cried.

Why, after all these years, was my fate still bound with Bill's? There was a time when I would have done anything for him but he had not deserved my devotion. I left because he was becoming erratic, taking drugs on the sly. I didn't wish to get dragged down and my instincts were correct. The next job they pulled was a disaster and they were caught soon afterwards. When we first met, you could have set a clock by that man. Each job was timed to the second, and the gang never left with less than five thousand dollars.

But Bill was still dangerous—the more he lost, the more joy he took in destruction.

## CHAPTER FOUR

# MARCH 1932

IT WAS IN motion. We had worked out everything for the Nanaimo job now, and Bill and I were staying under assumed names at the Metropolitan Hotel in Victoria, seventy miles south of our objective. We were travelling indirectly so we could not be traced. I was Mr. Roger Tremble. I repeated this to myself often so I wouldn't make a mistake. Yesterday I had tried out a big Durant Six from an auto livery on View Street, and it proved fast and powerful. If I wanted, I could buy a car like this after the job. I thought Bill would like the massive bumper on it because it could ram anything that got in his way. In retrospect, it was best that we stuck to rentals.

"Why's it called the Six when it fits eight people?" I had asked.

"It's not the passengers, it's the cylinders," the mechanic said, making me feel like an idiot. Bill would never have made such a gaffe.

Perhaps the mechanic felt sorry for me after that since he had given me the keys on the spot. He said they didn't open as early as I wanted to arrive the next morning, but no one would be renting it between then and now. He didn't charge me for the extra day. I felt bad about that kindness because we intended to abandon the car outside Nanaimo with the windows removed in case of a shootout with the police. I prayed it would not come to that.

As I walked to pick up the Durant from the lot, the wind shook the cherry blossoms from the trees, the petals already becoming a brown pulp on the sidewalk. Amazing how beautiful things could be ruined so quickly. A light rain began to fall so I opened my umbrella, tilting it down over my face. There was no one on the street since it was only 6:45 a.m., and this suited me. The fewer people who saw me, the better. But there was a crow that gave me the evil eye and unnervingly followed me block after block, cawing an alarm.

A thousand thoughts shuffled through my mind. Most of all, I hoped Lena would not get shot. It upset me that she would be the driver on this job, my former role, but she'd insisted. I had been promoted to go into the bank with Bill, because I was his top lieutenant now. But that did not give me the power to override any of his decisions, including the one about Lena, which I thought was reckless. Wasn't he worried about his girl? When she asked to drive the automobile all Bill did was laugh and rub his hands together. "What a wild one," he said. Then he handed her a twenty to buy a conspicuous hat.

"You're too pretty, everybody notices you. Got to hide your face. Not like these mugs." He jerked his thumb at us.

I was one of the mugs, not noticed. Lena only looked at Bill and glowed.

I was worried about our new strategy, which was not to wear masks anymore. Back at the rooming house, cigar smoke clogging the air, Bill had said that people only marked the most superficial parts of a stranger's appearance. We would change our overcoats and caps for other clothes after we escaped the scene. Bill would wear spectacles during the job and he said that was all people would remember, so when he removed them he'd be a new man. I couldn't help thinking of the Westerns I'd read as a boy where every outlaw used a kerchief for at least partial concealment. To show our faces seemed a needless risk.

"Nobody'll know none of us," Bill had insisted. "These thugs here, they just look like dark-haired foreigners. Italians or Greeks or whatever. All the same to the nice people. All we got to do is change our duds, and presto, we disappear."

"What about me?" Sho-nuff said.

"You're better off than the rest of us. You think they could ever pick you out in a lineup?"

Sho-nuff laughed. "First they got to find ten black men to stand together. Goddamn, I miss Chicago."

The gang was going to pretend to take me hostage. I was already a known "customer" at the Royal Bank but they needed me there to identify the manager in case the tellers refused to do so. I was nervous about this because it required acting on my part. Also, Ramon My One-Armed Friend would be the one to take me hostage. I didn't know why Bill chose him to do it, since Ramon hated me. I wasn't sure he would hold himself back.

I got into the Durant and the engine started with a purr. I drove up Douglas Street, where I picked up Bill a ways past the hotel where he was walking beside the road. He grinned and said the cop shop was just around the corner, so it was a good thing I came along before one of the officers did.

"I'm a wanted man," he said.

"In Victoria?" I said, despite myself, as he settled into his seat.

"No, no. California. Escaped from San Quentin, I tell you that?" He flashed his Clark Gable grin.

I shook my head and admired him all the more. He could do any impossible thing. Still, I was relieved when we left the police station and then the town behind, its northern boundary marked by the eight storeys of the Hudson's Bay department store, this small city's best try at a skyscraper. It did not take long to recede since the Durant went faster than any automobile I'd ever been in, and then the last clapboard homes and shacks disappeared also. We stopped briefly so Bill could put on chains before we drove up the Malahat highway, because we'd heard the mud was terrible through the mountains. The road was technically closed for repairs after the winter rains, but we had discovered that the crew was not working because there was some delay in equipment arriving from the mainland. That meant there would be no witnesses until we were well shot of Victoria.

The road was hazardous, not even hemmed in by guardrails as we switchbacked up Malahat Ridge. We were surrounded by a gloomy forest that suggested the lurking of wolves. Despite the chains, the tires skidded out on the corners, veering toward edges that dropped steeply into oblivion. My nerves were shot as we reached what I hoped was the summit and I pulled over. Bill asked me what the fuck I was doing and I felt my face twitch but I said as breezily as I could that I wanted to admire the view. Mount Baker in Washington was visible in the distance, a glittering white cone of ice.

"We're on top of the world, ain't we, By God?" Bill said, turning jovial as suddenly as he'd been enraged. He put his arm around my shoulder and gave me a friendly shake. "When we're back in Washington we'll live like kings."

With that encouragement I carried on, trying not to slide in the mud as we pointed downward to the bottom of the highway. We were going to pick up the rest of the gang at Yellow Point. We'd already made sure the whole area was nice and quiet; there were only a couple of dairy farms directly off the Island Highway and then it was just forests empty of everything except our scheme. This country was too solitary, like the people were just borrowing their corner of existence from the wilderness and had to fight not to be swallowed up by it. I thought of Lena again, since she was a product of this landscape; maybe that explained both her remoteness and strong spirit.

As we turned off the Island Highway I made myself focus on the job at hand. Bill had found two men, each driving identical Durant Sixes, to act as decoys and confuse the police after the robbery. Meanwhile we'd slip away on the *El Toro*, where it waited for us in perfect privacy at the harbour of an abandoned coal mine. I was pleased I'd thought of that part of the plan. Bill had slapped me on the back—while Ramon shot me a black look—and told me I was a smart man. However, the overarching scope of the plan was all Bill's. It was amazing, really, how his mind worked like the intricate cogs of a factory machine. There were fifteen men involved; cars, trucks and boats; an international border crossing; and various hideouts. We'd bought guns as well as stranger things like carpet tacks and panes of glass we had smashed in steel buckets. These last were to throw on the road if the cops tailed us. Thinking of that part made me queasy, but I reminded myself that Bill was experienced and he didn't seem worried at all.

Bill took the wheel of the Durant just outside Nanaimo and I got out to wait for a trolley that would take me to Commercial Street, where the Royal Bank was located. Soon after I boarded, hanging on to the straps to stay steady until I found a seat, the trolley passed through a district of coal miners' shacks that were small and dirty. To think that a handful of men lived in hilltop mansions built on the dangerous toils of these thousands. The miners could work themselves to the grave and never get ahead—this society we lived in was, as Bill put it, *fuck-eyed*. Robbing a bank, I told myself, was not wrong in the face of this. We were stealing from the masters, not the masses; the payroll was insured. The newspapers always mentioned that fact when they chronicled other heists, presumably to reassure the people. I was reassured, anyhow.

There was a growing movement against the robber barons who grew rich off other men's suffering or by finding loopholes in the law. My father was one of them; I had seen his name in the *Times* just before the Crash, when he was promoted to vice president of an investment firm on Wall Street. I wondered what became of him, now that so many of those companies had collapsed. Yet you never heard of much personal hardship among that crowd. It was regular folk who went broke from their advice while the millionaires plumped up their stocks.

On the other side of the trolley, an elderly lady smiled with frail benevolence. I bet she'd never harmed a fly in her life. Before I thought what I was doing I smiled back at her, but then I sunk down and let the brim of my fedora hang over my eyes. I didn't want to be remembered. But I needn't worry about that, I told myself; I'd never been memorable.

I alighted kitty corner from the bank, in front of the drugstore, where they were in the midst of changing the window display. I paused for a moment at the lurid sight of the undressed manne- quin. I felt equally exposed, but it was time to buck up. I was Mr. Roger Tremble, businessman, on his way to the Royal Bank. I had to be inside the doors at 2:25 p.m. Then I would wait in line, while the others would arrive at 2:30.

I pulled out my pocket watch and saw that there were precisely two minutes remaining—we had synchronized our timepieces in the morning. Mine was gold and inscribed on the back in capital letters, BY GOD. Bill had given it to me. The others had their various whimsical gifts from him but none were as fine as this watch, I thought. Fastidiously I wiped the rain droplets on its glass face against my vest. After waiting for a gap in the traffic to cross the muddy street, I dodged between some horse-drawn conveyances, which you rarely saw in Seattle now. Staring down again at the hands on my watch, my heart pounded as I noted there were only thirty seconds left. Taking a deep breath, I pushed the bank's heavy doors open at the correct time and returned the watch to my vest. Good, there were only four customers inside. Fewer witnesses to what was to pass.

Muddy footprints trailing behind me, I stood behind the last person in line. My suit was damp from the rain and I brushed it off with my hands, which left them clammy and uncomfortable. The moisture slipping down my face and collecting on my brow was no doubt from the rain also. I leaned forward to see behind the counter. Where was Mr. Clarke, the manager? His door was closed and the windows dark, but he should have been back from lunch by now. I had recommended this time for our job based on my earlier scouting trips. I told myself to stop tapping my foot, since I didn't want anyone to hear the noise and stare at me, thus remembering my face.

I focused on the back of the woman waiting in front of me. Her short bob revealed the cockleshell hollow of her white neck and it looked soft and vulnerable. When I finally heard an automobile pull up outside, I knew I shouldn't turn around, but I couldn't help myself. There was the big Durant Six and at the wheel was Lena, her face mostly concealed by a wide-brimmed hat with a long red feather arcing off it. Lena. I wanted to smile and wave at her, like a boy being picked up at school.

Six men burst from the automobile, two of them stopping at the door to stand guard and the others storming inside the bank, waving revolvers and shouting for us to get on the ground. Even though I knew this was supposed to happen, I was momentarily afraid of them, they looked so vicious. As I lay obediently on the cold polished floor with the other customers, I thought I felt their shudders transmitted through the stone; but despite such distractions I had the presence of mind to angle myself toward the vault. Moe trained his gun on us while Ramon, the biggest of the men, swaggered like the leader he wasn't while he and Bill pushed through the swinging gate to the tellers' side. From my previous instructions they headed straight for the manager's office, but when Ramon tried the handle it would not open. Bill tried it too, with the same result, and then he turned round and stared down the only man still standing in the back area. The lady tellers had already hit the floor.

"You Clarke?" Bill asked, shoving his gun into the man's ribs.

"No," the man said in a remarkably steady voice, given the circumstances. Bill sought my eye and I nodded affirmation as imperceptibly as I could.

"So where the fuck is Clarke?" Bill asked.

"He's at the dentist's."

"Mary, Mother of Jesus. Who might you be then?"

"Jordan. The assistant manager." He tugged nervously on his collar. Bill swatted his hand down and pinned it to his side. Meanwhile Ramon had walked over beside one of the tellers, and as he pushed up her skirt with his boot, she gave a little shriek.

"Leave the girls out of it, eh?" Jordan said.

"We never said we'd do nothing to the girls. You open the vault and everybody's happy. We can all go home."

"I can only open the outer door."

I dipped my chin again at Bill.

"Don't just stand there. Do it now or I'll blow your fucking brains out."

I wondered if Bill would do that, really. Either way he looked almost jolly. I heard every click of that dial as Jordan turned it slowly. This was not going as it should. Dentist appointment—how could this be? Every other day I'd been in the bank, the manager was back from lunch punctually by two. He had opened the vault for me, smooth as pudding, and he'd put my deposit inside for my "business," which I'd told him was a new lumbering operation to the north.

I heard an angry roar. "Fuck. Leave it," Bill said.

"You sure?" Ramon said.

"That shit's too heavy. Put it back. Eye on the prize. We'll wait."

Wait? How long? Until the manager came, or the police?

They had to be talking about the silver. I'd glimpsed it in the front section of the vault during one of my visits, and I bet there were a few thousand dollars there. I think I would have taken it but Bill had a singularly focused mind. And it's true it would be hard to run with the weight of all that metal.

"Lie down in the vault," Ramon said.

"Please don't close the door. There's no air. I could die," Jordan said.

This was hardly an argument to sway Ramon, and I could imagine his indifferent shrug when he said, "*Qué sera, sera*." Oh, that was stupid of him to talk Mexican. It might help to identify us if that time should come.

I felt a wave of cooler air through the bank like the change of weather at dusk on the sea. Someone had come in.

"But could I finish my cigarette?" I heard the man ask. What a bizarre question—maybe he thought it would be his last one. A black rage possessed Ramon's face as he stormed over and I feared what he might do: perhaps this man would become unfortunately acquainted with Ramon's prosthetic.

"Only if you give me one," Ramon said, suddenly benign. The bank was so quiet I could hear the scratch of the match across the emery, and the flare of the cigarette made an audible hiss like a disapproving audience.

"Your new friend there can lay down with the others," Bill said, his heels clicking on the floor as he advanced to examine his newest specimen. His voice had an edge to it that made me think he would discipline Ramon for his strange behaviour, and I hoped it would be severe. "Make yourself comfortable. We're all in this together. It's a dirty day for a dirty job, but we need the money."

"We don't want to hurt nobody," Sho-nuff said.

"Speak for yourself," Ramon said.

Bill said nothing else to Ramon and I was disappointed. I was a poor judge of human nature, I supposed. I never knew what Bill was going to do.

The tiny advances of my pocket watch, which rested between my chest and the stone floor, echoed in my soul, aging me. Three more people entered the bank and I wondered how far this would go. Bill decided they should stand in a line and "look pleasant," so that if anyone should glance inside from the street all would appear normal—the windows were high enough that those of us lying on the floor would not be visible. The three new men were stunned and obedient. However, the next person who walked in the door was a woman clutching a bundle and as soon as she realized what was happening, she turned hysterical. "Shoot me and spare my baby," she was shrieking over and over, "oh shoot me."

Bill walked over to her. "Just be calm," he said. "Nobody talked about shooting, lady." Though of course the fact was they were all holding guns. "That a boy or a girl?" Bill was strangely conversational, like it was a cocktail party or something, not a robbery. He seemed to be enjoying himself.

"A girl," she said, quieter now, but her voice was still quavering.

"There now, that's real nice. You should be glad," Bill said, putting his arm around her shoulder. She was young and pretty, a blonde. She looked up at Bill now and her face changed, looking almost happy; she must have registered how handsome he was. "If it were a boy he might be doing what we're doing some day." He sounded almost sad for a moment. He led her to a chair behind the counter and let her sit down to wait more comfortably.

Sho-nuff whistled a tune, its peppiness jarring given the situation, but at least a couple more minutes passed that way. Yet another man came into the bank, but it still wasn't Clarke. This was either a farce or a tragedy; I didn't know which yet. At least I appeared to be a customer, so I was all right if this job should fail. As soon as the thought crossed my mind, I was ashamed of it.

Ramon had a twitchy look that didn't bode well. He was no doubt getting as strung out as I was, but the results would be very different. "What you got there, mister?" he said to the new arrival.

"A deposit."

"Dump it out on the counter. You can make your deposit with us." He poked his revolver in the man's chest and the man did what he was asked, shaking out a small canvas bag. Some coins clattered onto the floor and Bill strode over, kicking them aside.

"Stop fucking around."

"Can't I take the bills? Looks like a couple hundred at least."

"No more of this chicken-feed stuff. We'll search the offices. This is getting fucking ridiculous."

With his fake arm Ramon punched through the manager's window, the glass shattering and tinkling, and then he opened the door from the handle inside. The rest of the gang, meanwhile, ransacked the cashier's cages. I didn't know what they thought they'd find except for a few paltry hundreds and some silver that Bill wouldn't even let them take. But it was a way to blow off steam I supposed; certainly the pressure of doing nothing was unbearable. Something moist was flowing along my cheek, I realized, and in a moment I saw bright red droplets hit the floor near my eye. Blood. I must have got hit by a shard when the window broke. I hoped it wasn't serious; the fact that it didn't hurt made me think that it might be.

There was a shout from the far corner, triumphant.

"It's here," Sho-nuff said. "Help me fill the bags."

The other men hurried over except for Bill, who stopped where the assistant manager was lying. He stepped on his chest. "Why didn't you tell us the money wasn't in the vault?"

"You didn't ask," Jordan said, choked and slow from the lack of air.

Bill laughed. "I like that. Gumption. But why ain't it in the vault? This a trick? Is it marked? Tell me true now." He clicked his revolver and pointed it at the man's head.

"We were counting it, that's all. It was going out to the mine later today."

"For my curiosity. Exactly how much is there?"

"One hundred and one thousand, two hundred."

Bill whistled. "Thank you kindly. Boys, you done back there?"

The three of them each carried a bulging sack over one shoulder that weighed them down on that side. That is heavy from money, I thought, giddy.

"One more thing," Bill said, waving Ramon over. "Just so's none of you pull something funny, we're going to take a hostage. Don't call the cops, or we'll kill him."

Ramon grabbed me roughly off the floor and made me stand, twisting my arm behind my back so that I yelped.

"Careful now," Bill said. "That one looks injured already. But you folks don't worry. We get out of here okay, we'll let him go."

With his arm around my neck, Ramon dragged me gagging outside and shoved me in the car, and they all piled in quickly after me, the sacks of money heaped on the floor. Lena lurched the car forward as they were still slamming the doors.

"What on earth happened, boys? You should have told me I had time to get a manicure."

She was saucy as Bonnie Parker, Lena was. Nothing fazed her.

"You wouldn't believe it, honeylamb." Bill pinched her cheek. "Just drive fast as hell, and I'll tell you later. But we got it. We got everything we wanted."

She gave a great whoop and pressed her foot harder on the gas pedal. The Durant surged. She navigated the strange curves of the downtown streets, the bank at its centre like a vortex. I was pressed against the door of the car as we sped through a corner, and the handle was painful in my ribs. I managed to straighten as we raced past a tall white tower, which I'd seen on an earlier survey of the town. It was the original Hudson's Bay fort, where the traders protected themselves from the Indians while extracting everything they could from them in furs. Yet more plunderers sanctioned by the law. It was baffling to me. Sometime if we were alone I would ask Lena if she knew how the government decided what was right or wrong, because she seemed a very educated person.

It only took a minute to leave the brick buildings of downtown behind, and then we were streaking through the coal miners' district that had so depressed me earlier. But nothing could depress me now; not even the young woman in a dusty calico dress who stood at the side of road with her shoulders hunched over. This moment was a pinnacle, and we'd risen above everyone and everything.

The car revved down a notch.

"Take this," Lena called to her, and with a single motion pulled the stupendous hat from her head and tossed it out the window; it sailed perfectly toward its target. It was the most glorious gesture I'd ever seen: Lena's white hand, flicked up in a regal wave.

"Thank you," the woman's mouth formed as she caught the hat, her face beaming with the miracle.

Then I heard the sirens.

## CHAPTER FIVE

# LONG WAY TO TIPPERARY

I WAS ON radio intercept, and I was relieved to put on the headset and shut out the rest of the world. I had a particular operator that I followed, and his voice had become as familiar to me as a dear friend. It was a lovely, sonorous voice, and for this I had nicknamed him Caruso. He was currently based out of Formosa, but at any time I might find him somewhere else in the vast Pacific. We each were assigned an operator because we needed to memorize every quirk of their inflections so that when they were transferred to a new location, and given a new codename, we could still recognize their voice, or even the way they delivered their Morse code. The stutters were unique as fingerprints. Whenever the signal was lost we spun wildly through all the frequencies until we found our man, somewhere out there on the airwaves. We were connected forever, although the knowledge of this was only on one side. It was a little lonely.

I jotted down the name of a ship I hadn't heard Caruso say before, which had been happening more often lately. I sensed that the fleet was converging, that something big was going to happen. I'd check with the clerks if there was a file on this ship. I laid my headset on my desk and walked down the hall. I wasn't pleased to see Montague rush over to reception, but at my request she disappeared among the rows of steel cabinets. I had to admit she was efficient, as all the girls they hired were. But there was nothing more boring than mere efficiency. These clerks had to examine every decoded message and generate red files matched by sender or receiver, or mention of the same person, unit or ship, and then create linked histories for them on the chance that we codebreakers should ask for them. Such thankless tasks were thought appropriate to the female worker—good training for marriage duties after the war, I supposed. Only my degree saved me from this tedium.

Montague returned with a file that was disappointingly slim. "Sorry, that's all we've got," she said, tucking a loose strand of brown hair behind her ear. "We always add everything Decrypt gives us the minute it comes in. We're totally up to date right now. It's pretty slow back here lately." Her sentences ran together in a hurry, defensively. She was leaning over the counter with her arms folded in an obvious attempt to conceal a newspaper.

"Slow enough that you have time to read other things," I said.

She smiled sheepishly, but also seemed to be bursting with some private excitement. "Only when all my work is done. I'm following that bank robber case. It's a good distraction from the gloomy war news. There's a picture today, and there's a girl in it. Can you imagine?"

My knees threatened to buckle underneath me, but I willed myself to stand tall and speak naturally. "Could I see it?"

She turned the newspaper right side up and slid it toward me. I remembered that job immediately because we always used a different car and they stuck in my mind. To this day I can't see a Packard limousine without remembering the night I left Bill. This one was a Model T. The photo was blurry but I recognized it immediately. How stupid of me to panic. Had there been a clear photo of me I would have been caught long ago.

The girl, me, was at the wheel of the car. A couple of the guys, Moe and Ramon I believe, were hanging off the outside running board. This was the one time we nearly got caught. But not quite. We were very good then. They called us the Clockwork Gang.

"You're right, Montague, it's quite a distracting story. Thanks for the file. I'll have it back by the end of the day."

Leaving the room, I walked with a measured step to the women's latrine, locked myself in a stall and put my head in my hands. This would not do. The past had become too volatile, threatening to burst out like lava—it needed to stay quietly underground, the bedrock of my life that no one would see. I had to take control of the situation.

I went to the Captain's office and, not needing to feign a look of sorrow or exhaustion, told him that my aunt in Calgary had died, my last relation, and I needed a week's leave for the funeral. He took a sip from his teacup and patted my hand. "Certainly, my dear, take all the time you need. It's quiet down here, at least for the moment."

A STRONG EASTERLY wind hampered the progress of the HMS *Venables* to New Westminster, and the voyage was so choppy I felt quite ill. They say that the fear of death changes people and makes them seek forgiveness. But Bill had shown no sign of that so far. I wondered if he would die the way he lived—he had revelled in his crimes as proof he was superior to other people. I supposed that would be for the best, the way things were. Such madness could give him strength to face the news I was bringing: that there would be no pardon. My only hope with Bill was brutal honesty. He was a crook but above all things he despised lies, which he viewed as a form of cowardice.

In front of the public market at the quay I secured a cab, a Model T just like our gang's in the newspaper picture. Back then the car had been a mark of privilege but now it was just old and shabby, a remnant of the Depression. Those days were done, and perhaps I was equally obsolete. I clutched my leather satchel tightly until the car door was shut; the docks were famous for thieves. In fact, I wondered if I had been marked out. As the cab pulled away I caught a glimpse of a dark-haired man, the same man I'd seen staring at me on the ferry deck. I usually did not travel with much cash as a precaution against this world of rogues. Bill had been born to that but, for a time at least, he had raised himself so far above them all.

I adjusted my dress carefully as I stepped out of the car and walked past the guard through the prison gate. When Bill was brought out for me, I scarcely recognized him. He was emaciated, his hair was thin and it was as though he was trying to disguise himself for a robbery with the odd spectacles he wore. Though he was only ten years older than me, he looked to be in his late fifties now.

Discomposed, I sat down across from him in a hard wooden chair. I didn't know what to say and wished that he would speak, to give me some hint about his frame of mind. Instead he whistled fragments from "It's a Long Way to Tipperary" and stared at the far wall, his glasses askew and the reflection on the lenses making his eyes big, shiny disks, cruelly blank. The visitors' room was quiet today, too quiet, with only two other prisoners present in opposite corners. Each held the hand of a girl and whispered earnestly. There was a wall of mirrors that I supposed was one way only, with guards on the other side observing this intimate misery. I would rather that than this entire lack of interest, as if I was a stranger, as if I was affronting Bill by coming, even though it was he who had summoned me to action with his message.

"Don't you know me?" I asked.

"What's the difference between a joke and a lie?" His leg was jittering something fierce.

I leaned forward and gripped the arm of his chair, which was smooth from decades of prisoners' hands rubbing nervously there. But Bill would not do as others had done, even down to the smallest detail. His hands were folded in his lap—as though the last thing he would ever do was reach out to anyone. "Bill, it's Lena. I need to talk to you."

"Got any coke?" he whispered.

I took a deep breath and drew my hand away. So this was it. There was nothing left of Bill's heart or soul or whatever you wanted to call it. The drugs had taken him over entirely; the process of destruction that started ten years ago had reached its end. I didn't know what I'd meant to say to him, anyhow. All that was left of this visit was to try to ensure the safety of my own neck.

"Bill. I tried to do what you asked, but I failed. That connection you mentioned—it's now broken. There's nothing else I can do. I'm very, very sorry."

He gave me a stare that seemed suddenly lucid and it filled me with fear. He was the best judge of character I had ever met, but he had not the slightest bit of empathy. Was he assessing my effort as inadequate and searching my eyes for the best way to harm me? He had been very good at finding people's weaknesses. Uncanny even, how he would nestle like a rat in your softest place.

He returned to his whistling, and under the circumstances it sounded like staccato madness. This visit was a failure in every way and quite possibly a serious mistake.

"All right. Goodbye, Bill," I said. I did not look behind me as I walked across the room, my steps echoing hollow on the cement in my high heels, and I avoided the guard's eyes when I passed him at the door. Hurrying down the hall, I brushed my cheeks to make sure they were dry.

After I exited the prison gate and it clanged behind me, I looked for the dark-haired man and was almost disappointed not to see him. Let there be robbers, let me be beaten, let me have nothing and forget who I was. Bill hadn't even cared that I came. The memory of him, I realized, had kept me going through these loveless years. It had been a warning, it had been a promise, but now it was a void. Everything was strangely blurry.

Aimless now, I took a trolley to the CPR train station because I remembered it was beautiful. I sat in front of the telegraph office, listening to the messages come in Morse code, familiar to me as a lover's voice, but they were either dull business cables or disastrous news from the front in Europe: sons and husbands killed. I pulled a Spanish shawl from my suitcase and wrapped it around me. I stood up and squared my shoulders, and went to the sales window. I asked for one ticket on the next train.

"Next train where?" the fellow asked.

"Anywhere."

It was Montreal. He remarked that, being so far and all, it was expensive, and I remarked back that it was no matter, and I wanted a first-class ticket. Montreal was perfect: I spoke French, and I could bury myself so that no one would ever find me.

"Been there before?"

No, I answered, exasperated at his penchant for small talk. I counted out the cash and pushed it under the grille. Now that I'd decided to go AWOL, I just wanted to curl up in a private berth and have everything go by in a blur out the window until there was no more Lena Stillman. In Montreal I would buy a new dress and listen to jazz in the company of honest men.

## CHAPTER SIX

# MARCH 1932

SHO-NUFF WAS SQUISHED beside me in the getaway car, and with that grin on his face he looked like he was having a country lark, a little Sunday drive. This was annoying. The sirens were wailing closer, and no one but me was concerned; or, I might as well admit, afraid. I wanted to ask Bill when we were going to dump out the tacks and broken glass to foil them, but nobody else was saying anything and I didn't want to jump the gun. Bill hated when you anticipated something he should do. Finally I leaned forward to whisper to Lena.

"Those aren't police sirens, By. It's a fire truck," she said so everybody could hear, and I wished she hadn't done that. Ramon made a sneering comment about people who were "chickenshits."

"Sirens probably sound different in America, don't they Bill?" Lena said.

And Bill agreed.

To hear her defend me was worth the initial humiliation—I figured Lena didn't mean to do it, because with the wind roaring through the open windows it was natural to talk loudly. And Bill took my side, so I shouldn't care what Ramon said. He might be brave but that's because he had a turnip on his shoulders instead of a proper brain that could worry about things. Of course I didn't say all that.

We'd turned onto some back roads, and I wished there were some more goddamn paved roads in this country so we could move faster. I was still chilled by that siren even though I knew what it was now. Visibility was bad here. The road was lined with huge cedar trees that snuffed out the light like in a fairytale with a bad ending. I hadn't scouted out this part of the escape—Cruickshank did that. So I was alarmed when we pulled over at a dock with a few boats tied up to it, and smoke rising from the trees suggested cabins were nearby. I hoped I hadn't made an error with my choice—the harbour had looked good on the old map I found, and people in Nanaimo had told me the coal mine was abandoned. Was Cruickshank blind? Quiet Yellow Point, where we'd first arrived, seemed more suitable than this place to make our escape.

Ramon and Sho-nuff heaved out the sacks and carried them down the dock to the *El Toro*, which was conspicuous among the old tugboats and battered dinghies. If we were seen, we'd be remembered. I followed behind Bill, the dock swaying unnervingly under my feet. I wished for steady ground.

"Bill, you think anybody's up there? With the smoke and all?"

"We don't got to worry none about them. We got confusion well sowed. Cruickshank paid people up and down the island to say they did see us. These people here been paid to say they didn't. They don't like the cops no how. It's the craziest goddamn place, a cult run by this feller who calls himself Brother xii. Believes the world is going to end."

"Nonetheless he likes his money. He took ours happy enough," Cruickshank said. He was slapping us each on the shoulder in greeting as we paraded one by one onto the boat. Sho-nuff untied the rope from the dock and jumped aboard as Cruickshank started the engine.

"I heard if you join the cult you got to sell everything you own, convert it into gold and give it to Brother xii," Cruickshank said, loud now to be heard above the motor's noise as we left the shore behind. "Got it buried around here somewheres, people say. What you suppose you do with gold after the world ends?"

"I don't know, but that's one to keep in the back pocket," Bill said.

We were silent and reverent with thoughts of riches while the boat picked up speed, the wind blowing Lena's hair. As she brushed it away from her luminous face where she sat above us on the gleaming mahogany bow, she was like some Greek goddess of the sea come to life. "That reminds me," she said, looking as always at Bill. "You never told me how much you got."

"More than one hundred grand," Bill said.

She clapped her hands together, delighted. "This has to be the best job you've ever done."

"By a long shot, darlin'. You're my lucky charm. But it ain't over till it's over."

At that everyone turned pensive, and I buttoned up my overcoat. The wind felt cold now and ominous clouds hung low, brushing against the tops of the mountainous islands. Bill stared at me funny.

"We should take By's talk about sirens as a premonition," he said. "Everybody change your clothes. We need to look different now."

Moe went into the cabin and came out with two sacks. We placed our overcoats and hats into the empty one, and he gave us new outerwear from the other. He put some rocks in with our old clothes, tied the sack closed and heaved it into the sea with a splash; it looked like a body as it slumped into the waves and sank.

Cruickshank slowed the boat as we came alongside a strange island made of sandstone that looked sculpted into tears; the grooved surface was pale and barren.

"Got to watch for rocks under the surface here," Cruickshank said.

Now that the engine was quieter I thought I heard another sound coming across the water, but I didn't want to be responsible for another false alarm. Unfortunately, only a few moments went by before I saw I was right this time. The dark form of another boat had appeared and seemed to be heading toward us.

"Shit, shit, shiteree," Bill muttered. "They were in Cufra Inlet. Should've known that. Concealed myself there a million times."

"I had to go this way, boss. It's the only way to navigate the channel." Cruickshank sounded defensive—as well he might, if his foolishness led to the end of our caper. I knew from the start that Cruickshank would be a liability. Bill hadn't needed to take on another partner, since I was plenty capable of giving him the help he needed.

As the boat drew closer, Bill's face relaxed. "It's the *Kheunamet*. Constable Gorman's boat. Crooked as a dog's hind leg. Wait, that's you, Cruickshank," Bill said, grinning slyly. "Ain't that the, what you call it Lena, entomology of that name?"

She smiled at him uneasily but then she nodded.

"Har, har," Cruickshank said.

"More than one breed of crooked cop, thank the Devil," Bill said.

The squat boat had pulled alongside the *El Toro*, and Bill raised his fingers to his cap in salute. I would never have picked Gorman out as police since he didn't wear a uniform and his yellow sou'wester had no insignia. He was a pudgy man who looked like he could scarcely arrest a hungry vagrant, let alone a boatload of strong men. Bill passed something into his hand, leaning across the water, and then we separated.

"He can't have heard anything," Bill said, watching the *Kheunamet* pull away. "He would have asked for a bigger tip."

Cruickshank pulled the throttle back and we took off, weaving through the islands, Bill muttering them off like a rosary: Wise Island, Hall Island, Secretary Island.

"Jackscrew Island," he said, thumping on the gunwale. "Pull up here. We'll wait in this here cove until it's dark. Then over the border to the good old US of A. I'd say that calls for a drink. Isn't it great to be alive?"

Cruickshank cut the engine. Sho-nuff threw the anchor into the clear, green water below us, and a seal poked its head up curiously and then disappeared. There was a ramshackle cabin visible on the shore.

"Don't be such a nervous Nelly," Cruickshank said. He must have seen me looking at the cabin. "There used to be some old coot in there, but he died a few years back. Take a pull of this, it'll calm your nerves."

He handed me a bottle of Seagram's whiskey. The bottle had not yet been opened so I did not hesitate to drink some down after pulling out the cork. I disliked their habit of passing the bottle around because it was unhygienic. The liquor burned down my throat and warmed my stomach and I did feel rather better. I wouldn't worry myself about germs anymore. After pressing the cork back in so it wouldn't spill, I held out the bottle to the group, the liquid glinting amber in the flash of late-afternoon light piercing out from beneath the shale of the clouds. Sho-nuff took it from me. Next was Lena, and I was surprised because I'd never seen her drink before.

She caught my stare. "Seems like I crossed over some threshold today. I'm in it with you boys real deep now."

"Darlin', that's a good thing, ain't it?" Bill said. "Whyn't you sound more like celebrating?"

I'd never heard the word "celebrating" sound so ominous.

"Sure Bill. Let's." She took another big drink.

"Whoa there, girlie. Takes a while to hit your brain," Cruickshank said. "Careful or you'll be tipping into the sea."

"That sounds like a good idea." Before any of us could think twice about what she meant or stop her, she threw off her shoes and jumped overboard. I waited tensely at the edge until she rose to the surface sputtering, her wet hair smoothed over her head so she looked sleek as the seal. "The water's fine! Come on in."

I thought Bill would scold her—the water had to be freezing, she'd catch her death—but instead he just laughed. "She's got spirit. That's why I love this girl."

I should have known by then not to expect a typical reaction from Bill. That's how he was. Normal things made him angry and crazy things made him happy. But someone here had to be sensible. Lena was shivering, and I begged her to get back in the boat. She cut smoothly through the water toward me with a perfect breast-stroke. A faint triangle of her motion widened out behind her, the memory of her presence, and I wondered if the ripples of her would remain, though smaller and smaller, and be transmitted across the ocean until they hit Japan. Her teeth chattering, she held out her hand to me. Looking over at Bill to make sure he wouldn't mind the liberty, I allowed myself to grasp her slender hand. I pulled her into the boat and let go reluctantly. I told myself I worried she would slip—the deck was smooth varnished timber and she was dripping with water.

"Moe, throw her a towel," Bill said. Moe lifted up a bench seat and handed Lena a jaunty navy striped one that she scrubbed herself with.

"I was going to give you this later but I think you could use it now," Bill said.

The rest of us watched as he went down into the cabin. He returned with a huge box in his arms that read "Pappas," and he untied the red ribbon on it himself. He pulled out a brown fur coat that he draped over her shoulders, queenly.

"Oh Bill," she said, snuggling herself into it. "You shouldn't have. What if this job hadn't gone off?"

"I had no doubts in my mind."

She went up to him and gave him a deep kiss. I turned my head away.

"Come on. Save that shit for private time," Cruickshank said, and I was grateful. Such displays were unseemly. Ramon was right about one thing: you bring a girl into a gang and it throws everyone off kilter.

"That water was awfully cold," Lena laughed. Bill took the hint and ushered us all into the cabin. With the door closed behind the last of us—except for Sho-nuff, who was taking the first watch—only a weak light came in through the portholes, so Bill lit a few lanterns.

"I got champagne," he said, almost shy. He pulled a green bottle the size of a fire extinguisher out of the cooler.

Lena giggled. "Where'd you get that? I've never seen such a big bottle."

"It's some Frenchie shit. They don't go halfways."

"Neither do you, Bill." Her eyes glowed with admiration. I thought to myself, I should learn how to be bolder in my actions.

Bill twitched his head and Cruickshank responded by going to a cupboard and pulling out some glasses, real crystal, I thought, as they tinkled against each other. He held a cluster in his hands, a brittle bouquet. Bill popped the cork and I flinched at the gunshot sound. He filled the glasses, the foam overflowing onto the table, and Moe made us laugh by licking it up saying, "Waste not, want not." Bill admonished him to take a drink proper like his mama taught him, and Moe retorted that his mama never knew nothing about the drinking of champagne, and we all laughed again. I finished my glass in one go and Bill filled it up again, grinning at my excess. Cruickshank held up his glass and said, "Cheers to the mastermind," and we all clinked our glasses together with a sound like church bells. After finishing up the bottle our giddiness subsided into exhaustion. We each took a spot on the benches along the side to lie down while Bill and Lena went forward into the cabin where the beds were, to teasing commentary that I did not take part in. I tried to nap as the others did.

I must have succeeded because I woke in the dark to Lena shaking me, her form only the barest outline, telling me we'd crossed the border and it was my turn to go up on deck to watch for trouble. I hauled myself up the stairs, hanging tight to the brass railings because the boat was lurching. To my surprise, Lena followed me and stood beside me as I stared out to sea.

"It's choppy now," I said.

"There was a small craft warning for the Strait of Juan de Fuca. That wind comes direct from Japan. Cold, isn't it?"

A wave pummelled the boat and Lena grabbed my hand, then let go of it with a laugh.

"I'm not cold at all," I said. And I wasn't, though the salt spray hit my face—it felt fresh and fine.

## CHAPTER SEVEN

# NO RETURN ADDRESS

A COUPLE HOURS out of the city, where the Fraser River narrowed and I felt suddenly hemmed in by the canyon walls outside my window, I walked to the bar car, holding myself steady against the wall as the train jolted and swayed. I ordered a gin and tonic from the barman and carried it to a booth where I could sit alone. Carefully, I stirred my drink with the glass swizzle stick, a surprising touch, but I was in first class and could apparently be trusted with delicate things.

I felt responsible for the disastrous meeting with Bill. I was less sure now that he had meant to threaten me. Perhaps he had just wanted to see me one last time, and I'd come bearing the news that ended his last hope of a pardon. So typical of any interaction with Bill, that the fault should not be his. He had a gift for that kind of deflection. Couldn't he for once have been more like other people? Contrite, regretful, loving even? He owed me that much at least.

I had been only twenty years old when I met him. Back then I thought I was all grown up, but I was still more of a child than an adult. I hadn't been able to see outside each vivid moment. When Bill came into that bank and fixed his eyes on me, that was it. It was like being electrocuted—your hand is on the socket and you can't let go or even think to do so. But that doesn't seem quite right. I still remember the feeling I had that day, of escape and freedom, that has never been matched since.

Back then, I had two years behind me studying linguistics at the University of British Columbia, during the time that Father was sick. It started not long after he lost his job as a postman. I think the purposefulness of that work was what had kept him going. When you lose the thing that is your glue, whatever it is, well of course you come undone. His job had seemed so stable, too, even when the hard times first hit. Government paycheque. But with the Depression, folks didn't send so many letters. No more stamps to lick, they just ran their dry tongues onto their lips in the memory of it, and stared at letters past. Still, he insisted I carry on with my schooling while his savings lasted. There had been some lady professors at the university, and I didn't want to abandon my dream of becoming one. But when Father died penniless, I was very lucky to get the job at the bank.

That's what Mr. Sampson told me, anyhow, when he ran his hand down my back and onto what I'll call here my ass, now I'm thinking of Bill and the way he talked. Mr. Sampson was balding and about fifty years old, portly, with a gold pocket watch chain stretched across his belly, and he was the greediest bastard that ever lived. He'd eat a whole chicken in front of a hungry child and not blink. I saw him do it too, when he insisted I join him at the Vancouver Club, and a little boy pressed his nose against the window. I stood to go give him a nickel, but Mr. Sampson yanked me back down and said he didn't invite me there to eat alone for his four dollars.

He had made it clear that if I didn't surrender my virtue to him soon, perhaps there was some other young lady who would like my job equally well. Though I hated the work, handling money for smug people who had not been touched by hard times, I could not afford to lose it. It was the only way I could imagine getting back to the university someday. I felt quite desperate, frankly.

And then the bank got robbed. Three men with masks on and automatic shotguns rushed through the doors and one of those big guns was pointing at me; I was a teller. My hands shaking, I put the money in the burlap flour sack held out to me. I remember seeing the picture painted faintly on it, White Knight Brand, and thinking it peculiar, in that weird slow way things have when you are scared.

Mr. Sampson blazed out of the back room brandishing a pistol—what vinegar he had in him suddenly when he thought he was losing his money. Bill's men panicked at that, and Sho-nuff put a gun to my temple and told me to come round to his side. Then they backed out the doors with me as their shield. I expected Mr. Sampson to shoot me to get his money, but he did not, and I'm still surprised by that. Perhaps he was a coward when he came to thinking of blood on the floor. I've heard it's dreadfully hard to get out of marble because the rock is porous. Not that he had to clean it personally, but the bank's state reflected on his management.

Then we were outside, the men about to leave me on the board-walk, when Bill Bagley tore off his mask and gave me that crazy grin. My, he was handsome. As they started up the car I called out, "Take me with you." And Bill grabbed my hand and hauled me into the car as they drove away. As the wind swooped back my hair, I was elated. These people had seized the money that had been as elusive to me as water in the desert. I had just discovered the oasis.

A bit later I felt some familial obligation and wrote to my aunt in Calgary, my only remaining relation, and told her I'd been promoted, that they sent me to Toronto to work in the head office. I doubt she ever read about the robbery and my disappearance. She lived quite inwardly and had no truck with the news. The Bible carried all the news she needed to know; it was Eternal Information, as she said. I sent her money sometimes for her church missionary fund, because it meant the world to her. Though personally I'd always thought it sounded a lot more fun to be a heathen.

Bill was a kind of philanthropist. He spent his money wildly on gambling and drink of course, but he also sent a good deal of money to the orphanages, and was quick to press a nickel into a pauper child's hand. In fact, all the boys had their good sides. Byron was sensitive and thoughtful, while Sho-nuff was always willing to show me the ropes. Moe would spend hours building perfect fires from rain-soaked logs so we were comfortable when we slept in the woods. Ramon was more alarming but his bravery could not be questioned. They were as good as most people, I thought. If they were sometimes greedy, at least they were honest about it. Not like my bank customers, pretending that saving was a moral virtue, when in fact they were simply hoarding money for their own comfort and letting the rest starve.

Going along on the robberies, the blood surged splendidly through my veins. And afterwards, I never felt bad—I recalled Mr. Sampson's arrogant face, and how the bank money was insured anyway. We would redistribute the wealth. I picked my own charity, donating to the Sisters who helped the young unwed mothers, and I felt no guilt, even when I got my first fur coat. It looked very nice on me, like I was a movie star. I enjoyed being out in public, no one guessing my secret life.

Bill bought me beautiful dresses, and he had a tuxedo, and we'd go out dancing on Saturday nights. When we were in Seattle, Bill's favourite place was the Bergonian Hotel. He liked the high-class environs, he said. He liked to use words like that sometimes, and if I had to guess I'd say he picked them up from me; otherwise he spoke coarsely, since he'd knocked about on the streets growing up. His father had been a terrible beater from what little he told me, and he was grateful when the drunkard disappeared and he had to raise his own self up.

Bill was the first man I'd ever been with. Sure, I'd messed around with boys at the university, because the roar of the Twenties had reached even that quiet campus in the forest at the end of the world. I admit my upbringing gave me the old-fashioned notion of saving myself until marriage, but when I took up with a gang of bank robbers, to have such scruples seemed ridiculous. The people I met followed their own pleasures, which was an appealing example, and Bill did not have to pressure me. He was actually a gentleman and, when I first travelled with them, ensured that I had my own room. He treated me gingerly, and looking back I suppose I was a foreign creature to him, being nothing like the women he'd known. But after a few weeks he stayed up with me late in my room and when I didn't ask him to leave, we both understood what it meant. It was wonderful. After that, being near him was all I wanted.

I'd started another gin and tonic when the train pulled into Spences Bridge, a small town in the sagebrush drylands where little prospered. But the platform seemed busy, chaotic even. Newsboys were running back and forth, holding up papers I could not see from this distance. Crowds followed them, clamouring.

"Something peculiar going on," the barman said in a Scottish brogue.

I shoved open my window, and the boys' shouts streamed in: "Extra, Extra, Japs bomb Hawaii. War on America. War on Great Britain."

On Canada, too. I needed to return to the bunker.

I downed my drink and rushed back to my berth. My personal troubles were nothing compared to this. The Japanese threat on the Pacific coast was immediate. The Examination Unit would now be of vital importance, as would trained Japanese linguists and codebreakers. I had behaved like a coward, running away, and this calamity—so large and outside myself—made me snap out of it. I grabbed my satchel from the rack over my seat and hustled past the conductor who stood at the door. He touched my elbow to help me down the stairs.

As the train's puff of smoke disappeared, the platform emptied of its unusual commotion. The wind rushed up the canyon, the only sound. Spences Bridge was a town with big dreams during the gold rush era, but now its faded hotels perched on hoodoo cliffs with silent nerve. I crossed the walkway over the tracks to switch sides for the next train back.

CAPTAIN BROMLEY-SINCLAIR HELD both my hands in his as he stood back to regard me. "My dear, you are a sight for sore eyes," he said, though in truth he himself was the sight. He was wearing his silk paisley smoking jacket, to which he had added bedroom slippers since the last time I saw him.

"I was only gone for a week," I said. "Though it did feel longer, with all that's happened."

"I hope you've had time to get back on your feet after the funeral." He looked at me with concern and I felt like a fraud.

"I'm fine, sir."

"You've come back just when we need you. Things have gone absolutely batty around here. Damn Japs are sending God knows how many messages."

I'd somehow forgotten how clammy it was down in the bunker, and already my bones felt cold. It was like winter existed perpetually inside oneself. The room was stuffed full of people I didn't know at desks that hadn't been here before, and I couldn't see Marguerite anywhere.

"They've brought in some Wrens from England to supplement us," he said. "And some good men also. By air transport, no less. The scale of everything has changed. I should mention, my dear, that Marguerite has been transferred to Washington, to be our liaison there. They appreciated her abilities."

The war had taken away my only friend. I must have looked upset, because he patted my shoulder as he sat me down at a desk already heaped with papers. With all the new junior staff, the Captain said, I was redeployed from radio intercept to codebreaking exclusively. This was where he needed the brains, he said, and this praise gave me a surge of happiness. The Captain hurtled off in his manic way, though he stopped at the desk of Lieutenant Hughes to converse with him. I grabbed the top sheet of paper and stared at the garbled letters, which swam before my eyes. My mind must have gone soft in my time away.

On the way back to Victoria, I had managed to miss the boat out of Vancouver by five minutes, which meant I had to spend an extra day there. It was a ridiculous error. I had skulked about the city, somehow worrying I would see Bill on the streets. When I was finally on the ferry, the wind lashing my face as I stood on the deck, I stared into the ocean's grey depths. What happened at the surface was irrelevant; it was all blackness underneath. Bill had been that impenetrable. Even in his last days, he had given me no resolution. Cold now, I went inside and a man in the cafeteria struck up a conversation with me. I was glad when he asked right away what I did because I could answer that it was confidential for the war. While he looked like he didn't believe me—what could a woman do that was so important?—it strangled his efforts.

The messages the Captain had started me on were quite simple. It was the Water Transport Code. We already knew the main code groups and the content was rarely a surprise. A ship's location and movements, latitude and longitude, supplies needed and such like. Now I knew I could get through my pile on this shift and I lost myself in the work. I hoped I would still be one of the best now that they'd brought in new codebreakers from England. They'd no doubt think themselves superior to colonials like me. As I stole a look around the room, I was annoyed that the hats issued with the British women's uniforms were much more darling than the Canadian ones—a beret rather than a goofy little homburg. I'd show those Brits. I'd make sure the Captain gave me the JN-25 messages to work on tomorrow. They contained the most vital information.

The radio intercept was more variable in importance, but I liked it because everything was happening in real time. I hoped I would still get to do some listening work. Now there would be so much more to hear because the Japanese would undoubtedly come closer to our coast. Perhaps they would even attack? I brushed the thought away. Surely they had more important targets.

By the end of my shift my head was awash with letters and numbers as I carried the pile of completed messages to the Captain's office. I wanted him to know what I'd accomplished. As I reviewed the information on the ship's movements, I realized there was something different about the room. I asked him what had happened to the map. He always used to put coloured pins on it to indicate what the ships were doing, and as each of us added our day's information, we could visualize what was happening out there. This was a comfort when we were clinging to the edge of the last island between us and the Japanese.

"I'm afraid there's been a division of responsibilities now, with all the new hands on deck," he said, sounding briefly nautical. "The map is in a restricted room. It's on a need-to-know basis."

"Doesn't it help to have all the information in front of us while we work? If we see the directions the ships have been going, we can make informed guesses about some of the new place words. They transliterate so strangely sometimes."

"Yes, I know," he said, his smile rueful. "I mentioned that. But the powers that be are sticking their noses in our business now, and I can't do anything about it. We have become rather too important for my liking."

WALKING UP THE stairs to my house in Rockland, I felt a sense of dread to see something sticking out of my mailbox. The parcel was postmarked from Seattle, but there was no return name or address. There was no sign of anyone nearby, but it would be easy to hide among the massive fir trees, ferns and salal that sheltered my house from the street. I locked the door behind me. Kicking off my boots, I tore open the brown wrapping while I was still in the front hall. Inside was a hardcover ledger of the kind accountants used, with sheets of rumpled paper stapled at the end that were not flush with the rest. I opened the cover.

"For Lena" was written in a familiar handwriting. Byron. When I saw the year in the corner, 1932, I panicked. This was an accounting of another sort: a journal of the gang. This was a story that should not exist with me in it.

Given the dedication, he had always intended me to have it. I knew he had a soft spot for me. So why had he not delivered the book before now as a signal that he was all right? He had vanished from the earth completely after the Harrison job. When Bill was captured, the newspaper had not mentioned Byron at all. No doubt he fled Bill's increasing lunacy, as I had, and he achieved an admirable secrecy. There was no obvious reason he would want to stir up the past now.

The timing pointed in another direction. I returned from a visit with Bill, received a threatening note from him, and now this. He must have a copy of it and wanted to hold it over my head. That he knew everything everyone ever did, and he had the proof. It was another show of his power to do what he wanted even when behind bars. It was completely nerve-wracking; just as he intended, I was sure.

Taking a moment to draw the curtains, willing my hands to be steady, I sat down in the parlour to read the journal. I hadn't remembered Byron keeping one, and it was peculiar to see my name in his private recollections. I felt like I was prying not only into his affairs but into a stranger's existence, this Lena Stillman.

## CHAPTER EIGHT

# MARCH 1932

SLOW AND QUIET we approached the Bellingham marina around midnight, well after respectable citizens had gone to bed. There were no lanterns left alight and no beacons on the docks, but Cruickshank was familiar with the area from his years chasing after rumrunners (or at least pretending to do so) and could navigate almost by feel. I asked him what the trick was.

"Nobody never had trouble screwing in the dark, now did they? You just slip it in," he said.

I did not approve of his leering tone but I wouldn't care for him to see my expression either. Embarrassment was not a manful reaction. I busied myself with the ropes and jumped off the boat onto the dock. When I looped the rope around the metal post I struggled to make a good knot so that I would not be the cause of the *El Toro* floating away. The coarse line chafed my palms as I yanked on it and I cursed under my breath. Sho-nuff leapt onto the dock beside me to take over the business, and I tried to make out how he did it.

"It ain't a natural thing," he said, and I was grateful for this admission. "I was a crewman on Lake Michigan. It was Bill gave me the chance to be a captain, back in his smuggling days, but Cruickshank runs the *El Toro* because it's his baby." He rolled his eyes. "He don't know shit, is my opinion."

"Can this boat outrun the police?"

"It's the fastest boat north of San Francisco. They're a bunch of bumblers up here anyhow. I gave them the slip in these waters many times." He jerked on the hitch and then, satisfied, strode away from the water. I followed after him.

"I want you in the same car as me. You sound like good luck."

"Sho nuff," he grinned.

Bill had laid down a plank for the rest of the gang to file off the boat. "Quit yammering, you two," he said as he brushed by. "This ain't no church social." Ramon sniggered. I hoped someday I would get up the nerve to punch him in the face. But I reminded myself that, for now, we were a team. At the end of the dock, everybody paused and stood instinctively together in a circle, facing outward as when surrounded. Surely if there was any danger to see, we would see it.

"By God, come with me and we'll get the cars," Bill said. "Moe, you take everybody up there to wait behind that shack so we can leave quick-like."

We marched up the path together until Bill and I cut left. We'd parked two touring cars in a garage down the road last week. Bill knew the owner, just as he seemed to know someone useful in every obscure corner—Bill used to supply him with stolen cars before expanding into the more profitable banking line. Bill could still start any car in twenty seconds flat without a key. As we walked silently along the verge through the long, wet grass, my feet were soon cold from water soaking through my boots. My eyes had adjusted to the darkness now, and the moon, nearly full, outlined the black trees edging the road. An owl called and I wondered what unlucky creature was about to die.

Reaching the garage, Bill put his keys to the padlocks and we each lifted a door. I flinched at the creak it made. If I'd realized how loud it was I would have oiled it when we were last here.

"Remember, don't turn on the headlights," he whispered, throwing me a key, which I missed. I had to feel around under muddy leaves to find it, and wiped it on my trousers. Bill took the Cadillac and left me with the Ford—even in flight he had a sense of his proper due. He started his engine and it echoed ungodly loud inside the garage. As he pulled out, I started mine to follow him down the road.

There were no houses visible out here; the landscape's unwelcoming character was our refuge if not a comfort. I realized now that the coastal rainforest I'd always lived in had never suited me—had always repelled me, in fact. Once I had my share of the money, I thought, I would escape to a new life somewhere open and golden. I tried to envision whether that was a desert island, or maybe the African savannah. I decided the beach would be more peaceful; there were no predators there. I shook my head to clear it of my ill-timed daydreaming—we had already arrived at the shack where the gang waited. I needed to focus: this was the most important undertaking of my life. While a bunch of the guys piled in the back, Lena stood expectantly outside my door. I found I could not move or speak. She was looking at me, finally, and this was a moment I wanted to last.

She opened the door herself, grinning, her white teeth shockingly bright against the darkness inside, and waved at me to move over.

"I'm the driver now, remember?" she said. I slid onto the passenger seat, elated to be in the same car with her.

The top was up in case of rain, but we'd previously removed the windows to prepare for a shootout, so the wind blew in cold and fierce as we picked up speed. The car jolted terribly over the potholes. Lena told the boys in back to make sure the tacks and such were at arm's reach, just in case, and the guns also. We had a couple of Tommy guns—Bill had said we needed a bigger armory against the American police, who were more savvy in the ways of crooks than the Canucks were. I wished he hadn't said "crooks," because it sounded unpleasant.

"This is the first time I've been to America. How exciting," Lena said over her shoulder.

"It's not so shit hot," Moe said. He was slumped low in his seat with his fedora pulled down to his eyes. "Think I want to get me a cabin in Canada when we're done. More elbow room up there."

"Elbow room!" Sho-nuff said. "That's for sure. You could walk round with your elbows out for your whole life and never hit nobody. You planning to join that Brother XII cult?"

"No way. I'm not giving him my gold. Maybe I'll start a cult, though. Sounds like a good gig."

"Nobody'd be fool enough to join it."

"Boys, be nice now," Lena said. Moonlight glinted on her hair.

In front of us Bill had slowed and Lena followed suit. There were some bright lights up ahead, a roadhouse. So as not to attract attention we put on our lights and took a more leisurely pace until we passed it. As soon as we were on Chuckanut Drive, we raced up the curves into the mountains. The corners were blind but Lena never slowed on the approach; in fact, she cut into the other lane to shorten our line and I squinted my eyes shut. Any doom that was coming, was coming, and I didn't want to know. We had a long way to go still and I wasn't sure I could take it; we were headed to Cruickshank's ranch on the Olympic Peninsula. We would detour through Seattle first, which concerned me because there were so many people who might see us. But Bill said he had some perfect hideouts there, and the more people there were about, the more you could disappear among them. That was true; there were six in our gang and no one noticed me, I thought, looking at Lena's profile.

My legs were getting cramped from being bent up halfway to my chest, since a sack on the floor was in the way; but I reminded myself it was full of money and the inconvenience could easily be borne. Briefly a sheet of silver glinted in the west. It was the ocean under the moonlight, and I was comforted by how it asserted its existence even in the obscurity of night.

I had a sensation of descent now, gradual at first, and then Lena took us through a hairpin turn that made my stomach heave. There was another roadhouse, glaring light upon us as we passed, and soon the forest opened into a flat expanse of farmland; we were out of Whatcom and into Skagit County now.

"Lena, I feel like a duck in a barrel here," I said. "Isn't there another road?"

"We'll be turning onto the Bow Hill Road soon. We're going to stick to the mountains as much as we can."

"Don't that route lead straight through some town, the woolly one?" Moe asked.

"Sedro-Woolley," I said, glad to know something for a change.

"I don't know about that," Lena said, a trace of irritation in her voice. "I'm just following the route Bill told me."

Sure enough we turned and hugged the forested hills again. This was the right thing, just as small birds never fly across the open if they can help it, for a hawk has room to manoeuvre there. We turned onto a larger road briefly, to cross a river, and passed some houses. Luckily there were no lights on anywhere; good folks were deep in dreams. Despite the late hour I wasn't sleepy at all, and my senses were keenly humming. Something made me look out the back window.

Three cars were driving over the bridge we'd just crossed. Their headlights were off also.

"Lena, try and shake those cars. See if they're tailing us."

She sped up until she was nearly on Bill's bumper and then she honked the horn, staccato anxious blasts. Bill too accelerated, then veered sharply left.

"What the hell's he doing going east?" she said.

"There's a road follows the Skagit River then pops out just above Everett, nice as you please," Moe said. "It's longer this way, but if they follow, won't be so many witnesses."

"Witnesses to what?" I asked, trying to keep my voice steady.

"This," Moe said, leaning out the back of the car and tipping out a bucket. It was the carpet tacks. "And whatever we got to do after this."

The first car shuddered to a halt. The other two drove into the brush and then regained the road, still following. A siren started to wail, the red light throwing everything around the car into sharp relief. Sho-nuff opened the glove box and pulled out a pistol, leaning out the side and squinting behind him. He let off two shots. The car with the siren veered off the road.

"Good shot," Moe said, thumping his back.

"Nice of them to light up the target."

"Still one left."

"They ain't following."

"We don't know that yet," Lena said.

The road hugged the river but despite the tight turns she stuck close to Bill's bumper—they were like a choreographed team. I wondered if anyone would ever focus on my existence with a fraction of the attention she put on that piece of chrome. But of course I had nothing to do with the life-and-death importance of that moment. I was the most useless member of the gang right now: I couldn't shoot. I could just sit here, hoping the night would conceal the twitching beneath my eye. In my mind I urged Lena forward, faster, so fast we could pass Bill and leave him behind. But as always we were constrained by the need to follow him; he was our lodestar. I had a sense of becoming smaller and as I stared out into the surroundings I realized that the deeper blackness around me was the looming of mountains, jagged and cruel.

We slowed a moment as we reached a junction, and then travelled along a smoother road at a faster pace again. Moe swore under his breath, "Motherfuckers." There was the third police car. They must have kept to this better route and despite their setback they'd nearly caught up to us, knowing that the valley was a funnel that would lead us back to them. Moe reached to the floor, pulled up a Tommy gun, shouldered it and let off some rounds wildly. I put my hands to my ears—the noise was unbearable at close range. A bullet casing hit the side of my head and I winced with the pain. Moe whooped as the police car spun and stopped on the road behind us.

"Got those motherfuckers."

"Naw, they just chickened out," Sho-nuff said. "We crossed the county line. Good excuse for them to drop the chase."

"Bet you five bucks. We'll find out next time we read the newspaper."

Sho-nuff shook hands with him.

As the silence around us thickened, I found myself becoming dreamy again. I hadn't thought of the fact we'd be in the newspaper—page one for what we did. My father's name had been in the newspaper, too, for his progress to the vice presidency of the bank in New York City. I didn't suppose my own name would be in there for him to see, but I liked the idea of being immortalized in some way. Maybe by the description my father would sense that it was me; a father should know that sort of thing, shouldn't he? His creation of me was a permanent connection, no matter that he tried to break it.

My reverie was broken as we pulled over, though the reason was unclear since we were still in the middle of nowhere. Bill stepped out of his car and strode up to congratulate the shooters, slapping Moe and Sho-nuff on their backs. We were nearly at the town of Darrington, he said, and if we sat tight for a few minutes he'd go siphon some gas for our cars; it was still a good while until we hit the coast.

"Change of plan. I know a Chinaman lives on Deadwater Slough, just north of Everett, and we can get a boat off him. We'll get to Cruick's ranch that way. Seattle's too hot for us. Damned Mounties must have called us in. That ain't usual procedure across the border."

"What we did ain't usual neither," Sho-nuff said.

"Amen, brother, for that." Bill grabbed a couple jerry cans out of his trunk and disappeared into the blackness.

"I swear that Bill knows every inch of backcountry from here to California," Moe said. "He got a map burned in his brain."

We waited silently until Bill returned. When he handed me one of the sloshing jerry cans so I could fill up Lena's car, some gasoline splashed on my hand, cool and then gone. Screwing the cap back on the tank I realized that the sky was subtly no longer black but deep blue, and I could more clearly make out the mountain peaks.

Bill told us to conceal the cars in the brush and we'd sleep in shifts until nightfall returned and we could complete our getaway.

"We should be safe here," he said. "This is a lonely stretch of road."

I agreed with him silently, completely, as he put his arm over Lena's shoulder and led her over to his car. Without being asked, the rest of the boys from Bill's car crammed into mine so we were heaped unwanted over each other like abandoned corpses after a war.

CHAPTER NINE

# THE BOOK CODE

HEADING TOWARD THE bunker I gripped my hat to my head so it would not fly off, and cursed once more the brimmed homburg of the Canadian uniform. I was glad of the distraction of it, though, because if I looked out to sea I was forced to acknowledge the anti-submarine nets that were now strung across Esquimalt Harbour. They had the effect of making me feel less secure, rather than more, though this was illogical. It was an improvement over the military embarrassment of the antique cannon on the bunker. It had been built in the last century to scare the Indians away from Fort Victoria, but the armaments had never been updated. If the Japanese hit the West Coast, I knew better than anyone the ferocity of their attacks.

I had left my house in Rockland and moved into the barracks. The Captain considered it too dangerous for me to make the trip back and forth into the city from the base, in case of air raids. Anyhow, I was tired from the irregular shifts. They had bumped us from eight hours to twelve, and I frequently worked nights. I dropped into bed at odd hours and woke, disoriented, to the tang of fresh cedar—the timber for the new barracks had been cut only a few months before. The boards let in the perpetual cold wind off the ocean, and I still used two wool blankets at night even though it was May.

I woke up frequently to thoughts of Byron's journal, which I had secured in the attic of my house. The trunk had a Hobbs antiviolence lock, which was impossible to pick without destroying it. Any lesser attempts would be revealed by the key, which would afterwards turn in the opposite direction. Even when I slept I kept the key on a chain around my neck. Before I moved to the barracks, I sat on my parlour window seat, with a big fire roaring in the fireplace, and relived the heist in Nanaimo that made our fortune. Bill's belief in our invulnerability back then had been contagious and it had all felt like an adventure. He was at his peak of experience and cunning and that's how I wanted to remember him. When I had finished the journal, I laid sheets on the furniture and closed up my house. As I opened the door to leave, I paused on the threshold when I heard a scrabbling in the shrubbery by the porch. From my experience hiking in the mountains, I knew it was the largest and most dangerous animals that make the least noise. Perhaps my haste to investigate was rash because even in the city, cougars had been known to stalk people. I thrashed through the salal but found nothing and no one. Despite that, when I lay awake in the barracks, I imagined vicious creatures prowling around my house, trying to find secret entrances.

I thought I was developing an ulcer but nonetheless I was eager each day to get to work. We were very close to cracking the complete JN-25 and our success was crucial because the Allied soldiers were doing badly. After Japan's furious advance this winter, the British had lost most of their holdings in the Pacific and withdrawn their troops to the European theatre. It was shocking. It was Britain's worst naval defeat in centuries—which also left Canada's Pacific flank exposed, and here I was standing on it. The Americans, and to some extent the plucky Australians, were still patrolling this ocean but we were not their priority. The Canadian government was mobilizing a new regiment here at the base, though no one would reveal where they were going to fight. To soothe the public, the government had also created the Militia Rangers to patrol the home coast, but I had little faith in these old men and back-woods boys who weren't fit to serve overseas. Canada's size was overwhelming. A thousand Japanese troops could hide in a single mountain valley and we'd never notice them unless they went to the Empress Hotel downtown for tea. It was all very well for the Brits, on their little island in the Atlantic, to forget about us halfway round the world. Yet for the English king our young men were pouring out their blood on European ground that they had never seen before in their lives.

I ducked my head as I descended the steps into the bunker—I had hit the low door frame a number of times in my distracted state—and my eyes adjusted to the stuttering artificial light. There was a dreadful roar now that we'd acquired an IBM tabulating machine. The Captain had spent months haranguing the Prime Minister himself to get it. The machine took up an entire room but it could sort messages in one day that would have taken weeks for the clerical staff to do. It aided our decoding to discover recurring patterns in the messages as soon as possible. Then we could focus our efforts on finding the foolish errors people made. This was the most dependable thing in our work. Every advance we made we sent to the Americans as per our agreement, though we were damn well certain they were not doing us the same courtesy.

I sat down at my desk and smack in the middle of it was an unfinished crossword from the *Times of London*, evidently left by the man on the previous shift. What was he doing, wasting his time like that? As I put it in the bottom drawer, I remembered how I had loved to do the crossword with my father; we would read the clues out loud to each other. It had been excellent training for codebreaking, but it held little appeal now, being too similar to the work we did. Since the puzzle was in English and had proper clues, it would be child's play. Perhaps it would be soothing after all, especially if I could fill in the answers the last fellow had missed. I opened the drawer, tore the page out and put it in my jacket pocket.

I opened the blue folder to read the day's Magic Summary. It showed an increase in the amount of Japanese traffic, which suggested their campaign was ramping up. We still had no idea of the important details, because they had an extra level of code on the place names and dates that we had yet to strip off. This was what I applied myself to. I felt the pain in my stomach like a bullet hole. Something was going to happen in the Pacific soon, and we needed to know where and when or all the rest of our work was useless. The death toll in the Pacific had been horrible this winter, when the Allies lost Hong Kong, Singapore, Guam, Sumatra, the Philippines, and downward to all the small islands I had never heard of before. The Examination Unit had not properly foreseen the attacks, and I felt each loss of life as a personal failure.

I pushed my chair away from my desk and walked down the corridor to the file room. Josie, one of the new British Wrens, rushed over to reception and saluted. I was glad it was not Montague on duty. At my request for five files Josie disappeared among the rows of steel cabinets. She had a quick mind—she didn't need to look anything up. With her pug nose and stocky arms, I could imagine her selling fish on the piers. Her opposite number was Madeleine, who had soft, milky hands and a polished accent. She was quite happy to let Josie do all the work, but if you button-holed her, she was also capable. Evaluating the girls for war duties was perhaps the most egalitarian thing the Brits had ever done. They needed a certain kind of organizing aptitude and they'd take it where it came. But the girls they sent us for codebreaking were from Oxford or Cambridge and lorded their qualifications over us all.

Josie returned with the five files, making the big pile look easy to manage with her fishmonger arms, and she grinned at me from behind the stack. I smiled back at her faintly as I held out my hands for the load. Josie had an inclination for chitchat that I regrettably couldn't share—the clerical girls did not understand the stress we were under. From a past encounter I knew that Josie was one of our Communists, a piece of information she'd have done better to keep to herself. But Reds were persistent as Christian missionaries, always hoping for converts in unwelcoming lands. She stacked the folders onto my arms, and I moved as quickly as I could under their weight because I was eager to get back to my desk.

In a dream last night I had envisioned the breakthrough for the substitution cipher. I had been in Alaska and a Tlinkit man, wearing both a priest's robe and a transformation mask, had inscribed some figures in the snow where we stood near the frozen seashore. E 43:24. His mask was a beautiful thunderbird, and the beak opened to reveal the false face; I had the strange sensation that it was myself underneath. When I awoke I knew what the number was from: Ecclesiasticus 43:24. My years of Sunday school had apparently left their residue. I climbed quietly out of bed and opened the bedside drawer belonging to the girl next to me. She had a Bible stowed there, which I saw her reading at night. Sitting back on my bunk near the window with the moonlight streaming in, I flipped through the pages until I found what I wanted. "They that sail on the sea tell of danger thereof; And when we hear it with our ears, we marvel."

The files on top were starting to slide off my pile so I was relieved when I arrived safely at my desk and thunked them down. I got lost in them and next I looked at the clock, five hours had gone by. I was hungry, but that did not matter. I had solved the cipher from my dream, though it was so out of character for the Japanese I could hardly believe it was true. Usually they worked from randomized tables or numeric substitutions created by their Purple machine. This was a book code, in which numbers reference a page and line, and the letters found there spell out the message. In this case the book was the King James Bible. My five hours of cross-checking dates from old messages confirmed my five seconds of inspiration—they matched events that had actually occurred. Soon I had found two new dates for the Japanese attacks—June 3 and June 4. That was only two weeks from now. I had also found two sets of letters, AO and MI. These location indicators were surely correct, as they had in the past followed the same substitution code as the dates. The only thing left to do was confirm what places the Japanese meant by the two letters.

I had to tell the Captain. Rushing down the hall toward his office, I collided with Lieutenant Hughes. He laughed at me, grabbing my arms.

"Sorry, I didn't see you there," I said.

"I don't usually have that problem, being kind of a beanpole. Where are you off to in such a hurry?"

"Nowhere," I said, not wanting to share my hunches with him. I wished he would let go of my arms. I didn't need this distraction now. All I could think of was my arms—it felt as though all my nerves were concentrated where his hands touched me. I looked up at his face, annoyed.

There was a dark circle under one of his eyes. A black eye, I realized, fresh. I was satisfied to change the subject to one that might be uncomfortable to him. "Were you in a fight?"

"Yes," he laughed easily. "I'm a little impetuous. This is a poor introduction, since we haven't been officially introduced. I'm Link, by the way."

"Lena," I said, hesitating before shaking the hand he offered. "Was it about women or politics?" I asked.

"You don't think it could be sports?"

"I don't see you as someone to fight about that."

"It was about women, then," he said.

I felt vaguely disappointed, but held myself back from asking anything further. It would have been more worthy of him to fight about politics. I liked people with convictions. "I need to speak to the Captain, so I'd better go."

Feeling that Link was staring at my back, I was glad to round the corner. I knocked on the Captain's half-closed door, but pushed it open before I heard his reply.

"My dear, you're hyperventilating," the Captain said. "What is it?" He reclined with his slippered feet on his desk and crisscrossed his fingers together behind his head.

"The JN-25 date cipher—I've got it. The Japanese will attack on June 4, at MI, I believe that's Midway Island, near Hawaii. Before that another attack, June 3, but it looks like a diversion. It's directed at AO, but I'm less sure what that stands for. Aotearoa, the North Island of New Zealand?"

"Hm," he said, annoyingly noncommittal. "And how'd you get that?"

I hesitated. "It's peculiar, I know. But they used a book code. It's based on the Bible."

"The Japs are Buddhist or Shinto. Why'd they use the Bible?"

"Maybe it's so counterintuitive, they thought we'd never guess it."

"Well, that must be it. That's the same dates the Americans got."

"The Americans had it already? Why didn't you tell us? It could have saved weeks of work!"

"They needed independent confirmation. And they don't know AO either, so I'll pass on your supposition. But good job. I should say, hip hip hooray." He opened his desk drawer and pulled out a bottle of cognac, and poured two drams into his flowered teacups. He held one out to me and it looked impossibly fragile in his big hand. I attempted to transform my giggle into a cough. I took a few deep breaths before I spoke to compose myself—the Captain liked to think he was a serious authority figure in our minds.

"But I still have three hours left on my shift."

"Take the rest of the day off, I'd like you to rest your noggin. It's going to be a bloody madhouse in the next couple of weeks with those attacks coming."

I took a gulp of the cognac and it burned pleasantly. The Captain always had the best of everything, straight down to his shoes, when he wore them. They were made by the King's cobbler in London. "Say, do you know anything about the new fellow?"

"Which one?"

It was difficult to say his name, somehow. "Hughes."

"Want me to give him the afternoon off as well?"

He winked and I felt my face grow hot. "No."

"I'm just teasing, my dear. I wouldn't want to encourage anyone to break the rules about fraternizing." He paused to sip his cognac. "Hughes seems a good sort. He comes out for drinks with the lads sometimes, makes us laugh. He's from Toronto. His father ran some kind of business, import export, though I never know what that's supposed to mean. Hughes isn't quiet, but I know very little about him when I think of it. Funny that, how people in this line of work don't give a lot away. He's as secretive as you are."

"I'm not secretive. I'm just not very interesting. You know my father was a mailman."

I left the Captain's office angry with myself for awakening his curiosity with my misplaced question. There were more serious things to think about anyhow. The Pacific front was heading for some kind of crisis, that much was clear. I slotted the decoded papers into the cubbies that lined the hall for the clerks to deal with. It was peculiar how the blood spilled in war necessitated an equal torrent of words. I'd always thought of death as silent and secret but it was voluble as the dictionary itself.

I returned to my desk to double check it was cleared off, and I caught Link giving me a quizzical look. No doubt he wondered why I was leaving early, but I just shrugged. I had no wish to fraternize, as the Captain put it. Despite my success I didn't feel like talking to him or anyone. I didn't need credit for anything I had done. I just did what I thought I had to do in each moment. But I felt oddly hollow, like a vessel through which events merely flowed.

I jammed my hands into my pockets and tucked my chin into my collar as I opened the door to leave the bunker. To clear my head, I walked against the wind as I circled the rocky perimeter of the base, which was more like an island because it had only a thin connection to the rest of the Esquimalt peninsula. I looked west to confirm that no Japanese battleships, planes or submarines were within sight of shore. Seeing nothing, I wandered over to the bustle of the First Graving Dock, where men swarmed over an aircraft carrier being refitted for duty. There was a large hole in the hull that the welders busied themselves with. I didn't care to think how it had got there or what lives might have been lost when it was made, so I kept walking.

## CHAPTER TEN

# APRIL 1932

THE REST OF the getaway went without a hitch. We found the Chinaman, his shack raised on stilts in the slough and remote from any other soul. Bill asked for a boat, handed him a hundred dollars, and he guided us along his dock without speaking a word. The dory sat low in the water with all of us in it but it had a good engine and the Hood Canal was sheltered so we had no trouble making progress. We landed the dory at the wrong stretch of shore the first time and Cruickshank looked sheepish; but once we were settled in his lodge I told myself no one would find us here since even Cruickshank himself got lost. I don't know why he called it a ranch except that he was from Montana originally—nothing to do with cattle went on there. The building looked more like a hunting lodge and was shoved into the forest away from shore. The lodge was surprisingly beautiful inside, with soaring timber beams, manful displays of deer antlers and a snarling mountain lion head arrayed on the walls. Bill made us sit tight at the ranch for three weeks, which made me feel claustrophobic, but at least there was a billiard table and we were well kitted with good food and drink, including more French champagne.

Cruickshank had a fast boat stowed there and we made good time to Seattle at last. Though I was nervous to be seen in public, we would only go to the speakeasies and I comforted myself that no law-abiding citizen would disport himself at these places—though I could not ignore the idea of stool pigeons. I told myself to relax and quit looking over my shoulder when Bill spent a day, with just me, visiting his favourite tailor and haberdasher. He said that none of the other men appreciated quality the way I could, and he had me fitted up with new outfits as well as himself. He tried to convince me to wear the broad-patterned cravats he was buying but I drew the line there. I could imagine the field day Ramon would have if he thought I was aping Bill. But at least I wouldn't be seeing Ramon for a while. Bill had suggested the gang disperse for now so we did not attract attention, though in truth he loved to be the centre of every room, especially with Lena on his arm. I was pleased I was the one chosen to remain with them. The first time I saw Lena all dressed up, when the three of us went out together to the So Different, I drew in my breath. No one else in the crowded room could compare to her. She wore a floor-length silk dress that draped over her curves. Her whole back was revealed, and when I helped her into her seat I could not help but brush her skin.

"You look a little pale, By God, like you could use a drink," Bill said.

"Surely," I said, injecting bluster into my tone and willing colour into my cheeks.

Bill thrust out his arm to detain a waiter. The man looked annoyed until he realized who Bill was and turned all smooth and deferential. Bill ordered three double bourbons.

"That's a bit much for me," Lena said.

"Who said any of it was for you?" Bill said, a shark-like grin coming over him that did not bode well. "So what'll you have then? Don't spoil this."

"I'd like some caviar. I've never had any before."

Bill laughed and gripped her around the shoulders. "That's the spirit, honeylamb." He gave her a shake and when he removed his arm there were white marks where his fingers had pressed. He didn't understand how delicate Lena was. A rage came over me that I'd never felt in my life, but I tamped it down. Meanwhile Bill had summoned the waiter again to make Lena's request, but he said they did not have any caviar and Bill stood up so suddenly he nearly flipped over our table.

"Let's get the fuck out of here and go somewhere with class, like the Bergonian," he said.

"Bill," I said, soothing, "Bill. You know what we talked about. We're not going out to those places right now." My cowardice of being caught made me paradoxically brave enough to stand up to him. "I like it here. Why don't we send someone out to get the caviar?"

"Good idea." He sat down, complacent now, but shot the waiter a black look before speaking to the man again. "Why didn't you think of that? Tell Mahone to come over here."

The waiter wrung his hands but darted off to do what he was told. Mahone was the owner of the speakeasy and a thug through and through. I didn't relish him spending any time at our table. Soon the crowd parted before Mahone to make way for his majestic mass. He greeted us with the innocent smile of the truly deranged. I was nervous until he left but he left happy because Bill said he'd buy a round for everybody in the place.

"You sure you want to do that?" I asked. "That's a lot of dough to spend on these lowlifes."

"Amigo, this is the time to share our good fortune," Bill said. I wondered if his use of "amigo" was to remind me he could replace my company with Ramon's if I was too much of a wet blanket. "Deserving or not deserving, I like to make people happy. Who are we to judge?"

Lena squeezed his hand and I rued my narrow mind.

Mahone stood up on a chair—I was surprised he could manage it but he rose smoothly as a Zeppelin—and the room went silent. A large pistol was visible on a holster around his sizeable waist, so perhaps people were concerned. But when he announced the free drinks and pointed to our table, everybody cheered and clapped. I couldn't help calculating in my head how much that would cost—certainly hundreds of dollars. Bill could have bought a car for that price. But the caviar appeared within ten minutes and Lena nibbled it with delight. She said she could eat it breakfast, lunch and dinner from now on, and Bill said, "For you Lena, anything." They kissed and made a spectacle of themselves but they didn't seem to care.

Throughout the evening, people came over to speak to Bill and pat him on the back. If they weren't already his friend they made sure to become so. I sat there pretty quietly, drinking double bourbons. There was a band playing music that must have been jolly, because people got up and danced.

Bill insisted we were in the clear, and he pushed for our debut in "high-class environs." He was fixed on going to the restaurant at the Bergonian Hotel, so finally we gave in to him. This required a new round of shopping, and he presented Lena with a diamond bracelet that made her gasp. Bill seemed set on burning through his money—though as leader he had a bigger pile than the rest of us, so it would take him a good long while.

Just as Lena shone above everyone at the speakeasy, it was the same at the Bergonian. The rich ladies were nothing to her. I stole a look at her sideways with pride and wonder as we three entered the restaurant, with Lena between us, and she took my arm as well as Bill's. All the men looked up from their dinners, their forks suspended in the air. Their overwrought wives were like fussy poodles, yipping to regain attention. After the maître d' sat us, we ordered sirloin steaks. Even Lena wanted one—she could eat as good as a man. However, as we waited for the food to arrive, we became fidgety sitting on the Moroccan leather chairs. Perhaps it was because we had no alcohol—we'd grown used to it at the So Different. I was becoming an accomplished drinker.

Bill spotted an underworld pal across the room and, after he nodded at him invitingly, the man came over. I sank into my chair with embarrassment—the man's swagger was conspicuous as a pirate's. Why did Bill insist on his "high-class environs" and then associate with such trash? The man leaned in confidentially, muttered in Bill's ear and pressed something into his hand before returning to his table. Soon afterwards, Bill got up and told me to follow him. We went into the washroom, which had a private lounge. On top of the black granite counter Bill poured out some white powder. He pulled a silver cigarette case from his pocket and used it to push the powder into two stripes.

"Take a whiff of this, it'll knock your socks off," he said. He plugged one nostril, leaned down and breathed it in like snuff. His shoulders twitched and then he stood up straight, grinning.

I hesitated but then asked myself, why do I always hesitate? It was a trait no one admired. So I did as he illustrated with the other pile.

"That burns," I said.

"And? Anything else?"

"Not really." But then something *was* happening: an electric current shot up to my brain. "Hold on, wait a minute. Wow."

"What I tell you?" He slapped me on the back. "Let's go out there and show them what's what. You and me, we're in this together, By God."

As we re-entered the dining room my eyes were dazzled by the multitude of crystal chandeliers. How had I not noticed this before? And the music the orchestra was playing—while before it had struck me as fusty background noise, now the notes flowed through me like quicksilver.

"What took you boys so long?" Lena put down her fork with a clatter, and I saw she was almost done with her steak.

Bill and I exchanged glances and I suppressed a laugh, cutting into my steak to divert myself. I put a piece in my mouth but the meat was cold now, oozing blood, and suddenly I didn't feel like finishing it.

"Fucking fat rich people," Bill said, staring about the room. "All they do is eat, eat, eat, talk, talk, talk."

"Well, I enjoyed my meal, except that I ate half of it alone," Lena said in a low voice. Bill, I thought, watch yourself.

"I'm back now, honeylamb. How's about we dance?"

She didn't answer but she took the arm he offered, and he escorted her onto the floor where a few couples were already dancing. As he weaved between them, I marvelled at his grace; I'd never seen him dance before, because at the speakeasy we were always too busy drinking to bother. Yet why should I be surprised to find him with one more superior accomplishment? After a couple of songs they returned to the table, Lena breathless and laughing, her eyes sparkling. I supposed it was the drugs that ignited the heavenly chorus in my head—Lena, lovely Lena, forever and ever coming back to me, amen.

"You see Bill out there? He was amazing."

"May I have the honour?" I asked. For once I would do as I wanted and not look to Bill for permission. I was electric with the thought: I could take on the world.

"You don't mind, Bill?" she said.

He waved his hand dismissively, an impatient but fair god. Lightly I guided Lena's elbow until we reached the floor, which was more crowded now; then I clasped her in my arms and felt the warmth of her body against mine. I believed I could die then, happy, to the strains of "Blue Danube." We whirled around the floor, the chandeliers above us sparkling and refracting in Lena's eyes. I was thinking how, after all, I wasn't such a bad dancer, when the waltz was suddenly over. She was heading back to the table so I followed her, reluctantly.

"That was fun, but I'm beat now," she said as we sat down.

"You'll need to pep up," Bill said. "We're going to the speakeasy next. Got some business with Washtub."

She sighed. "It's going to seem like a dump after this place."

"The high and mighty shall fall," he said, his tone righteous and loud as a street preacher's. At the surrounding tables, heads turned.

She glared at him as she snapped shut her purse. "What is wrong with you?"

"It's all right, Lena," I said. "Won't it be nice to have a drink?"

"I guess so." She offered her arm to me and turned her back on Bill. He followed us out of the room like a chastised puppy, or at least that's how I imagined it. I could get used to this triumphant feeling.

## CHAPTER ELEVEN

# THE SECRECY DIRECTIVE

AS I FOLLOWED the shoreline away from the barracks, the hazy afternoon sun sinking in the sky, I waved to the sentry from a distance. He didn't need to watch me, since I had no plans to leave. I wanted to stay away from the rest of the world. I wished the Captain had not given me this break because it left me too much time to think. I'd gotten cold during my walk and when I retrieved my jacket, I'd seen something that shocked me to the core. On Montague's bedside table across from mine there was a newspaper folded open with an article circled. They had set the date of Bill's hanging: June 23. It was only a month away.

In Byron's journal, Bill had sounded like a tyrant from near the beginning, but that was not how it seemed then. During that golden period after the big job I remembered laughing a lot and Bill being at the centre of everything. Byron's observations made me feel I should have seen Bill's dark side much sooner than I did. He certainly wasn't ordinary, or restful, but I thought then that there would be plenty of time to rest when I was dead. I had learned that from my father, who had lived quiet and friendless despite his kind heart—until his heart ceased to beat. What mark had he made on the world? Bill, on the other hand, lived with gusto. People loved him for that and, I had thought, Byron most of all. Why didn't Byron write more of Bill's generosity? Like the time we were walking down the street and an old woman begged for change, but Bill insisted I give her my fur coat instead. I took it off wordlessly, enraged, but then the next thing we did was take a cab to Salvator P. Trippy's salon and Bill bought me an extravagant full-length ermine. His charity was random, but so was everything he did, and for a while that was heady and addictive.

I walked over some smooth rocks near the surf and leaned down, my eyes drawn by the bright colours there. In a little pool there was a purple blob, its tendrils waving in the underwater currents. Curious, I poked it. The translucent strands closed around my finger and I snatched my hand away. Strangely detached, I tried to remember if such creatures were poisonous; I thought not.

It kept bothering me, what Byron had written about Bill having a child. I had never heard that. I think Byron must have been mistaken, and the woman herself wrong or a liar as Bill said. I did not think he would abandon a child. After we'd been together a while he'd wanted us to have one, but I told him I was too young and needed to live first. He had grown angry and said, "Of course, don't be a damn fool. I meant when these days are behind us. This ain't no family life." Something in my soul was frightened at the thought of him as a father, but I did not know it then.

Of course Bill had to introduce Byron to cocaine. Since Byron was always jittery around me, I hadn't noticed the difference in his behaviour when it started. I suppose that's how he got the nerve to ask me to dance that night at the Bergonian—I'd forgotten about that. All I had remembered was Bill, so excited that we were finally going to the hotel ballroom, where he could live the glittering life he had dreamed of when he was a kid on the streets. It was disappointing to learn the experience had been hijacked by drugs. Could it be that Bill was uneasy in that aristocratic setting?

I didn't think they used coke too much, at first, though it was hard to tell with Bill because he was by nature so erratic. I was surprised that Byron tried it. He seemed to have a stronger moral compass than the others in the gang, but Bill could put anyone under his sway. After all, he'd turned Cruickshank from a cop into a criminal, and myself from a bank teller into a robber. We had been like coins spinning on edge, two possible faces, but Bill tipped us over. At the So Different, everyone came by our table to see him, and Bill made private loans to anyone who asked. He never kept track, either. For someone whose passion was gathering money, he kept no accounting of it.

I stood up from the tidal pool and stared out to sea. The sky hung low over it, glowering with dark clouds. The whole scene looked empty and desolate. But in my mind the ocean was a teeming place, full of enemy ships whose communications crowded the ether. While I knew the Japanese Combined Fleet was thousands of miles away, I was plagued by the fear of submarines. The Germans had made some hits on the Atlantic coast and the Japs could do the same here. If a submarine came near to shore, we'd never know until it raised its periscope, and then it would be too late.

I turned my back on the endless horizon that led to Japan and walked back toward the barracks, kicking rocks as I went. Returning past the First Graving Dock, I paused as a figure loped toward me. It was an old man, grizzled, in Navy whites; despite his advanced years he had only a single chevron on his sleeve, Able Seaman. "Ma'am," he said in a hoarse voice. "You Lena Stillman?"

I nodded.

"I got something for you."

He handed me a sealed envelope, and I knew immediately who it was from.

"What's it about?" I said, hearing the exhaustion in my voice.

He shrugged. "I'm like an old treasure chest, sealed tight at the bottom of the sea." He kept standing there, grinning at me. It seemed strange to offer him money, but was that what he was waiting for?

"Can I do anything for you?" I asked faintly.

"No, ma'am. I was only told to see you read it."

I didn't know what else to do but comply, so I opened the envelope.

That shaky hand. The writing did not follow any line across the page, but shot out in a wild diagonal.

You're worthless as everybody else. One day you'll end up the same as me.

I couldn't stop shivering now that the wind had gotten so cold. What did Bill mean? That I'd end up in jail? Surely he wasn't planning to rat me out now. Ramon's Spanish came to me: *venganza*. Revenge. Perhaps Bill still had a taste for it even in his last days. I could see him in his cell, immoveable as the Sphinx; around him flowed years, decades, it could be centuries even, but he would be unyielding.

I carefully folded the paper and put it in the envelope, and then into my pocket. Perhaps, I thought suddenly, these will be his last words to me. Yet I knew I would destroy this message at my first chance. I smiled, calm and steady I hoped, at the sailor. "You have seen me read it. May I ask your name?"

"Shively." The horrid little man saluted and scurried off. I watched him return to the First Graving Dock until he was lost in the crowds there. I would watch for Shively's name on the lists of those lost at sea.

THE EXAMINATION UNIT was in an uproar. Eight days before the invasion of Midway and the still-unknown location, the Japanese changed the JN-25 code. We were assigned more shifts and the Navy issued us with amphetamines to stay alert, but after what I had seen of other drugs I wanted no part of them. I restricted myself to coffee, though I must have drunk a cup an hour. I had a pain near my heart and sometimes thought vaguely of asking the doctor if it was an ulcer as I feared, but so far I was too busy. I think the Captain was a little liberal with his pill ration; I had never seen him with such energy. He paced up and down the hall, smoking his pipe endlessly. I don't know if Link took the amphetamines, but I don't think so. He looked more tired than the others, though it was hard to see his desk clearly through the cigarette haze that permeated the bunker.

The Japanese had altered the JN-25 twice before in the war, just before they launched a big offensive. If this latest switch was standard procedure, they would create the new version with the Purple machine. This would not disturb us because now we had a copy of the machine. If they had discovered this fact, it would be disastrous, because they would invent a new one and we'd be back to square one. We'd never catch up before the attack.

A hand thwacked another sheet of paper on top of the ones I'd been studying and I looked up in annoyance. But when I realized it was the Captain, I smiled.

"Cat's already left the barn on this one, but here's the latest directive from High Command," he said, pattering a nervous drumbeat on his thigh.

"Horse, you mean?"

"Aren't there cats in the barn also, catching the mice? Let's not split hairs, my dear, just read it."

DO NOT TALK AT MEALS, DO NOT TALK IN THE TRANSPORT, DO NOT TALK TRAVELLING, BE CAREFUL EVEN IN YOUR HUT. DO NOT TALK BY YOUR OWN FIRESIDE.

"DO THEY THINK someone leaked our progress with the code, and that's why the Japs changed it?" I asked.

"Frankly, I don't believe High Command thinks at all. Just a reinforcement of necessary caution."

I continued scanning the document. "'If one day invasion came, Nazi brutality might stop at nothing to wring from those you care for secrets that you would give anything, then, to have saved them from knowing. Their only safety will lie in continued ignorance of your work.' A Nazi invasion, in Canada?"

"Anything's possible," he said. "But even if they took the East Coast, they'd have a devil of a time getting this far. Just like in Russia—they haven't captured Moscow yet. But this is a national directive, and as usual they've forgotten about us in the west. They left out the Japanese threat. I've heard some harrowing stories about how they treat their prisoners." He glanced at me. "Don't worry, my dear, the Americans stand between us and them."

"There's a lot of empty sea between each carrier group. The Japanese subs can always get through."

"Well, that's what we're here for. To find them."

I sighed and he patted my head, then snatched the paper off my desk and waved it in the air. "Only one copy, and I've got to eat it after you lot have seen it." As he zipped over to Link's desk, I wondered if he was actually serious. I watched Link read the directive, his brow furrowed, until he noticed me and I looked down, embarrassed.

I focused once more on my page of letter groups, searching for repetitions. Like the word *okosoto*, full stop. Careless operators used it too many times in one message, especially if they had to spell out words adopted from Chinese in *kana* characters. When I didn't detect it, I flipped through my stack again. My favourite was the repetition of an entire message after the short imperative, "Your message is indecipherable, please repeat." That was a good crib into the code—but so far I hadn't seen it. I lit a cigarette. I'd taken up the habit only a few months ago, after Pearl Harbor put more pressure on our work. On the dog shift just before sunrise, an enlisted man offered me a "tickler," one of their hand-rolled cigarettes, and I took it. With everyone else smoking in the windowless bunker and me breathing it in all day anyhow, why not? It was a relief to have something to do with my hands after sitting in the same place for hours on end. Though since that first time, I used my officer's ration to get proper factory-made ones. I breathed the smoke into my lungs and was grateful as an alert calm suffused me. I needed it—I hadn't felt like myself since that message from Bill.

Stubbing out my cigarette, I went through my papers once more, now hoping for a short cable; it could very well be "Quiet night. Nothing to report." I spent my days pondering things of little consequence that in the end could mean a great deal.

CHAPTER TWELVE

# MAY 1932

"I'M SICK OF sitting around," Bill said. "It's time we called the gang together."

We were in the Claremont Hotel, where he had summoned me into the sitting room of his suite. It was all white and gold with antique French sofas and mirrors, just how I imagined the Palace of Versailles would be. Lena looked just right here. We'd been staying at the Claremont since last week, when Bill thought it was safe to leave the Panama, the shadier hotel we'd been lodged in. I'd said I was fine there, but Bill insisted I come with them and got me an adjoining room. So we didn't have to traipse about the halls, he said. But I wasn't pleased with this arrangement, as the walls were not so thick as one might hope.

"I thought we were having a good time, hon," Lena said, caressing his neck. She was in a silk kimono and sat close beside him on a loveseat, while I was across from them, leaning my chair against the wall. "Going out to the Bergonian and all, just like you wanted."

He shrugged. "Dreams pale when they come true, sometimes. You ever noticed that, By God?"

96

"No," I said, startled to be addressed on this point. I'd never expected dreams I had to come true. But when I thought about it, this time with Bill was kind of like a dream in its entirety, and the most exciting thing I'd ever known.

"Well they do, and that's a fact," he said, scowling and crossing his arms. "You'll learn that soon enough, when you've had more of life like me."

"I'm sure you're right, Bill. I didn't dream too big before I met you."

"You were just a pencil pusher until I saved you from that boredom," he said. "You ever been bored since you met me?"

"Never."

"And you, Lena?"

"Never, Bill."

He smiled at us now, like a proud teacher at his pupils. "So we need a new plan, to keep ourselves in that blissful state. I've been scoping out the First National Bank."

"Bill, really," Lena said. "After all we went through on the Nanaimo job? Shouldn't we lie low?"

"It's just a little something to keep us sharp."

Lena and I exchanged worried glances. Neither of us said anything more to oppose him, but I was ecstatic that our wills were aligned against Bill. I suppressed such a traitorous thought.

"By God, here's the addresses where the boys are." He scrawled on a piece of paper in his shaky hand and passed it to me. "Round them up, and have them meet us at the So Different at eleven o'clock tonight. That'll give us time to have a nice dinner at the Arctic Club before we dirty our hands with them."

"What should I do?" Lena asked.

"Just make yourself pretty."

She stood up abruptly, her face red. "It would be nice to be taken seriously for once." She stomped into their room and slammed the door.

"Women," Bill said, shrugging. He opened the humidor on the coffee table and lit up a cigar. "Want one?"

"Naw, thanks." I studied the paper he'd given me. "I'd better start finding the gang. Looks like they're all over town, so it could take a while."

"Right-o," he said, and I could have sworn there was a trace of an English accent to it. As I left he was puffing away contentedly, a plume of smoke about his head.

THE THREE OF us were waiting in the back room of the So Different, which Mahone was letting us use until midnight when the poker game started. Bill and I had ditched the tuxedos we'd worn to the Arctic Club restaurant and put on regular chumps' clothes, though Lena kept her ermine on because she was cold, she said. It looked so soft I wanted to reach over and touch it, but of course I'd never dare. Lena and I were seated at the card table with a space between us where Bill had been; his legs were all twitchy "with a damnable impatience," he said, so he stood at the door to greet the new arrivals. He grinned and clapped them on the back in turn. He led each man to a chair, putting Ramon beside me and I gave him a quick half-smile. Why did I bother? He just stared at me like an oaf. Once we were all settled, Bill contemplated us with the satisfaction of a collector regarding unusual specimens. "So? News?"

No one spoke while Moe looked at Ramon, wringing his hands.

"Out with it," Bill said.

"Was a copper sniffing around our hotel," Moe said. He and Ramon were staying in one of Seattle's worst dives, the Gold Rush. It was the underbelly opposite of where I had just dined, the private Arctic Club with its stained-glass dome glittering like the roof of heaven. Funny that the worst and the best should be named after the same thing—men's lust for fortune in Alaska, the greed that launched Seattle. Money could do unpredictable things to men's souls.

Moe cleared his throat. "He was asking for William Gladstone."

My eyes must have bugged straight out of my head when he said that. William Gladstone was the alias Bill had used at the hotel in Victoria right before the Nanaimo job.

"Good thing the clerk kept his mouth shut, or I'd have put a shiv in him," Ramon said, making a twisting gesture with his good arm.

"Luckily William Gladstone never checked into the Gold Rush," Bill said. He was staring up at the ceiling as though it were the sky and a source of weather that could give him a forecast of what was to come. "What did the cop look like?"

"Medium height, medium brown hair, skinny as a scarecrow," Moe said.

Cruickshank stubbed out his cigarillo. "That must be Detective Brooke. Damn his boots."

"Who's that?" Lena asked, running her hands up and down the chain of her purse. I hadn't noticed her get up but she was standing a little apart from us now, near the door.

"Hiram Ulysses Brooke. The *second*," Bill said, a strange look of satisfaction on his face. "Fancies himself a real Sherlock, that one."

"This sounds bad," Lena said. "Shouldn't we cancel the new plan?"

"Why is the *chica* part of this meeting anyhow?" Ramon said.

Bill gave him an acid look. "I thought everyone knew that's how it is." He glanced at Lena as if for approval but she was staring off somewhere else. "If you don't like it, you can go," he said. Ramon gripped the edge of the poker table as though to raise himself, but he stayed seated. "Moving on. To address my dear lady's concern— old Brooke only asked about William Gladstone, not Bill Bagley. He's five steps behind us. I'm not worried. He's never been able to pin anything on me."

"He gave us a little trouble in California," Ramon said.

"Look at it the other way. We gave *him* trouble."

"But it seems he didn't learn his lesson. I would like to teach him good this time." Ramon rubbed the hook on his false arm and grinned.

"Okay, Ramon. But we're here to talk about the job I thought up, a real easy one."

As he explained his scheme for First National, around the table the men stayed silent. Bill's words skittered around and his sentences went in circles, ending where they began. But Bill had always led us right before. I was ready to follow him into battle because he was my general.

Then Lena spoke up.

"I'm worried about this idea of going in all blazes when we are becoming well known to the public and the police," she said, moving from where she was standing by the door to sit by Ramon, of all people.

"Remember that I worked in a bank. These people are easily lulled by routine. We should obtain blank cheques from another bank, and write the order for the holdup on it, so there is no chance to raise an alarm until the last minute. I'll go in with Ramon, as though we are a couple, so we don't raise suspicions. He will have the gun." She caressed his good arm.

"Now I am liking the *chica*. I can be the lead man." He grinned.

"Ramon and you?" Bill grit his teeth. I wished I was sitting beside Lena so I could protect her from Bill if need be. He had an animal rage in his eyes.

"Also, we should hire some people—Bill, of course you know best who can be trusted," she said calmly, placating him, "and they can stand outside the bank to give false accounts of us to the police."

The rest of the men were silent, but I sensed they were leaning toward Lena's idea. Bill's scheme had not had all its usual details—it was in fact as full of holes as his tax returns were before I worked on them. He had perhaps overdone the cocaine, I thought, and surely I was not the only one who had noticed Bill's jitterings.

"I'll keep the car running outside," I said, not looking at Bill.

"Well then, it's all settled," Bill said, rubbing his hands together, as though his authority had not been sidelined. "I knew you'd all like this First National job."

Mahone came into the room and whispered to Bill, and Bill announced it was time for us to bust up and let the poker players in. "Though personally, I'm going to stay. I feel an urge to gamble.

Anyone?" Some of the boys stayed with him, while myself, Moe and Lena left. I let Moe get ahead of us in the noisy club before daring to lean in close to Lena. Her perfume was heady, like Oriental flowers, I thought.

"Things are changing, aren't they," I said. "You've never gone against one of Bill's plans before."

"Neither have you, Byron. Maybe we're finding our independence at last."

## CHAPTER THIRTEEN

# HIGH ALERT

THE RADIOS HAD been silent for twenty-five hours. We expected the Japanese attack at any moment, and we still didn't know where AO was. The tension was terrible and one of the codebreakers, the quiet man named Olson, had snapped. He stood in the main hallway of the bunker crying and raving, so incongruous in his pinstripe suit. The military police came for him, and the rest of us followed silently to the surface and watched the policemen grip Olson's arms as he thrashed. I blinked in the bright sunlight; I'd forgotten it was afternoon. Link whispered to me that the man drank an entire fifth of Scotch every day. He'd once caught Olson sneaking out of the barracks with a pile of empty bottles in his arms. It helped him work, Olson had explained. I wondered if the Captain knew about that. I recalled how Olson always muttered to himself as he paced the corridors, but most codebreakers were unusual in one way or another. The policemen shoved Olson to the back of a van and drove away. I wondered where they would take him—an asylum, I supposed. There was such a thin line between genius and madness. A line that never existed for Bill, which I should have seen.

A Wren popped out of the bunker and ran toward us, breathing heavily. "The Japanese are attacking. Radio intercept has got them, they're bombing Alaska. The Aleutian Islands. The Captain needs you back inside."

Alaska—that meant we were the closest signals intelligence unit to the front line. As we rushed to our stations, the sigint bunker's steel door clanged shut behind us. But my frenzy for action was soon stalled. At my desk was still the same pile of papers as before, and they were now useless. I wished I was on radio intercept, with access to the raw information the moment it came in.

Link flopped into the desk beside mine and held his head in his hands. "I can't believe we didn't get it. It's so obvious if you think how they transliterate into romaji. AO was from AR-OO-SHAN. God, I hope the generals had other intel. My brother's in the Navy. The real Navy, not like us. I wonder where he is right now."

"I didn't know you had family serving." He looked so worried I wanted to go over to him, but I didn't know what I would do when I got there.

"My wife does too."

"Oh." My head felt peculiar and I gripped the arms of my chair to stay steady. I'd been working too hard lately.

"I guess we never talk about personal things in the bunker."

"No, we don't." While this was true, after we'd been in close quarters for months, it was depressing to think we were still just strangers to each other.

Link's wife must live in another city because he'd been staying in the men's barracks as long as I'd known him. So when the war was over he'd go back to her and live a normal life. The kind of life I suddenly wished I could have. I stared at the opposite wall. It was maddening to wait when at this very moment the battle was raging. In another room, the signals were coming in furiously. But out here, nothing. A blank. Even the IBM tabulating machine was stopped for once, and that made the bunker eerily silent.

"Fuck, I can't stand this," I said. Link looked startled and I realized I'd never sworn in front of him before. But I was no lady;

everyone used to swear all the time when I was in the gang so I had forgotten for a minute to hold back. "I'm going to talk to the Captain."

I flung open his door without knocking, and he was popping some pills into his mouth. He had a bucket of them sitting on the corner of his desk. "Got to be alert more than ever," he said.

"We're going crazy out there. Can't you give us something to do?"

"You're so impatient, my dear. Must keep a cool head in battle. I was just about to tell you lot to work on the JN-14s. I'll have Josie run them out to you. There's so much coming in, intercept doesn't have time to decode it. They're just copying it verbatim. Find me a nice long list of *chimbotsu*, won't you?"

I saluted him smartly and rushed off to tell the others about our easy assignment. The sigint unit in Australia had broken the JN-14, a naval code used to report fleet movements and casualties, about six months ago. All we had to do was refer to the book. A *chimbotsu* was a destroyed Japanese ship (while *gekichin* referred to an Allied sinking, and that was a word we never wanted to find). But the messages we got from Josie had no *chimbotsu* at all. Instead they showed the Japanese, over the course of the following hours, taking the islands of Attu and Kiska without opposition in a heavy fog.

"Jesus Christ on the cross," Link said, running his fingers through his hair so that it stood up on end, giving him the look of a madman.

I didn't answer because I was deep into a transmission from Admiral Hosogaya, which ordered a squadron of thirty-two aeroplanes to attack the American base at Dutch Harbor. The next communiqué detailed fifteen planes lost en route due to the fog, but the other seventeen dropped their bombs over the settlement. Of course, from the Japanese reports we did not know how much damage they had inflicted on the ground, or how many lives were lost. We lived a one-sided war, through the eyes of our enemies, and had to wait for the newspapers to learn the official Allied version.

Right now I didn't care if they lied; I just wanted to hear something that would give me hope. I should have been able to help prevent this slaughter. I had failed to figure out where the Japanese were going to attack.

When I got Bill's last note, I had dismissed the part where he called me worthless as the words of a doomed man needing to lash out. Now it nagged at me. He used to include me in his magic circle, with the two of us smarter than everyone else, and that was something I had loved about being with him. But he had exiled me and I needed to prove I could succeed on my own. What was the point of this loneliness if I did not triumph at my work? I didn't brush my eye fast enough to keep a tear from falling on the sheet of paper in front of me.

"What's wrong?" Link said.

"I never told you, but I had a dream that helped me solve the book code. I was so stupid though. I missed the most important thing about it. There was snow everywhere, because it happened in *Alaska*." I felt a sob forming in my throat and pressed my lips together, sealing it in. "I should have figured out it was the Aleutians they were going to attack."

"Hey, hold on." He walked over to my desk and laid his hand on my shoulder, crouching down to speak privately and look into my eyes. "It's amazing you got the book code at all. It helped the Americans confirm Midway. That's going to be the main battle." He stood again and withdrew his hand. "Anyways, I don't think Admiral Spruance would have changed his plans based on a dream."

"How many people do you think died at Dutch Harbor?" I drew in a ragged breath.

"I don't know. A small number in the scheme of things. And I don't think anybody lives on Attu or Kiska at all."

"It must be the loneliest place on earth." I sniffed. "You got a handkerchief? God, I feel like such an idiot. I'm not usually emotional like this."

He pulled a square from his suit pocket and handed it to me. "What did you do before the war, anyways?"

"It was pretty high stress, so I should know how to work under pressure."

"That's all you're going to give me?"

I shrugged. "You realize our shifts have been over for twenty minutes?"

"I don't see you leaving. I'm going to get some coffee. Want me to grab you some?"

"Sure. I suppose the attack on Midway will start soon. It's going to be a long day. Or night. Whatever it is outside right now."

## CHAPTER FOURTEEN

# MAY 1932

THE FIRST NATIONAL job went perfectly, but that didn't seem to make Lena any happier. During our escape, she had sat in the car with a stony expression. Meanwhile Bill and the rest of us whooped with delight, our heads out the windows to enjoy the wind on our faces, howling like a pack of dogs. We'd done it. We had cleared six thousand dollars. Last year that would have seemed an astonishing sum to me—but now, I had to admit it seemed paltry after the hundred grand. But who could complain about more money? And I was starting to understand why Bill was only truly happy when he was doing something dangerous. The adrenaline that shot through you at those moments was a powerful thing.

A few days after the robbery, the three of us were sitting in the suite at the Claremont, and Bill asked Lena if she had any dough left in her purse because he wanted to go to the So Different that night. She pretty near blew a gasket.

"What the fuck happened to your money?"

I waited to hear Bill explain it to her and make it all right, but he just hung his head and kicked the leg of the French settee. She was starting to tear a strip off him when I interrupted.

"Lena, he gave his share of First National to the Protestant orphans' home, the one in Lake Forest Park. We went out there yesterday."

She still looked suspicious. "I thought you went to play poker with Ramon and them."

"Naw. That's just what Bill *said* we were going to do. I don't know why he wanted to keep what he did a secret from you and everybody."

"Fuck, if I wanted to talk about it, I would've," Bill said. "Keep your trap shut in future."

I was hurt that he took it out on me like that. I was only trying to help—and it worked out pretty good for Bill. Lena was all affectionate, hanging off him and cooing and caressing him. I was a right moron sometimes.

BILL HAD A way of piling up conflicting emotions in his wake. First there was the gift to the orphanage, and then, on the other hand, there was the visit to the pawnshop. I honestly don't like to think of that, and was ashamed to have been involved. But once something got underway with Bill there was no extracting yourself. I wished I could blame Ramon, but he only escalated what Bill started.

Bill had been going crazy with boredom in our suite at the Claremont, and he turned to me all of a sudden and said we had to go out. He ignored Lena's questions and protests. Me, I just went. First we stopped by Ramon's room at the Cherry, the hotel he'd switched to after the cop came around his last place. It only had one window that looked out onto a brick wall, and a lumpy bed that I sat on uncomfortably with Ramon after he had given Bill the only chair. Ramon had never seen our rooms at the Claremont, which was a good thing, because he would have become bitter at the contrast in our situations. I smirked at the thought.

Without any preamble Bill dumped out his coke on the bedside table and cut it into three piles. He snuffed his up and told us to "have at her," so I did. Then he said he had a plan. He knew about a pawnshop where a friend had left some expensive jewellery and that we should go get it. The friend had already been given some money for it on hock—he had in fact stolen it out of a house on Capitol Hill—so he wouldn't care if we nabbed it. In fact, this friend had tipped off Bill that only one old man worked at the shop.

"It'll be a snap," Bill said.

So we got on a trolley car all excited and grinning at each other, even me at Ramon as I thought of how easy it was going to be.

The pawnshop was located just off Skid Road. That fact troubled me momentarily as it reminded me of my mother. She always had a horror of the place. Our social standing without my father was precarious and in her mind it was as though, if we went anywhere near Skid Road, its moral downward gravity would take hold of us. But I told myself that its origins were innocent enough, being where the early lumbermen of Seattle "skidded" their logs down to the ocean for shipment. I didn't know how its lowlife reputation came into existence out of that, though I supposed the lumbermen weren't the most refined sorts. My thoughts stopped their strange spirals when Bill started whistling the contagious "Blue Skies" song from the Al Jolson talkie where everything works out right. He caught my eye, puffed his cheeks out comically, and I started whistling along. Why not have fun like Bill? It felt pretty damn good. Ramon soon joined in and we made a complete spectacle of ourselves, but we didn't care. Nothing could touch us.

Ramon yanked the trolley bell with a grin and we alighted, silent and stealthy now, on the lookout for Arenson's Pawn. We found it soon enough on a muddy, disreputable side street with windows that did not let you see inside because they were so dirty. As we stepped in the door and our eyes adjusted to the dimness, all you could see were shelves with overcoats and old shoes and junk like that. Bill gestured to me to check that the place was empty, which I did, while he talked to the owner all friendly like. As soon as I nodded the okay, Bill went straight to business, asking about diamond jewellery.

"Do you have something in mind for a lady?" the old man asked.

"Something in mind for myself," Bill said with a vicious grin.

Immediately the old man divined what he meant and went pale. However, he was stubborn and would not reveal the jewellery's whereabouts. Bill twisted the man's arm behind his back until he screamed but still he would not tell. In my mind I begged him to, so we could end this job and leave. The joy had gone out of it. Unbeknownst to me, Ramon had brought a revolver that he pulled from inside his jacket. Over and over again, he hit the man's head with the grip and there was blood everywhere. It was awful, but I was afraid to intervene against Ramon's rage for I didn't want it turned upon myself. Crying, the man at last revealed where the jewellery was—in a safe box underneath the counter.

With blood running down his forehead, which he wiped with the back of his hand, he threw the key onto the counter. Bill told me to open the safe box, so I picked up the bloody key and was nauseous from the feel of it on my hand. Frantically I looked around for a rag and settled on an old coat to clean it with. Then I shoved the coat underneath the counter before Bill had time to say anything. My hands were shaking so I was glad the old safe opened easily. Inside there was a diamond necklace and a ring that I held up for the boys to see before slipping them into my pocket. Bill pulled a length of twine from his coat—he was always prepared with such necessities—and he tied the man to a chair. Since it was the end of the day we hoped that no one would discover the man until morning, but at the very least this should give us time to flee.

We deked through back alleys that Bill seemed to know well until we came out onto Skid Road proper, near the bottom of the hill, and we jumped into the back of a delivery truck where we lay down flat so the driver wouldn't see us. When the truck slowed after a while, we got out and walked the rest of the way back to the Hotel Cherry to inspect our haul. Neither of them seemed upset at what had just happened.

"That's a real nice set," Bill said as I laid out the jewellery on the bedside table. "But there's only two pieces for three men. We'll have to sell it somehows and split the money."

"Naw, that's all right," I said. "You two keep it."

"You're a strange man, By God. You just in it for the thrills?"

"Guess so."

"I won't argue with him," Ramon said. "Can I have the ring?" He put it on his pinkie finger. "Fits perfect."

"Go ahead," Bill said. "I know a lady who'll look real nice in this necklace."

"You sure you shouldn't sell it anyways?" I said. "It's pretty flashy. Somebody might recognize it."

"Without risk there is no reward, By God. But if it makes you feel better, I'll tell Lena to wait until we've left Seattle to wear it."

"You don't think she'll worry where you got the necklace if you say that?"

Really, I hoped she would never wear it, because it would always remind me of my part in procuring it. I should have stopped Ramon from pummelling the old man.

"Lena doesn't fear anything. Certainly not ill-gotten gains." Bill grinned.

"Yes, that is a *chica* who follows the money."

"Shut the fuck up, Ramon. As if you're so high and mighty. Only By God here has the true spirit of adventure."

He slapped me on the back and I tried to smile like he expected. My mind, which had been electric earlier, was now left cold; and for a moment I wished I was dead. All I could think of was the old man tied to the chair, his head hanging down and covered in blood.

## CHAPTER FIFTEEN

# THE MIDWAY DOUBTS

"*CHIMBOTSU!*" LINK YELLED, standing on his desk and waving a sheet of paper.

The room erupted with cheers. Everyone rushed round him to hear more and I elbowed to the front of the throng. The bunker was packed because no one was going off shift—one of the Oxford girls had pulled a folding chair to the corner of my desk without asking. I found it difficult to concentrate with her there. I'd more success at smoking down cigarettes than decoding, I dare say. At least it wasn't her who'd got the *chimbotsu*.

"The *Akagi* sank off Midway Atoll, hit by two torpedoes and ten bombs," Link said, reading from the Japanese message. He rubbed his bloodshot eyes. "Eighty were injured but were retrieved from life rafts along with the rest of the crew. The *Kaga* sank, hit by three torpedoes and eight bombs. Ninety-four killed, including five officers. Rest of the crew was saved. The *Soryu* sank, hit by seven torpedoes and thirteen bombs. All hands went down with the ship."

Some people cheered again, but I was not the only one who did not. Of course we wanted to win, but to hear the losses from the enemy's perspective was a little too personal. I wondered how long it took the poor sailors to drown and what their last thoughts were. Were they full of regrets? Would I be, at the end? If anyone would not be, it was Bill. For him, no moment of life was wasted. Being with him had been like flying in a hot-air balloon, with everyone else far below us and unimportant. If the world crashed in around his ears, he would blame the world, not the fierce vortex of his actions. But in the end he was left in the centre of the world he had created, alone.

I had never thought I would be part of the rubble. After Shively's note, I couldn't decide if Bill just hated me and wanted me to know it with crushing finality, or if he planned to do me actual harm. Through Byron's journal I had learned more about what Bill was capable of. I had been disturbed by the vicious attack on the old man at the pawnshop. Bill had never told me where he got that diamond necklace, and I had not asked though of course I knew it was stolen. I had worn it with pride, a trophy of Bill's prowess. I had only seen what I wanted to see—a man who loved me with desperate intensity. I was young and having an adventure, and of course I could not imagine the years unspooling and Bill turning on me. That in the end I really was, to him, as meaningless and worthless as everyone else. If I had discovered the story about the old man back then, I would have accepted Bill's version of what happened. Such delusions were necessary for my love to exist. He would have said the old man brought trouble on his own head by not cooperating. Bill had never shouldered blame for anything, which at the time was part of his charm. It was the opposite of how I was raised. The few times my father spoke of my mother, it was only to blame himself: he should have called the doctor sooner, he should have let my mother know how much he loved her before it was too late. Every moment in life there were two choices, and he felt he always made the wrong one. The weight of it was exhausting.

Rubbing my temple, I returned to the stack of JN-14s on my desk. They were boring but I welcomed the distraction. We had to scour each message for the proper additive group, which was a secondary layer of "garbage" letters mixed in varying intervals with the real ones. Then, when we figured out that day's decoding table, it showed the correct code group to use for each syllable. I flipped to page 143.

"They could put a monkey on this, couldn't they?" the Oxford girl said from the corner of my desk, where she'd re-established herself after Link's announcement. She was a mathematics graduate named Cat Trelawney who thought herself above those of us on the language side. However, she had to sneak off to consult the Japanese linguists more often than I did, so I considered us equally matched.

I looked at her coldly. "It's all important information in the end."

"Right-o," she said, and returned to her work. Good.

These JN-14s were limited to charting the incremental shifts of ships and aeroplane squadrons—which were indeed important but not at all dramatic. Now that we no longer had map privileges, it was hard to keep track of the accumulated effect on the Japanese fleet's activities and, as I had foreseen, this hampered our guesswork. I continued to complain to the Captain about this but he insisted the order was unwavering. But once in a while the conference room door was left ajar and I could glimpse the maps on the wall, and I looked at them for as long as I dared to. I'd nearly jumped out of my skin when this selfsame Cat Trelawney came down the hall when I was standing there yesterday, but I'd managed a blustery greeting. Perhaps that was why she thought we were on friendly terms. I should have gone into the map room and closed the door behind me to avoid such passersby. But I hadn't wanted to commit myself that far, because if I was caught inside there would be no explaining it away. Only the Captain and occasional mystery visitors ever went into the room.

Montague ran over to my desk, and I gave her a feeble smile as she handed me a coded message. "Hot off the presses," she said.

She lingered, but I could not begin while she stood there. She wasn't permitted to see the decryptions until they had been cleared by the Captain.

"Thank you," I said, placing my pencil flat on the desk in front of me and waiting for her to take the hint.

"What's your favourite movie?" she asked instead.

I suppressed a sigh. "I'm pretty busy right now. Can we talk later?"

"Sure." Looking disappointed she left the room, and I immediately fell to examining the message she had brought. I walked to the wall cabinet to get the codebook for the correct additive table, and sitting down once more, I started in on the syllables.

Ge-ki-chin.

USS *Yorktown.*

I put my hands up to hide my face. I wasn't prepared for the sudden image of those dead men. The Americans had lost a ship, or at least that was what the Japanese believed. Their information on the enemy—us—was not always accurate, because battle conditions often forced them to scatter before they could confirm a sinking. But I felt in my heart it was true. The Japanese reports were more reliable than our newspapers, because the government wanted to keep the public from knowing our defeats. I reminded myself that as codebreakers it was our duty to bear what others could not.

"*Gekichin,*" I said in the loudest voice I could muster. Those at the surrounding desks quickly spread the word throughout the room: *gekichin*, they said, hushed, again and again like a fast river clattering over stones. I laid my head on my arms until I sensed someone standing over me. It was Link. Averting my eyes, I handed the sheet of paper to him.

"USS *Yorktown.* I don't suppose you could finish the rest? I'm rather tired. I've been working too long."

He nodded. "Why don't you go get some sleep?"

I picked up my pencil and stood to leave, becoming briefly annoyed when Cat Trelawney took over my chair. But I departed without saying anything. Outside the ground was wet with dew, which meant it must be morning. The base was unusually quiet and the First Graving Dock was empty. I wondered if our ship had been headed for Midway. I recalled the scripture from my dream: "They that sail on the sea tell of danger thereof; and when we hear it with our ears, we marvel." Everything else blurred, and I stared with a sense of panic at my pencil stub. There was only about three inches of it left, and I had considered it my lucky pencil. I had broken the Bible book code with it. But cryptanalysis was not an intellectual game; it had human consequences. People had died. And then with this pencil I had deciphered the *gekichin*. Everything circled back, didn't it? I threw the pencil into the grass and beads of water scattered in its wake. Despite the childishness of this act, I felt relieved as I walked away.

Hearing someone approaching from behind, I calmed my breathing and slowed my step. If it was Link, I wanted him to catch up. He'd seemed worried about me, which was nice. Hopefully he hadn't seen my little fit back there; I didn't want him to think I was unstable. I wasn't.

Instead it was Montague who rested her hand on my arm and smiled at me—this was deeply irritating, given her rank.

"Did you have a chance to think of your favourite movie? There've been lots of good ones the last few years."

*"Gone with the Wind,"* I said, though it was only the first thing that came to mind. I wondered what was the fastest way to get rid of her, since I was in no mood for this frivolous conversation.

"That's a sad one." She paused. "I like gangster movies. They have more zip. Did you ever see *Angels with Dirty Faces*? With James Cagney and Ann Sheridan? I loved her hair in that, so I do mine the same." But it is not, I couldn't help thinking as I stared at the frizzy mop swept back from her long face. "It's about two boys who rob trains and they get caught. Well, one does, and he's sent to reform school and becomes a crook for life. The other one escapes and becomes a priest. Then later they meet again, and the crook saves the priest's life by killing a man. But the crook is jailed for murder and gets sentenced to hang."

"That's a pretty sad one too," I said. Why did she have to go on all the time about gangsters and murders? What did she see in me or want from me?

"Yeah." She stared across the green fields toward the steel-grey sea. "Sometimes I wonder if I'm the only one who feels bad for that

Bill Bagley. Don't you think everybody has a good side, if they're given a chance to find it?"

"I wish it was true."

"But you don't think so?"

"No, I suppose I don't."

She fell behind me and walked on in silence. I was surprised to find I regretted having squelched her—she had a good heart. But if she wasn't careful life would kick her in the teeth, so I was protecting her, really, by discouraging these Pollyanna fantasies. Feeling pity for anyone like Bill could lead her into bad company and compromise her happiness for life. Pity meant weakness. Yet I couldn't help thinking of the men who died on the *Yorktown*, which made me wonder how I would ever regain my composure.

## CHAPTER SIXTEEN

# MAY 1933

WITH NEARLY A year gone by since the big Nanaimo job, the gang was idling. Nobody wanted to admit it, but there was dissent and unhappiness among us all. After we pulled three more holdups in Seattle, with only a small haul to share, some of the boys decided to decamp. Just temporarily, they said. Moe bought a cabin in the woods on Vancouver Island like he'd wanted, and was joining the cougar bounty hunt, he said, to keep his aim sharp for the next time we needed him. Sho-nuff announced he was going to buy a salmon trawler and be his own captain; Bill slapped him on the back and told him to drop by whenever he was in port, but somehow he never was. Cruickshank might as well have left because we hardly ever saw him. He was a member of the Sand Point Country Club and was always playing golf. He wore tweed and practised his swing with an invisible club like a twit.

Then there was Lena, who seemed distant. This was painful when we shared the same living space, a mansion Bill had rented on Capitol Hill. But I think the strain was between her and Bill—I hoped so, anyway. I didn't have the nerve to ask. Meanwhile, Ramon was the same crazy bastard as always, which became a comfort to me among all these other changes. We grew strangely closer over this time, like fraternal twins forced to develop in the same womb.

One quiet afternoon, Ramon chased the cook out of the kitchen for making some "bland fucking white fish soup that I can't deal with no more."

"I'm tired of it too," I said as the cook ran past me through the garden. I was putting together a picture puzzle of a Yorkshire terrier, which I'd found in a cupboard. I hated its smug little face as the pieces came together but I carried on anyhow—that's how bored I was. Ramon flashed me a surprising grin and said he would teach me how to make a Mexican sauce if I wanted.

"Absolutely," I said, and followed him inside.

"My mother showed me this." Expertly he held down some green peppers on the butcher block with his hook, and diced them with a knife in his good hand. "I was born in Tijuana, so it was natural my mother looks across the border for a better life. We left Mexico when I was twelve. But she made not much money as a maid. She taught me to cook so I could look after my sisters when she was out. She was always out. These little housewives in Los Angeles, they pretend to be like queens and work her like a dog. Bill he always pay the help decent, I don't have to worry about that with him." I gave Ramon a look but held my tongue about how he had just terrorized the cook. But it was true she was well paid, and now she would have the afternoon off. "Anyhow, my mother and me, and my three little sisters, we were hungry, my friend. Have you known real hunger?" I shook my head no. "It makes you crazy. My mother wanted school for me, but I had to work in a warehouse instead. Put some food on the table."

When he was fourteen years old, a forklift crushed his arm. One of the older men had sawed the bad leg off a horse once, so he knew what to do; Ramon's mother could not afford a doctor. He hadn't been a crook then, but with almost no schooling and unable to do physical labour anymore, he had no idea how to support himself.

"But then it worked out perfect," Ramon said. "Bill came along." He held out the spoon for me to sip the broth, spicy now.

"Good," I said, my mouth burning.

Ramon met Bill when he had just got back from the war and was in uniform still. Bill had been friends with one of the warehouse men and went over to his rooming house, where Ramon was hanging around. At first, Ramon had seen Bill the soldier as a model of American citizenship and looked up to him. But later that night they all got drunk and Bill burned an American flag. He'd climbed up a pole in somebody's yard and torn it down, wearing it as a cape for a while. They wandered into a railroad yard and came upon some hobos, and he threw it in their fire barrel. "Fuck the US of A!" he had yelled. The flames lit up their dirty grinning faces—it would keep them warmer a little longer that night. Then Bill tossed in his uniform too, laughing, until he was standing there in his white underclothes. I imagined him like some ash-smudged angel of demented mercy. I wished I'd known him back then.

Ramon stirred the soup as it simmered. "I realize that night, I will not end up one of these old men, broke and living on the tracks. I will be like Bill instead. I learn to read, I learn to steal." I admired his can-do attitude. My upbringing was much less disastrous than his, and yet I'd let it harm me much more. I was ashamed that I spent my life mourning my lost opportunities—even though I had both arms, and I had a father even if he had abandoned me. He'd left enough money behind for my schooling at the junior college, no matter that it was below my expectations. I could still support myself. Ramon's father had died in a mining accident and left him nothing at all, not even a bitter memory.

Bill, meanwhile, had been brooding in his room all afternoon. He only came alive when he sat in front of our fireplace at eight o'clock and read aloud the newspaper accounts of the Clockwork Gang—which we'd been named for our precision timing—and of Detective Brooke's hapless pursuit. Bill laughed at the wildly varying witness accounts of our appearances, though there was mention of a quiet man wearing spectacles. Detective Brooke seemed to have a good head on his shoulders, so I thought Bill should be more concerned. Brooke told the *Post-Intelligencer* that he had divined a "modus operandi" connecting our various bank jobs, and that he would use the latest science in fingerprinting and blood work to hunt us down. I wished I'd never heard that.

I was relieved when there was a knock on the door because I knew the distraction this would bring. Most nights some boys from Mahone's came by to play poker. Lena, who did not like gambling, retired upstairs; and then Bill brought out his coke. I had learned to bet aggressively, though I only won occasionally. I discovered the point was not winning, but taking the risk; it was Bill taught me that. No matter what wild bets he made he usually triumphed in our games, though at times this lack of challenge seemed to enrage him.

We did not go to bed until three a.m. and I still did not feel settled. An hour later, I woke up in a cold sweat because I had dreamed of Detective Brooke tailing us, wearing the overcoat I had used to wipe my bloodied hand at the pawnshop. None of the others seemed to be afflicted with such weaknesses, so at breakfast I kept my fears to myself.

When I was sure everyone had cleared out, I went into the living room to examine the paper Bill had left behind yesterday. Even though I hated the news, I needed to know if there was something important Bill had missed. I did not care to be surprised by this Detective Brooke even if Bill gave him no never-mind. I didn't find anything on that front but I did learn something interesting: there was going to be a new kind of criminal. President Roosevelt wanted to make some practices on the stock market illegal, since uncontrolled speculation had caused the Crash. He was spurred on by a federal investigation of Continental Trust's securities arm in New York—of which my father happened to be vice president. I pondered on that all day; pondered it to the bottom of the silver flask Bill had given me on my last birthday. When we went to the Arctic Club later, I don't even remember what we had for dinner; maybe it was quail. I admit I was more than a little drunk.

"What, might I ask, is the definition of a criminal? Is it just a useful scapegoat for society?"

Bill told me to shut my fool yap but he gave me a friendly grin, adding, "Fuck if I know."

Later that night, back in the mansion on Capitol Hill, Bill announced it was time for a serious powwow. We followed him into the drawing room.

"We have reached a state of terminal boredom. I have a new master plan."

"Bill, I don't even want to hear about it," Lena said. She was sitting on a velvet settee and twitching her foot up and down. There was a large gilt-framed portrait of her on the wall behind, looking angelic in a garden. Since it had been hung last month I had stared at it for so long that I had memorized each brush stroke. Bill had hired Seattle's best society artist and I was jealous of all the hours he spent with Lena, fawning over her beauty. I couldn't blame him though. From what I'd seen, most of the other rich dames had mutton faces.

"You're a fucking hypocrite, you know," Bill said, smiling. He went and sat down beside her, putting his arm over her shoulder like a C-clamp. "You've become used to the high life but you don't want to work for it."

"What we do is not what most people call work."

He slapped her face.

She put her hand to the place, shocked, but she didn't make a sound. She was a woman made of stone, brave and needing no one, I thought, as I ached uselessly to rush to her side.

"I know why you're acting strange. You're planning to go back to Dr. Phipps," Bill said. "Gonna leave this behind and get all high-faluting, like you're better than what you've done?"

Her foot, which had been twitching and twitching this whole time, stopped. "Where'd you get that crazy idea?"

"This," he said, grabbing her foot. "Your body says what your mouth is smart enough to hide."

Her face pale, she struggled to free her foot but his grip was too strong. "It is just a foot, Bill," she said, every word precise, and I cheered her on inwardly. She could stand up to this brute.

"Okey-dokey then, forget about the foot." He grinned and I became nervous for her. Whenever Bill dropped into homey expressions he was at his most dangerous. "How's about a letter?"

She stared at him with a cold hatred that would have made his soul quaver if he had had one. "You've been spying on me."

"What's mine is yours and yours is mine. We are one and the same person, darlin', joined til death do us part. Til death do us part."

"We are not married," she said, finally freeing her foot from him. "I did not make that vow nor did you."

"You're happy enough to wear my ring though." He pointed at the large diamond on her finger and she covered it up with her other hand, flushing. "There is a promise in that. Why are you hiding things from me? Especially about Dr. Phipps. You know I have a special interest in him."

"You shouldn't. He was only my teacher. Nothing ever passed between us."

"I think he might like it to. Why else would he invite you on a trip to Russia?"

"Did it ever occur to you that I might be useful to him in his fieldwork? That I have a talent for language?"

"Goddammit." Bill grabbed a fly that had been buzzing around his face and crushed it. "I never knowed a place so plagued by flies as this one. It's driving me mad." He swatted at the coffee table, where a mesh dome over the fruit bowl had flies crawling all over it, spoiling the display of pomegranates. The flies rose in all directions but soon resettled. He stared angrily at the window, a sashed bay from floor to ceiling, fifteen feet high, that overlooked a park across the street. As a child, I had walked on occasion down this very street, wondering about the rich lives within, though I never took especial note of this house among the Victorian piles built all of a kind. It was true that since we arrived more and more flies had been convening daily inside and then bashing themselves against the glass. I was worried for a moment that Bill might transfer his rage to me, as I stood by the brocade curtain with my hands in my pockets. But he was used to me always around, a pale presence, and as usual took no note of me. "Why the fuck do they come in when all they want is out?"

"It's just the heat," Lena said. "There's never been such a hot summer as this."

"You ain't never been to California. There's some heat that'll fry an egg on a sidewalk. But still nothing to this for flies. Woman, why do you keep distracting me? You'll answer to me for this Phipps business."

"It's completely innocent. How dare you go digging through my things?"

"If it was innocent you wouldn't hide the letter. Knowledge is power, darlin'. You've heard me say it a hundred times, and should have heeded the warning. Why else do I study plans of vaults and banks till I know them better than the men who designed them? I need to know what's in people's heads, especially if they take it to conceal things. I don't like surprises."

I thought of the very journal I was now keeping, writing about the gang when I was sure I was alone, in my old office building where I could hear every footstep echo up the marble stairs. I had started it in an anonymous accounting ledger during this period of drift, as everyone started to go his own way. It was a time of thoughtfulness, though to what end I did not know. For once I was a step ahead of Lena. I had noted Bill's appetite for ferreting out everything, and I kept a safety deposit box in the Mercantile Bank downtown. We had no other accounts there, and the manager was instructed to hand over the key only to me or my lawyer. The journal's existence scared me a little, but the pleasure of having a secret from Bill overpowered that cowardice. I had something that was well and truly mine, and Bill had no say over it.

"I couldn't stand it if you left me." He smoothed the hair from her face now, gentle as a kitten. I was angry at his sudden contrition, this unsettling change of mood—yet another of his manipulations—especially since Lena softened toward him and laid her head in the crook of his shoulder.

"I'm not going with Dr. Phipps," she said, and Bill gave her a hug that seemed almost as desperate as it did loving. Though it was just a second before his face expressed his old complacence, I sensed he might well and truly fall to pieces if Lena left him. There was a madness to him that only she could manage. For a moment I longed for the old days when I looked up to Bill as invincible.

She kissed him full on the lips. This display pained me and I left the room for my suite on the second floor. I put my head under the pillow to make sure I heard nothing more of their reconciliation, for I had learned these were fiercely loving times.

The next morning Bill told me to pack my bags, because we were going back to Canada. When I went outside, Lena was already sitting in the blue Packard limousine with a hatbox on her lap. She smiled at me with clear eyes, beautiful.

## CHAPTER SEVENTEEN

# MISS MAGGIE

THE BATTLE OF Midway had started only five minutes and five degrees of latitude off from the predictions of our sigint, which was gratifying. Usually we did not see the results of our work so clearly. I felt buoyed by the mood around me and wanted to leave behind my weakness with the *gekichins*. I would go to the heart of the action and monitor the battle as it happened. I gathered myself together, marched into the Captain's office and asked to join the radio team. He pursed his lips as though about to say no, so I reminded him I had done listening work before Pearl Harbor. There would be so much going on over the following hours, I argued, that we needed as many people as possible at the radios to monitor the fighting. These reports could help our Navy comrades at sea. The Captain ultimately agreed.

No one looked up when I entered the large room that had been newly commandeered for radio intercept. They were too intent on their work, staring into the space in front of them as though they could see clear to Midway. It was stifling with the heat generated from the equipment. Sweat already running down my forehead, I sat down at an empty chair, put on a pair of headphones and began spinning the dial. My hand froze when I heard a familiar voice: the Japanese radio operator whom I'd called Caruso. After some chatter I determined he was stationed on the *Kaga* aircraft carrier, and I wrote this down. He was ordering out the Zeros—planes superior to both British Tomahawks and American Wildcats—to attack the Allied ships. The response from the cockpits was enthusiastic, since the Japanese did not know that we expected them. There was a hum of propellers as they took to the sky.

"I am under attack," a Japanese pilot yelled into his radio. It wasn't in code—there was no time for that. He sounded very young.

"Squadron 4, Plane 7," I scrawled.

There followed an explosion and the whine of an engine in freefall—reflexively I covered my ears, pressing my hands uselessly to the headphones—and then the pilot's scream as he crashed into the ocean.

"Destroyed," I wrote.

I clutched my wrist to stop my hand from shaking. This was not a random incident. The pilot had died because of the intelligence I supplied by deciphering the book code, which confirmed the location of the Japanese attack. I had helped launch this ambush.

I could not bear to listen to Caruso's squadron anymore. More of them were sure to die. I spun the dial through static, hoping I wouldn't find anything else. But today my hand was a lodestone and I fell upon a broadcast in basic Naval Code: "*Hiryu* proceed to latitude 19°30'N, longitude 164°30'W." I hesitated to write down these orders, even though I knew this carrier-class ship was important. I was paralyzed by my desire not to cause any more harm. Anything I did would be wrong. If I saved one man, another would die. After arriving at this designated location, the Japanese would no doubt launch their aircraft to bomb the Americans. After sketching a line of crosses on my page, I finally reported the order to the head of the radio team.

At the end of my shift I went back to the Captain's office and, keeping my voice neutral, suggested that I return to decoding. The reason I supplied was that the Japanese were following their plan—which we already knew—to the letter. The radio reports were therefore superfluous and, during battle, the codes were not complicated enough to warrant my work on them. He again agreed with my request and dismissed me. As I walked back to the women's barracks, I was relieved he had not seen into my soul. I was a coward hiding behind the abstraction of paperwork, where the murders were silent and remote. I disgusted myself.

My feet suddenly felt heavy and, looking down, I saw that my shoes were coated with mud. It must have rained hard during the day because there were puddles all around, which I had somehow failed to notice. I was scraping the mud off on a boulder when I heard a rustle behind it. I moved slowly, quietly, around the rock and saw a pigeon hobbling on the ground. Lifting it gently, I saw that a metal band had dug into its leg and made a deep cut.

"There now," I said aloud as I took off the band. "You'll be all right."

Released of its burden, the pigeon flew from my hands, and I fell to examining the band. Attached to it was a small tube with a cap, which, curious now, I pried off. Inside was a rolled-up piece of paper. It had a coded message on it. Were the Japanese so close that a pigeon could make it to shore from one of their ships? I scanned the horizon—nothing. I cupped the paper in my damp hand to keep it from flying away in the wind, and studied it for repetitions. There were a few, but the message was too short for the pattern to be definitive—it could have been a result of randomization. I didn't know if I could crack this one in isolation. In our daily work, we tried to build up "depth," or a number of messages sent with the same code, so we had more elements to compare. I shoved the paper in my pocket and continued toward the barracks.

I should report this to the Captain immediately. But if the message was to be cracked, I wanted to be the one to do it. Not the insufferable Oxford girl, Cat Trelawney, who was probably still perched on my chair. After I slept and regained my edge I'd work on the code for just a little while. I'd give it to the Captain tomorrow if I couldn't figure it out. That was reasonable.

But I wasn't sleepy yet, so I went to the mess and ordered a coffee. I must have been sitting there alone a long while, blowing absently on my steaming drink, when Link came in and sat beside me. I emerged from my haze to take a sip and discovered that the coffee was startlingly cold.

"I have some good news for you," he said.

"What?"

"The USS *Yorktown* wasn't sunk like the Japanese thought."

"That's good," I said, affecting a smile.

"My brother-in-law was on that carrier. He's American."

"You must be so relieved," I said, and put my hand on his without thinking. I drew it away quickly. "So your wife is American too? How did you meet her?"

"It's a long story." He took a sip of his coffee. "But looking back, I wasn't really ready to get married." I felt an unaccountable surge of pleasure at this, but I didn't know what to say. I tried to keep my face neutral. "You don't wear a ring," he continued, "so I guess you never tied the knot?"

"I was sort of engaged once, but it didn't work out. Marriage isn't for me anyhow. Women can't pursue a career that way. I was studying linguistics before the war and my boyfriend couldn't stand the idea of it. That there was something important to me that wasn't him."

"He wasn't the right man for you, then." He stared at me. "I've never met a woman who wasn't interested in marriage."

"I'm sure I'm very strange."

"Anybody who winds up in this business isn't like other people. I've always felt the odd one out."

"What do you mean? You get along with everyone."

"I try." He smiled at me as he stood up to leave and I studied his face, but it was a smile like you'd give anybody, I thought. Leaving my cup on the table, I returned to the barracks. It was better to be alone without an audience.

Despite my fatigue I could not sleep for a long while and lay staring at the ceiling. I wondered why Link got married if he didn't want to. We all did things that seemed strange in retrospect, I supposed. Like my relationship with Bill. It had many bad elements, but I had learned a lot about myself. It was that time he hit me, in the mansion on Capitol Hill, that my need for independence crystallized. I knew I had to leave him, but I had to wait in silent concealment until the time was right. Under normal circumstances, Bill would hunt me down. But once the job he was obsessed with was underway, I could make my break. And Byron, who had been watching me so closely, had had no suspicion of my plan. I was pleased by that discovery when I read it in his journal. It was this escape that made me capable of being what I am now, and taught me to hide my thoughts from others. So while Bill gave me this past that could ruin me, through him I found the strength to conceal it.

I must have slept eventually, for when I opened my bleary eyes I saw Montague reading the news, sitting on her bed across from me. I closed my eyes again. I could scarcely bear the thought of calmly discussing the Clockwork Gang. But I had to face her eventually, so I made myself sit up. The front-page headline was so big I could see it from my bunk:

## PACIFIC BATTLE OVER—JAPS FLEE

Every few minutes Montague would peer over the newspaper and say, "Isn't it wonderful?"

"Yes," I said. It really was.

Finally Montague passed me the *Globe* on her way out the door. I paused on page three, where there was a lengthy piece about the *Yorktown*'s secret resurrection. After being hit by torpedoes, it was towed to Hawaii where fourteen hundred American mechanics had fixed the crippled vessel in a single day. This was an unprecedented feat. The repair of such a massive ship would have taken months before the war changed every scale and expectation. By the time I put down the newspaper, I believed that the British would no longer be the world's greatest power after the war ended. Yet somehow this did not disturb me. What real part had I in this past

Empire, any more or less than the American dominion to come? In fact, I cut out the article and tacked it to the wall above my bed, because the revival of the *Yorktown* was a comfort to me. It was sometimes possible to come back from the dead.

AT 1325, JOSIE poked her head into Decrypt to announce the Captain's order to muster in the conference room. We locked our papers in our desk drawers and proceeded down the hall. After the Captain thanked us for the extra hours we'd put in during the Battle of Midway, he cleared his throat.

"We have two important visitors coming to the Examination Unit, for whose benefit everything must be by the book."

His eyes drifted to the walls that were now purified of the maps we were never meant to see. I thought uncomfortably of the coded message I had found, and that I'd better report it to the Captain the first chance I got. But now was not the time.

"I will start with the more formidable of the two. Miss Maggie Newbigin from OP-20-G in Washington."

A murmur went through the room. Miss Maggie, as she was known, was a legend. She had made many decryption break-throughs over the last twenty years, and she was the top-ranked female codebreaker in the world. Though technically a civilian, she was second in command of HQ in Washington. By merit she should have been first. She had developed much of the wiring for the Americans' crib of the Purple machine, and all the Allied code-breakers now relied on it to decipher the JN-25. There were very few people, male or female, who had distinction in both decryption and engineering as she did.

"Yes, Miss Maggie is formidable," the Captain repeated, taking one of his pills. There was a sheen of sweat on his forehead. "She has many responsibilities, so we are lucky to receive her attention. She wants to personally congratulate our section for the work with the JN-25, particularly the Bible book code." His eyes flicked in my direction. "Before you meet her, I should mention that Miss Maggie has an unusual appearance. Try not to stare. She was in a terrible car accident before the war, but her religion prevented her from seeking corrective surgery."

People were so peculiar, I thought. This woman who rose through the ranks of men in a profession of logic was prone to a fit of irrational religion, even if it should mean her disfigurement.

"Our other visitor is Minister Middlebury. When he heard Miss Maggie was coming from Washington, he wanted to make sure our government was not short in its duties. He will inspect the unit tomorrow at 0930. Miss Maggie will be here the day after, at 0830. Dismissed," he said, fluttering his hand at us.

While the others trickled out of the room, I waited to confer privately with the Captain. This was an awkward situation. I was surprised that Constantine wanted to come after he had been scarce for so long—in fact, I hadn't talked to him since our argument over Bill's pardon. If I ever thought of him, it was with a flicker of annoyance that he never tried to reach me, but I had no desire to see him anymore. He was useless. When this visit had to do with my own commendation, how would it work to anyone's pleasure or advantage?

"May I speak of a personal matter, sir?"

"Of course."

"I had an unfortunate disagreement with the Minister. Would it be acceptable for me to report to the nursing station tomorrow with a sore throat I've felt coming on?" I coughed.

He nodded. "I have something to confess. The Minister does not know it was you who broke the book code. In my report to the War Ministry, I said it was another cryptanalyst."

This threw me utterly. "Why?"

"We need to throw about misinformation to smoke out a spy. I think he must be in Washington, in OP-20-G. Did you hear about the article in the *Chicago Tribune*?"

"Of course. Everyone was talking about it. It said that the Americans won at Midway because they were warned about the Japanese attack through signals intelligence."

"It's an utter disaster. The extent we're breaking their codes is supposed to be top secret. If they get wind of it, they'll change systems immediately and we'll be in the dark for months. The British government believes that the security breach was among the Americans because they have loose protocols. But don't ask Miss Maggie to believe that. Part of her visit is to investigate our unit."

"She's looking for a spy here?"

"Don't worry, my dear. Nothing will come of it. I have my plan in place now. For each advance we make, we're putting a different story out to each country's divisions, to see which version makes it to the press. Then we'll know the source of the leak. Unfortunately, this last incident is a little untidy. It was too late to keep the Americans from knowing that you broke the code. I had already reported it."

"You reported to OP-20-G before our own War Ministry?"

"All I can tell you is, I have my orders and I follow them. This is one case where I go by the rules, and you'd best do the same. This conversation is classified. Recall the penalty in the Official Secrets Act for a breach of that article. You are dismissed."

I walked out in a daze. I couldn't believe the Captain had invoked the Act—the penalty was death by firing squad. Our government had reached a point in the war where civilized ways no longer applied, and I wondered what exactly I was defending anymore.

## CHAPTER EIGHTEEN

# JUNE 1933

I WAS NERVOUS crossing the border to say the least. The last time we passed over, we had been on the run from the law. Maybe the Canadian police had our descriptions. Would we attract their notice? Ramon had a perpetually shifty look, even though Bill had supervised the purchase of his travelling suit, and he kept tugging at the collar. Just before we reached the guard station, I urged him to calm down.

"It's just this fucking fake hand," he said. "I can't stand it. Give me a hook any day." Bill had sensibly insisted that businessmen did not have hooks, and bought him expensive kid gloves, pearl grey, to wear over both the real hand and the fake one.

"I like your hook better too," I said.

Meanwhile, Cruickshank was hunched down in the back seat in his idiotic tweed, and concealed his face behind a golfing magazine while we stopped at the border station. Bill of course was cool, answering the officer's questions calmly.

"We're visiting friends in Vancouver," Bill said. "Just for three days."

"Profession?"

"Businessmen."

The border guard looked over our expensive car, nodded, and waved us through. Bill accelerated evenly to the speed limit and we motored through the quiet farmlands.

"It's proved again that money buys respectability," Bill said, craning his head round to grin at us in the back seat. "Lena, honey, pass me a cigar."

Lena opened the glove box. She clipped the end of a cigar with small silver scissors kept there for that purpose, lit the cigar and placed it between Bill's lips so that he needn't take his hands from the wheel. If Lena ever performed an intimate service like that for me I shouldn't take it for granted as Bill did. He was busy watching the road signs, though as far as I knew we had no plans. He turned into a place called White Rock and followed a waterfront road alongside a pretty beach, where he pulled over, the motor idling as we faced the sea, the sun warming my skin. Blue herons waded near the shore.

Bill spread his arms wide. "Life is beautiful."

My worries about the job evaporated, and I couldn't help grinning. I saw the world through his eyes, with birds singing, for us, the waves crashing and breaking, for us, and wished we could pause this moment forever. But Bill was a cog ever turning, and his fancy was caught by a hotel overlooking the pier, where he suggested we could get some liquor to enjoy the fact there was no Prohibition in Canada. The restaurant was empty, it being a weekday afternoon, and Bill had to go find the waiter, which annoyed him; but he pepped up as soon as the man brought our beers. The waiter put them directly into our hands, explaining that the bottle had a round bottom and would tip over if you put it down.

"I love this country," Bill said as the waiter returned to the kitchen. "It's got spirit. They invented a bottle that forces you to drink like a man. Or a full-blooded woman." He winked at Lena.

"Cheers," she said, holding up the brown bottle and guzzling from it. She giggled as she nearly forgot about the trick bottom and had started putting it down. She took another sip instead. "I'll be done this in two seconds. But I guess that's the idea."

Bill crooked his finger, beckoning us to lean forward. "Let me tell you about my plan."

"I'd love to know it," she said, "but maybe in a more private place?"

"Right, honeylamb." Bill had been contrite—as much as he was capable of it—after the incident at the mansion. "I'll just say we're going to enjoy ourselves at Harrison Hot Springs. The waters are very healing. At least that's what my rich friends tell me."

Lena sighed, but she didn't argue about it. We finished the beers quickly, as the round bottoms demanded, and we got up to leave. Ramon left a handful of American coins on the table, which gave me some unease. We would be remembered. Leaving the ocean-front town, we turned northeast toward Fort Langley, and when we arrived there an hour later we drove onto a small barge that would ferry us across the Fraser River. We got out of the car to stretch our legs, and the wind pushed Lena's hair into wild swirls about her face.

"How far is this place?" Ramon asked. "Do you know it, *chica*?"

"It's practically as far as Hope, I think. Where the mountain road starts." She pointed into the eastern distance.

"Well then, we'll stop just before we get to Hope," Bill said. "I've never believed in Hope, anyhow."

"What do you believe in?" I asked.

"I'm quite partial to fairy tales," he said, his face betraying no joke. I was careful to keep a neutral expression until I saw where he was going. You never knew with Bill. "They always have bad things happening to good people. Like that Little Red Riding Hood or the kiddies with the breadcrumbs. Shows that fate plays no favourites."

I stared up at the sky, which was clear except for some tall clouds building at the eastern head of the valley, as though it was a wall where the world ended. The barge bumped hard against the dock and we all faltered and grabbed the rail. We piled back in the car with Lena driving now and headed east on the Lougheed Highway, toward Harrison Hot Springs. The road followed the whipsaw curves of the Fraser, which was running high with melt-water. There was still snow on the peaks.

"I know an interesting fairy tale," Lena said, following my glance for a moment before returning her attention to the road. "Or an Indian myth anyhow, about these mountains. There's supposed to be a giant hairy beast called the Sasquatch that lives back there. Sasquatch means 'wild man' in the Salish tongue."

"What does it do?" Bill asked.

"Nothing particular. It just exists."

"That's a really fucking stupid fairy tale, then."

Lena looked hurt.

"I think it's interesting," I said. Bill stared me down, but I plowed on, feeling rather bold for crossing him. "Maybe Bill's sore. He doesn't like to think of any other wild man in these mountains besides himself."

Bill's arm shot out and I squeezed my eyes shut, expecting a blow. But Bill just laughed and thumped me on the shoulder, friendly-like. "Yes, By God, I am the original wild man, and don't forget it."

"Nobody is crazy like you," Ramon said.

We motored along quietly for a while, Bill evidently puffed up with pleasure at Ramon's regard for his lack of sanity.

"Is there a golf course at the resort?" Cruickshank asked out of the blue.

"You and your fucking golf," Bill said. "No. There is no golf. Just a fancy hotel with a safe where rich people leave all their valu-ables. I know for a fact that the Princess of Denmark is there this week. Also Dunsmuir, the coal millionaire, along with his wife. I'd like to pull one over on him personally, that fucking slave driver. There is a cool forty grand in cash and jewels stowed away right now."

I marvelled at Bill's information but did not doubt it. He had a genius for befriending the unnoticed people in important situations and prying everything of worth out of them, and they'd thank him for it too. Bill was always a dab hand with the kickback.

"Anyways, we're not staying there," Bill said. "That would be a dumb fuck move. Keep your eyes peeled for an Indian village when we get near Lake Errock. There's a man I knew a long time back. We'll stay there tonight. He's going to leave a canoe for us on the river near Harrison for our getaway."

"We're going to use a canoe?" I asked. I didn't know how to swim.

"Yep. Won't nobody expect us to be crossing the river that way. If there's a chase, they'll only be watching the bridges."

"You see how high the river's running right now?"

"It's one of them big war canoes, they can take anything. And Cruickshank's an old water dog."

"You expect there's going to be a chase?"

"Jesus, By God, be a man about it. Anyhows, this plan is solid and secret as can be. Much less security to worry about than a bank. And I got the night watchman sewed up."

Ramon pointed into the forest, having spotted the village from the smoke rising up from the shacks. Bill told Lena to carry on a bit further, because our hideout was secluded from the main village. We turned onto a muddy track and Bill instructed Lena to pull into the brush more so the car was concealed from the highway. The place had seemed deserted, but when we got out of the car a man was standing in front of us. He was barefoot and had approached silently through the jungle of giant ferns. He was a striking man, his features sharp underneath his derby and his wide face framed by an old-fashioned haircut, all one length at his chin. The brass buttons on his suit vest gleamed as he turned without greeting us while Bill followed him. They spoke together close and muttering, and then Bill passed him something that was no doubt currency to smooth our way.

"Not a friendly bugger," Cruickshank said.

"Best he can say truly he don't know us," Ramon said.

We perched awkwardly on the only dry hummock of land amid the mud while we waited for Bill to return.

"You want to borrow my galoshes, Lena? Those shoes are too nice to get spoiled."

"Thank you, Byron, yes."

I rummaged in the trunk and found them. Lena took off her shoes one by one, holding my arm to balance herself, and she replaced them with my boots. Of course they were too large but they would do, and I was grateful to be of any use to her.

Bill returned, rubbing his hands together. "It's all set," he said. "There are two cabins. One for the bachelors, and one for the happy couple. Couldn't be better."

Lena was silent as we approached the cabins. They were terrible rundown things, the cedar boards gapped and crooked and faded to grey.

"I'm going to visit with the boys a while," Bill said.

Lena left and we followed him into the bachelor cabin as he grabbed some cut wood stacked by the door. Inside there was a rusty tin prospector stove, and Bill started a fire in it.

"There, that's nice. Ramon, pull that table closer and let's have a game of poker."

"You bring any coke?"

"You have to ask? What the fuck else we going to do out here?"

## CHAPTER NINETEEN

# THE ENEMY

IN THE MORNING I visited the infirmary but of course they found nothing wrong with me. They merely advised a saltwater gargle and honey tea. At least my charade took enough time that Constantine should be done his inspection of the unit. I returned to the barracks with a newspaper and lay on my bed to read it while I drank my tea. There was talk of the Japanese bombing the West Coast, and Los Angeles was under blackout orders. We had detected no such attack plan, but was it possible they had intelligence we had missed? After what the Captain said, I supposed there were spies who worked their own secret channels.

I took the slip of paper from my pocket and rested it inside the crease of the newspaper. Even though the barracks was empty with everyone at the inspection, I wanted to remain unobserved should someone arrive. I focused on the code for a good twenty minutes, but got nothing out of it. I was ready to admit defeat until I thought of Bill's insult. I was not worthless. All I needed was another message of this type to compare it with. I should spend more time watching the seashore in case another pigeon went astray. I was putting on my coat when an announcement crackled over the loudspeaker.

"All hands report to duty, effective immediately."

There was no explanation. It was surely not an air raid, or the siren would have sounded. I restrained myself from running and adopted the dignified hustle of the sailors reporting to the docks or HQ. By the time I arrived at my own more obscure deployment in the bunker, I found everyone assembled in the conference room—including Minister Constantine Middlebury. What had I seen in him, anyway? He looked older and heavier than I remembered. The only thing handsome about him was his intelligent eyes, dark brown, though with no trace of the sympathy that is often attributed to that colour. I was glad that our affair was apparently over. I took a place at the back and stared at the floor.

"What I am about to tell you must not leave this room," the Captain began. "The government does not wish the public to be alarmed." He glanced at the Minister and cleared his throat. "A Japanese submarine has sunk an American freighter near Port Renfrew."

I gasped, a sound that disappeared into the murmur rippling through the room. The war had come to our very doorstep—Port Renfrew was a fishing village on Vancouver Island.

"The ship was called the *Coast Trader*. You are privileged with this information because we need to know if any hint of it was in the JN-25, and if not, how we can discover such plans in future." His eyes scanned the silent room. "Speak up, please, anyone."

"Sir," Link said, stepping forward. "We have never seen anything that suggested it. We have 80 percent penetration of the code now, so I don't think it could have slipped by."

"Third Officer Stillman," the Captain said, startling me with this form of address. "Your opinion?"

"I agree." I tried to look only at the Captain and not at Constantine, who was standing right beside him. I reminded myself to speak more hoarsely, since I was supposed to have a sore throat. "The Japanese use at least twenty codes that we are aware of, depending on the type of communication. There may be another one exclusive to the submarine deployments. The listening room would have to find it."

"Very good, Stillman, thank you. I will assign the listening room to that task. Minister, I trust you are satisfied with us. May I escort you to your car?"

I was glad to see the back of Constantine's expensive suit, and hoped it was the last time I'd be in the same room with him. As everyone else began filing out, I flopped into a chair at the conference table. Link lingered behind.

"It must have been hard for you to see the Minister," he said.

"Why should it be?" I tried to sound casual. I hated to think that everyone might know my personal business, because I had been as discreet as possible throughout the affair.

"I don't think it's fair that he gave a commendation to Cat for cracking the book code."

"He gave it to Cat?" The ever-so-superior Oxford mathematician! How could the Captain choose her of all people to be the red herring? I breathed deeply to control myself. "Forget I said anything to you about the book code. Apparently there's a new official version of what happened. Which is fine. We didn't sign up for this job to have roses thrown at our feet."

I chose to believe that Link's smile was merely friendly rather than sympathetic. Sympathy might have made me cry. I reached deep within myself to find the hardness I knew I possessed.

"Are you going to the dance on Saturday night?" he asked.

This non sequitur threw me off and I stared at my hands on the table. Surely it was a hypothetical question, coming from a married man. "Won't it be cancelled after the attack at Port Renfrew?"

"A dance is good for morale. It'll go on."

"I don't know if it's good for *my* morale. The last one I went to, I felt like bait in a shark tank. Too many men. And you know how we're not supposed to talk about what we do. It's awkward."

"You could talk to me instead. I've already got security clearance."

I imagined talking was the only thing I could expect, not dancing; but I wanted to learn more about him.

"All right then."

His smile was the only thing I could see, like lightning in an empty field. "You want to grab a coffee?" he asked.

"Sure."

I followed him through the warrens until we climbed the stairs into the daylight and I moved up beside him. The breeze was fresh, from the west, with a saltier tang than usual, and a smell of seaweed. It was a strong smell but I liked it—it reminded you that you were really alive.

"Nice to get away from that place sometimes," he said. "Clears the mind." His words seemed small on the wind, carried away before they reached me. He leaned in closer. "So you think there's a special code for the submarines?"

"Has to be. If the commands were in the JN-25, we'd have found them by now. I knew it was a mistake when they ordered us to focus so narrowly, even though it is the highest-level code. We need more personnel."

"Exactly. We work around the clock already."

"And we have a lot to think about." The mystery closest to my heart was of course the pigeon code because in its scantness—two lines only—it was nearly impossible to break. I was always drawn to the impossible. I wasn't sure if it was my strength or my weakness, but suddenly I was tired of doing things alone. Link could help me. We had the same clearance, as he himself had mentioned. Now that he had basically invited me to the dance, I wondered if we could have something more—and confiding in him would bring us closer.

"Link, I found something strange that I can't figure out. You have any ideas?" I found the slip of paper where I'd wedged it against the hem inside my jacket pocket. I handed it to him, careful not to touch his fingers. My pride demanded that I keep my composure, which felt difficult today.

He looked startled. "Where'd you get this?"

"It was on a carrier pigeon. It was injured."

His expression was wiped clean and then he smiled. "Maybe if you give it to me for a while, I can get somewhere with it."

"You don't think I should give it to the Captain?"

"Sure. Once we've cracked it. It was a raw deal that you didn't get any credit for the book code. You deserve this."

He took my arm to guide me around a large puddle swamping the path and I found myself wishing that it would rain eternally, so that he would always need to do this. I was happy to be beside him and to have confided a piece of my silent heart, which left a little more room there.

## CHAPTER TWENTY

# JUNE 1933

AFTER THE FIRE had warmed the cabin, we'd relaxed by playing poker and sharing Bill's coke. I was feeling pretty optimistic about the Harrison job even though it was different from anything we'd done before. Bill still had the old magic. He had already paid off the night watchman, and he had purchased dynamite to blow up the safe, of which he was informed of the exact make. He had practised destroying one just like it when we were in Seattle.

"You're a deep one, Bill," Cruickshank said, between sucking on his pipe. "The rest of us just out for larks these last few months, and you worked out everything for a new job. Even the dynamiting! It's not something you can nip off and do anywhere, like lawn darts. How'd you manage it?"

"Mahone had some construction projects going. I helped with the demolition."

"You're a deep one," Cruickshank repeated, chuckling in a patrician manner. I wished I could shove his pipe where the sun didn't shine. "But for once, I think, that's not enough to win the game." He laid down a straight flush. I shook my head in disbelief as he scooped up all the chips. "To the victor goes the spoils, boys."

"Merry fucking Christmas," Bill said. "Enjoy it while it lasts." He threw his cards face down on the table and, knocking over his chair as he stood up, left the cabin for the darkness outside.

"Guess he'll go console himself with the *chica*," Ramon said.

"Shut up, *animal*," I said, using the Mexican pronunciation. Ramon had taught me various insults in his language, of which this was the tamest.

The boys shifted their chairs closer to the fire as I cleared the table. Curious, because Bill so rarely lost, I checked his hand. It was a royal flush. Though I was puzzled, I said nothing about him being the true winner. He had his whims and his secrets that were more important to him than most. I mixed his cards into the deck without letting anyone else see them.

With Bill gone our energy for any other pursuit to pass the time left us, and we decided to go to bed. I blew out the kerosene lantern but left the fire going, which was the cabin's one comfort. The cots were terrible: old canvas army surplus heaped with lumpy hay, and there was only one moth-holed wool blanket apiece to cover ourselves with. My blanket was too short, so either my feet or my shoulders would be cold unless I curled into a ball, which I did.

"That Indian wasn't so hot on us," Cruickshank said from his cot. "Can we trust him?"

"Maybe you *blancos* better watch out. Me, I am his brother," Ramon said.

"He didn't treat you like a brother. You're a damn sight paler than he was. You live or die with us, I'd say."

"Nice conversation," I said. "How about we all just go to sleep?"

They were quiet then and in a while I heard Cruickshank gently snoring. I couldn't sleep myself. Through the grease-paper window the glow of the moon penetrated the room like a spotlight, shining straight onto my bed while the others were in slumberous shadows. My thoughts drifted to my lonely childhood, something I usually tried to avoid.

Outside I heard the distant sounds of people yelling. As the ruckus grew louder, I recognized the voices of Lena and Bill. Still

I could not quite make out the words, but they were definitely fighting. I worried about what Bill might do. His anger had been expanding recently, and Lena was more often included in it than in the past. My hands were sweating. I wished to go out and calm them, but I didn't dare interfere. Bill hated that.

When Lena shrieked and sobs followed, I couldn't hold back any longer. I jumped into my boots without tying them and, grabbing my overcoat off the hook by the door, I threw it over my long johns. The moment I opened the door I saw her standing on the path between our two cabins. She glimmered white in the moonlight, her dress blowing round her knees. She was clutching her face. I ran to her.

"What happened? Are you all right?"

She shook her head, keeping the side of her face averted. "Bill and I are through. I'm leaving."

"Are you sure?"

"Yes. He's a monster."

I took her in my arms and she sobbed into my chest. Her vulnerability made me feel, for once, strong. "I'll go with you." In the silence that followed I imagined sympathy for my words and this urged me onward. "We'll start a new life. I love you, you know."

She drew away from me, her face still turned. "Byron, I'm sorry. But I don't think of you that way."

A white heat of shame washed over me. "Can't you even look me in the eye when you say a thing like that?"

She turned full toward me, removing her hand from her face. There was blood flowing down her swollen cheek, and it looked black as oil in the moonlight.

"Oh my God. Lena. Did he do that to you?"

She nodded and as she began to weep again, my heart was filled with a rage that instructed me, in the absence of love, to obey what hate demanded.

"Where did he go?"

She pointed up a path that led into the forest. Leaving her there, a wan signpost at the dirt crossroads, I ran into the darkness. I would find Bill and make him pay.

## CHAPTER TWENTY-ONE

# A NEW ASSIGNMENT

AT 0800 WE codebreakers lined up in the bunker's main hallway with our best military posture to be inspected by Miss Maggie Newbigin of OP-20-G. Though a civilian, she had mastered a sterner eye than any admiral. When she passed me, I was glad that for this exercise we were supposed to stare straight ahead, because that rid me of the difficulty of focusing or not focusing on Miss Maggie's deformity. There was a white scar running from her left cheek to her chin, and that side of her face sagged like a curtain missing hooks. It was hard not to raise my hand to my own face to reassure myself it was all right. It was the same place where Bill had injured me years ago.

I would hate to see Miss Maggie in anger because even in her approval, I felt like we had done something wrong. She gave grudging praise to the work we were doing, and paused to commend Cat Trelawney for cracking the Bible book code. Miss Maggie then announced she would speak with us individually throughout the day. We would meet with her in the conference room at the time appointed on a sheet hanging outside the Captain's office. After she released us, we rushed there to check our times. I was scheduled for the later afternoon. I worked as best I could until 1530 but got nothing worthwhile done, and I was certain Miss Maggie would know of it. I wiped my hands on my skirt—this one was regulation length, unlike the one I usually wore with the secret tailoring—before I entered the conference room.

"Sit down," she said, checking a sheet. "So you are Third Officer Stillman. The one who broke the book code. Very good indeed. It will be noted in your file. For the eyes of the highest security classification only, I am afraid. No parade for you. No, there is never a parade for the likes of us." She gave me the shadow of a smile.

I quelled myself from saying something about the commendation that would be received by Cat Trelawney, rather more public if not quite a parade. She would have the honour of a medal to wear on her uniform.

"You are being considered for a promotion, you know. Very few women have received the rank of Second Officer. They don't like to raise us too high. But before that happens, we need to be sure of your loyalty."

"Of course I'm loyal," I said, wondering who had thrown it into question. Wasn't it obvious I would do anything for the Captain?

"So tell me then. Is there anyone in this unit who seems suspicious to you? Who asks too many questions, or is seen in places they shouldn't be?"

"Not that I've noticed, ma'am." I regretted my stint in the radio room: that sounded like just the sort of thing she was talking about.

"I would like you to make it your business to notice. You will report anything of the sort."

"Yes, ma'am." The idea of a promotion pleased me; I would be one rank above Cat Trelawney.

She looked now not at me, but at the back wall, where the pale square of a map's former presence was evident. "I believe you are one of those women who fills their heads with nonsense about men."

"Not at all, ma'am."

She waved her hand dismissively. "I don't require your dissembling. Go ahead, mix with all the men you like, as long as you can keep quiet yourself. This is useful to us. We like to know who is weak."

"I can keep quiet."

"Now you are telling the truth." She stared at me over her steel-rimmed spectacles and I feared what information she had in the file that rested under her hand, bearing my name. It was thicker than the one the Captain possessed. "I would particularly like you to talk to three men. Sub-Lieutenant Charles Bouvette, Sub-Lieutenant Robert McCormick and Lieutenant Link Hughes."

My hands curled around the armrests of my chair. Link. "Are they under suspicion?"

"Everyone is under suspicion." I stared at her with the irresistible question in my mind: including me? Was she assigning anyone in the unit to probe my weaknesses?

"If I may speak frankly, ma'am, I don't care for what sounds like spying on my colleagues."

"You seem to mistake the nature of this meeting. My requests are not optional. Your qualms also strike me as ridiculous, given the nature of your work. You must erase these last artificial lines in your mind." She opened the file with my name on it and read silently for a while. I felt my armpits grow damp and hoped no mark showed on my jacket. "We like people with secrets. We find it makes them obedient." She stared at me, the good half of her face in a smile, the other side inert. It was dreadful, like a fishhook had yanked up the corner of her face. "Desires change, but fears never do."

I swallowed, hard, hoping this was empty talk—the sort of thing that skillful manipulators pulled. Making you think they knew things they didn't, so you would crack. "I have nothing to be afraid of."

"You were discovered looking into the map room. That's a red flag. You could be the spy. Do you know what the consequences are?"

My mind fluttered, a bird trapped in a room, but quickly I found the window. I was in trouble, but I was not a spy; the truth was on my side. I drew in my breath. "We always had access to the maps before. It was a bureaucratic move that I thought ridiculous. It helped us do our work better, to have a picture of fleet movements." Only one person could have ratted me out about the map room: Cat Trelawney. Had she been spying on me already, or had she merely spilled the information under Miss Maggie's questioning today?

"Let's assume that's true, and you merely have rogue attitudes, with the best interests of the war effort at heart." She scanned the file again, flipping pages. "Let's talk about your relationship with the Minister."

"Minister Middlebury?" Now my shirt was sticking to my back. She had a catalogue of my life. But she couldn't know about before.

"Were you sleeping with any other Minister?"

"Of course not."

"I doubt you were foolish enough to love him. An old man. What did you hope to gain?"

"I was looking for security, and he bought me a house."

"That's all? You could have got so much more out of it—selling sensitive information and such like. That's what someone clever would do. Come now, didn't you?" She looked at me almost sadly, like a priest urging confession, knowing that he will not like what he hears, but must hear and must absolve.

"I don't need money."

She smiled her horrible half-smile again. "Yes, that's right. Your savings are impressive." She tapped the file folder, which she had shut. "What about the visit you made to this fellow in prison, Bill Bagley? The bank robber."

I just stared at her.

"Don't try to deny it. We know everything."

Everything. My whole fate was contained in those three syllables. Miss Maggie had had me under surveillance from the very start. That man I saw twice on my way to see Bill, on the ferry and at the docks—at the time I thought he was a thief who'd marked me, but he must have been her flunky. I'd been a fool to visit Bill. But I had been desperate to ensure his silence, and I had believed in those days, before Japan declared war, that my unit was a forgotten fragment in an obscure part of the world. That what I did was of interest only to myself. But now my work was at the centre of the war and I had delivered to Bill the means of undoing me. He must have told them what they wanted to know.

"We find your skills extremely interesting, and useful in these difficult times. Good under pressure, good at keeping secrets. Flexible morals."

I looked at her angrily but dared not defend myself. She would find a way to use anything I said against me. My jaw throbbed with the tension building from my shoulders and piercing into my head. I had never thought that about myself, never. My morals were just not like other people's, because unlike the somnolent majority I saw society's problems. In my youth I had been misguided, and picked the wrong way of lashing out against an unfair system. But I had left the gang behind, and found a greater ease in my soul. The war had provided an enemy I could fight with my country's blessing. But now that role would be muddied.

"I will take your silence as agreement. Let's be clear how this will work. Your loyalty is not to your Captain or your colleagues, but to me. I think you understand now that I run this show. What you will do exists outside your unit and even outside most of your government. This is the highest classification. So, this is your assignment. You will report back to me, in detail, about the three men I mentioned. Everything, big or small, you learn about Bouvette, McCormick and Hughes. I can't tolerate any holding back."

"Yes, ma'am." I tasted the iron bitterness of blood on the inside of my lip—I must have bitten it.

"Nothing further, Third Officer Stillman. You are dismissed."

## CHAPTER TWENTY-TWO

# JUNE 1933

THOUGH I RAN until my lungs burned, I could not find Bill. I followed the path Lena sent me on through the forest until it petered out to nothing. Standing there, panting, nowhere left to go, I asked myself with a helpless rage: Why do so many paths do this? Does everyone in the world make the same mistake over and over, thinking they are going somewhere and dead-ending all the same? In the process, we each wore the useless path deeper into the ground to lead others onward eternally.

I dry-heaved into the salal bushes. I hadn't run so hard in years.

I collected myself and doubled back, my pace slowed now from exhaustion as I searched for Bill along the highway and then in the main Indian village, where no one was up except for a few mangy dogs that nipped at my heels. I hit one across the bridge of the nose and then I gave up the hunt as hopeless. Walking back to the cabin I passed the place where I'd last seen Lena, which was empty now. The car too was gone from its place in the shrubbery. This would cause us some difficulties.

I crept back into the cabin at the first blue hint of dawn, the men still snoring as it was around 4:30 a.m. It was close to midsummer and there was a longer bleed of daylight in Canada than I was used to. I climbed quietly into bed and curled up under the too-small blanket. What was I to do now? The burning aspect of my rage had subsided and there was only a tight black ball now, embers faded to charcoal. I had no other life but this. I was part of the gang in such a way that extraction was impossible. Bill organized our every move and like a voodoo amulet kept us from harm.

And I had to admit that I would like some more money from this job and then I would be set up for life. My motivations were base. I was a pathetic person and it was no wonder that Lena did not want me. God, the way she looked at me! There was no emotion in her eyes at all. I might as well have been a stranger.

I could not sleep, and fixed my gaze on the ceiling where a mouse scampered across a beam. Its tiny feet gripped the rough board wall easily as it made a zigzag dash to the floor and then disappeared into some crack.

The grease-paper window glowed suddenly bright: true morning. The boys stirred in their beds and Ramon sat up and rubbed his eyes. He was not conscious of me awake and watching him. Drawing his suspenders over his shoulders he shuffled to the door and went outside, no doubt to visit the privy. Some moments later there came an angry roar, and I heard a banging on the other cabin and some shouting.

Ramon burst through our door.

"*Puta madre*! The car is gone! The *chica* is gone! She fucking stole the car!" He punched the wall. "Now what? We're stuck here in the middle of fucking nowhere."

Bill had stepped into the cabin behind him and watched this show with an impassive face. "It's true boys, she took off. Calm you down, Ramon. We don't need her. Dead weight. I've got it figured already. I'll get the Indian to take me across the river and I'll find us another car in Chilliwack. Easy peasy."

He had called her a dead weight. I couldn't believe it. God, the man was unfeeling. How did Lena love him? Still in bed, I kept my face turned to the wall because I did not trust my expression.

"Make yourselves some breakfast, boys. I won't be long," Bill said. "We'll be heading to Harrison by lunchtime."

BILL WAS TRUE to his word and back by lunchtime in an old Chevy sedan. Ramon complained of it because we'd had a Packard limousine before, but Bill told him to shut up, it was for the best, no one would notice us in this car.

"It's ubiquitous," Bill said.

"That is one of the *chica*'s words," Ramon said. "I don't know what you mean when you talk like that."

"Don't ever speak of her again, understand?"

"Okay." Ramon held his hands in the air in apology.

"Just get in the car. Let's go."

No one took the driver's seat until, angrily, Bill told me to sit there; we had been used to Lena doing that job. Low branches scratched the roof as the car jolted crazily along the dirt road, and I gripped the steering wheel tighter. The suspension was nothing like the Packard's, but no matter. We turned onto the highway and, though it was just gravel, at least it had been graded flat and the going was easier. As we sped up, wind blowing fresh through the car, Ramon asked Bill to tell him more about the job, and Bill began to sound cheerful again.

"It's a Concordia safe, model 1911. I can blow the door right off the hinges in five minutes." He turned round to stare at Ramon in the back seat. "Remember, this is not a real holdup. I've paid off the night watchman. We're going to tie him up so it looks right, but we're not going to beat him. So keep your temper under control."

"Why are you talking to me only?"

"Okay, everybody stay under control. I know it's a challenge. By God is a fucking madman."

Everybody laughed.

Why couldn't Bill just leave me alone?

We crossed a bridge over a wide river that surged away from the overbearing mountains. It looked cold and relentless; eventually even water could cut through stone. We passed an old mill perched over the rapids and I slowed at a crossroads where there was a small cluster of clapboard buildings. Bill told me to stop at the general store and he went inside. When he came out he was grinning and holding a large pie.

"Let's have us a picnic," he said.

Not sharing his enthusiasm, I followed his directions down a short dirt road, at the end of which the river was visible. When we pulled over there was not a soul in sight. The place had every kind of emptiness. There was no wind but the urgent river rushed loudly over solitary boulders. The sun failed to warm the rocks we sat ourselves on; they had a deep wintry chill emanating from inside.

Bill had only one fork, so each man ate his share in turn from the pie dish. I thought how if Lena was here we surely would have had plates, napkins and a blanket to sit on. And a full lunch, for that matter. This was a bachelor scheme, indulgent yet incomplete. With Lena we would have laughed more, and I missed how she had illuminated each second of my life. Nothing seemed worth much, now.

When the apple pie was finished—after I'd waited for the last piece—Bill flipped over the dish and poured his white powder on it and sniffed a line. He invited us to do the same, and I was glad of the distraction. Our pit stop done, we drove on.

## CHAPTER TWENTY-THREE

# THE SUSPECTS

I TOOK EXTRA care readying myself for the dance, though there was only so much I could do since I had to wear the uniform and oh, those dreadful shoes. In the morning I made a trip to my house in Rockland to retrieve some nice things. The sentries patted me down on my way out. Security had been tighter these last few months, and they searched us every time we left now, especially those of us in the Examination Unit. We were paradoxically the most and least trusted people on the base; we had access to highly classified information, and would cause a lot of damage if we turned. I was not the spy, but to absolve myself I was forced to spy on my colleagues until I found the traitor and presented him to Miss Maggie. But even then would I be free of her? I thought of the Russian doll I had as a girl, which I had played with obsessively, opening each layer to find the perfect yet slightly smaller doll concealed underneath until finally there was the tiny one you could not open, solitary and exposed. There'd been a satisfying sense of completion to it. Miss Maggie was equally intent on prying open my life and I had to hope she had not truly reached the last layer.

I wished now I'd changed my name after I left Bill. But I had never been identified when I was with the gang, so I believed myself safe after I lay low with my aunt in Calgary for a year. Bill had taken so much from me—scouring my heart of soft feelings—that I had wanted to keep my own name, at least, after I escaped. Also, I needed it to resume my studies at the university. But I should have known Bill would not rest until he'd ruined my new life without him, no matter that years went by.

The night before the Harrison job was when I made my break, when Bill was most fixated on something besides the loss of me. He had gone to the boys' cabin to play poker, which usually lasted for hours, so I waited until deepest night when there would be no witnesses. But when I left our cabin I ran into him, in a rage already, on the path; he must have lost their game because he was returning much sooner than I expected. He was so addled I'm not sure he realized I was meaning to leave—I had not dared bring a suitcase, just a single change of clothes in my purse—but he picked a fight with me anyhow. That night, as well as hitting me, he grabbed me round the neck. I knew I had to get away then or he might kill me. Byron probably saved my life; Bill had dashed into the forest like a maniac when he heard him coming up the path.

I wish I had not let Byron down so openly but he forced my hand. Poor man. I had not realized his pining had developed into love, but it was not to be. I had no appreciation for goodness then, but thought it only dull. Despite the violence I had faced, my love for Bill had not died completely. I believed there was a "real" Bill underneath somewhere who was better. For a long while I half hoped he might quit the drugs and come looking for me when he finished his sentence, but he never did. He surely would have found me had he tried.

A block from my house, I passed a Chinese servant out on an errand—or pretending to be. There could be people watching me right now. I wondered if it was possible Miss Maggie's snoops had discovered the journal in the locked trunk in my attic. The idea made me sweat. If they had that evidence against me, spelled out on paper, I was truly Miss Maggie's slave. But with the precautions I had taken with the lock, I didn't see how they could. And if they didn't know now, it seemed unlikely they ever would. They would have ransacked my things while I was unaware that I was under surveillance. Still, I worried now about the condition of my house as I walked down my street in Rockland, which was silent and almost hostile in its decaying wealth. It had once felt peaceful to me, back when I was naively setting myself up as an esteemed member of society; as though there were second chances.

When I stepped through the door, the place seemed abandoned. Dustsheets covered the furniture, just as I'd left them. My former secure life was gone and I was an interloper here. I shivered in the draft coming down the chimney. I couldn't detect any physical disruptions, but I went upstairs to the attic to be sure. The Hobbs lock was secure as always, so I descended to my bedroom, where everything also looked to be in its place. I opened the dresser and tucked into my military packsack the last remaining pair of silk stockings I had bought before the war—I had surrendered the others to the salvage drives. From my vanity table, I retrieved some lipstick and perfume that Constantine had bought for me in New York. I had the uncomfortable thought that I was engaging in entrapment. But I didn't believe Link was guilty of anything, so I would have nothing to report. I was only going to talk to him because I wanted to, not because Miss Maggie told me to. The other two men could take their chances with me. If one of them was a spy, he had already chosen the risk.

At eight o'clock, the scheduled starting time, I entered the door under the hand-lettered sign "Maison de Danse." Someone on the base had had visions that were not fulfilled; the place remained a workaday gymnasium. At least there was a good sprung floor, and coloured spotlights had been rigged from the ceiling to cast a rose glow. But right now, no one was dancing. There were a few office workers from HQ lined awkwardly along the far wall, and that was all. How could I have forgotten? The young sailors went out first to get drunk, gathering courage to ask the women to dance. I didn't see Link anywhere, though surely he was not out with that crowd.

Having progressed only about twenty feet into the room, I stopped and lit a cigarette. At least I was still close to the escape route if necessary. God, I hated these dances. I'd only come because Link invited me and he wasn't even here.

I was almost glad when I saw Montague making a beeline toward me.

"You look so pretty tonight," she said.

"Thanks." I searched for some compliment I could give her in return. "I love your shoes." And they were beautiful, in dark blue suede with peep toes and high heels that made her skinny legs go on forever like a model's. I'd never noticed this about her before— maybe she'd find a date tonight after all.

"I just had to wear them." She giggled, and I realized she was drunk. "What do you think the punishment is for a shoe infraction?"

"I wish I'd committed one too. I hate these shoes," I said, nodding at my feet.

She laughed again, a little hysterically. She was not just drunk, but very drunk.

"Do you think that Bill Bagley will escape from prison?" she said.

I wondered if this constriction in my chest was what a drowning person felt as water poured into their lungs. "What makes you think he could?" I managed to say.

"He's escaped so many times. Once he was on the loose for eight months down in California. He got a hacksaw blade into the jail and cut through the bars."

I remembered that story because Bill liked to tell it to any new audience. It was from before I knew him and it was a masterpiece of his best planning. Back then I listened to the tale with delight, but I should have taken warning from it instead. As with everything in Bill's life, it ended badly. They wouldn't have captured him if he'd stayed in hiding. But he couldn't resist a new spree of robberies and got caught when the getaway car broke down.

Montague was staring into the group of dancers. "There's something about bank robbers I find so romantic. Maybe I just want an adventure right now."

"They'll watch a man like Bagley really closely. He won't get out." Montague started to protest but I cut her off. "Listen, I'm going to get a drink. See you around." I felt sick to think that Bill could actually escape one more time. Then, his schemes to harm me would have no restraint. I just wanted him dead so I could finally be free. The thought shocked me; I had wanted to forgive Bill, perhaps even remember him as darkly heroic, but he had made it impossible.

I knew I'd been strangely abrupt, and was grateful that Montague was unlikely to notice. A drink. I really did need one. I went to the far wall where a canteen was set up and ordered a whiskey that I downed in one go. Fortified, I scanned the men standing across from me. Still no Link, but I did see Bouvette. He wasn't handsome so I'd never paid him much mind before. He was one of the *kana* Morse operators. In my opinion such men as him should be sent for duty overseas. His work recording Japanese cables was simple enough that any smart girl could be taught to do it in a few months. Josie, for instance, seemed considerably brighter than him.

I walked by him and, locking eyes with him before moving on, I leaned against the wall only ten feet away. He took the bait and came over to say hello. He pulled a pack of Marlboros from his inside pocket, holding it toward me.

"American cigarettes," I said. "Nice. Where'd you get them?"

"That's my little secret. Go on, take one."

"Thanks. This is just ration junk." I stubbed my old one out on the ashtray stand. He handed me a cigarette and lit it with an engraved silver lighter. I breathed out the smoke and smiled. "Much better. You know, it's funny, but I never smoked until after I joined the unit."

"Me neither. It's either crazy boring and you need something to do, or it's a mile a minute and smoking helps with the stress."

"It can be pretty intense." I paused, wondering if I should probe him about his work, but decided it was too early. "Bouvette—that sounds French. Are you from Quebec?"

"Born in Montreal. But I moved to Ottawa when I was a kid, when my dad got a job for the feds."

"What department?"

"Foreign Affairs."

I was momentarily deflated. It seemed unlikely that someone whose father had a cushy government job would bother to be a spy. On the other hand, some people would do anything to lash out against their parents. Bad seeds—I couldn't discount that. In fact, he would be at a premium as a turncoat with his connections.

"I would love to visit Montreal," I said. "I even booked a train ticket last year but then Pearl Harbor happened. So all hands on deck, as the Captain says." Bouvette grinned.

"I wanted to listen to jazz," I continued. "And I've heard the penance at Mount Royal is something to see. The women on their knees, going up the stone steps. Perhaps I would have done it myself. Sort of a peculiar combination, I guess."

"Not at all. Montreal is the perfect place to both sin and be forgiven. We Catholics like a bit of both."

This seemed like a pretty good opening, and I was starting to credit Bouvette with more know-how than I expected. The handsome men weren't the only ones who succeeded with the ladies. But I didn't have a chance to answer Bouvette because Cat Trelawney had shoehorned herself between us. She linked her arm through his.

"I see you've met my date," she said, with a defiant look at me.

"Of course I've met him. He works in the Examination Unit."

"I haven't noticed that you talk to many people. Except Link. He's married, isn't he?" She had tried for an offhand tone, but her jibe was transparent.

"I believe so." Well, I could give as good as I got. I smiled at her sweetly. "Congratulations on your commendation, Cat. That was really great work you did on the book code."

She at least had the good grace to blush and stare at the floor. "Thanks."

"She's a real brainiac," Bouvette said. "Went to Oxford and all."

"Yes, she's talked about it." Ad nauseam, I thought.

"Anyways, somebody ought to break in the dance floor," she said. "Bouvie?"

Cat tugged on his arm and he shrugged at me apologetically. "See you later."

A swing band had started playing on a stage set up beneath the basketball hoop. They were good, especially the lead clarinet, who leaned into his playing like he meant it. The gymnasium had gotten busier and more couples made their way to the floor. Watching them, I leaned against the wall to finish my cigarette. Bouvette was fast on his feet and Cat was having trouble following him. So she wasn't good at everything. She did look lovely tonight though, her raven hair done in a roll over her forehead and pinned up at the sides. Bouvette didn't interest me personally—his plain face had only the virtue of dimples and a strong chin that I'd noticed for the first time when we spoke tonight. But it would be some satisfaction if my attentions to him were an irritation to Cat Trelawney. Whether or not she was snooping on me, she clearly wanted to get under my skin. Her friendly attentions had changed.

"That an American cigarette?"

The question startled me out of my thoughts, but I didn't need to look to know who it was. Link's voice was low, distinctive.

"How did you know?"

"The smell, it's fantastic. Where'd you get it?"

"Bouvette," I said, gesturing toward the floor.

"He's just a Morse operator, isn't he?"

"Yeah. You can finish this if you want." I held the cigarette out to him.

"That's all right. You keep it."

He stood beside me silently a while, staring at the dance floor.

"I thought you said you would talk to me if I came out tonight."

"You're right. I'm sorry. But I am performing my job as watchdog. No other man is bothering you while I'm here."

"True."

"Like Bouvette did."

"Actually, I talked to him first."

"Did you."

"Does that bother you?" I smiled at him.

"Not at all," he said, but I thought, pleased, that it did.

"Turns out he's from Montreal." I stubbed out the cigarette. "I once believed that men from Montreal would be consoling."

"You changed your mind?"

"I never went there to find out, but I'm an eternal optimist."

"No, you're not."

"What do you mean?" I felt a gathering outrage that he should presume to know anything about me.

"To be an optimist you have to look to the future. But from what I've seen, you only live in the present."

"That's not so bad, is it?"

"The present's pretty good, but it could be better. Do you want to dance?"

"Sure."

I had never dared expect that he would ask me to dance. I followed him as he deked between the other couples since the floor was crowded now—the band had started playing Glenn Miller's "In the Mood." He took my right hand in his. I closed my eyes for a moment, sinking into the warm feeling of his other hand resting in the curve of my back until the first gesture of his lead spun me away from him. Unfortunately, swing was not the most intimate of dances. But I had to admit it was fun—by the end of the song I was out of breath and laughing.

"You can really dance," I said.

"Lessons. From my mother," he said, blushing a little. This was charming. "She was crazy for dancing. Competed a bit when she was young."

During the pause in the music we returned to stand against the wall, and he was much more talkative now.

"She also loved music, classical especially. Bach's Brandenburg Concertos was her favourite. Kind of embarrassing now, since it's German and all. But to me, art takes no sides in war. Is that stupid?"

"Bach's from so long ago, he has nothing to do with the Nazis."

"I'd like to play the record for you sometime, if you want."

"That would be great," I said, surprised. He had never been so friendly to me.

I spotted McCormick, the third of my assigned men, across the room, but I brushed the thought aside; I could talk to him some other time. Link was assigned to me also, wasn't he? I'd take pleasure in clearing his name.

The band started a tango and Link asked me again to dance. I wanted to, but worried I'd clomp around like Cat Trelawney. "I don't know if I can do credit to a tango," I admitted.

"Come on, all you have to do is follow me."

Back on the floor among the crowd, he pulled me close until our bodies were touching from shoulder to thigh. Any tango I'd seen, there were a few inches of air between partners—Link must have sensed my surprise.

"This is the Argentinean style," he said.

I wondered at his lack of discretion until I realized that no one from the Examination Unit was nearby. We'd never be noticed unless they literally bumped into us because the hall had filled with hundreds of drunk sailors and HQ clerks we'd never met. It was a soothing anonymity. I did my best to flow with Link's movements, but there was no room for error in our position. Soon I stepped on his foot and I laughed, embarrassed. "This is hopeless."

He murmured into my ear: "Dance as if you were making love to me here on the floor."

Had he been drinking with the sailors? I struggled to concentrate on the tango, flustered by the words "making love." At last I gave over to the dream of his suggestion and, melting into him, felt us move as one.

"When this song ends, I'm going to the creek, near Craigflower Road," he said. "Meet me there, but wait fifteen minutes before you leave."

I stared at him. It was a well-known rendezvous for men and women seeking privacy.

"Will you come?" he asked.

"Yes."

After he left, I went to the washroom to fix my makeup while I waited for the fifteen minutes to pass. Evaluating the face in the mirror, I felt a stab of nervousness. It seemed to take more effort to be pretty than it used to. Most of the Wrens were only twenty years old—but I reminded myself that I was still as slender as any of them, and I had no lines about my eyes. Well, one or two but only if I smiled too hard. That was a rare enough occurrence that no one should notice.

Why was I worried? Link wanted me.

What about his wife? I paused from smoothing dark shadow above my eyes. Well, that wasn't my dilemma. During the war plenty of people forgot those they left behind. She must be one of the forgettable ones. I parted my lips and applied my Max Factor Clear Red.

Surely no one who'd seen me when I was with the gang could identify me now. I had never worn makeup then. My blonde hair had been in a bob, and now it was dyed dark brown and waved down to my shoulders. Clothing styles had changed dramatically—and Bill was right when he said people only noticed the superficial things. From that one grainy picture of me in the newspaper, a distant blur in the getaway car, no connection could possibly be made. Miss Maggie could have no credible witness from any of our jobs or I would have been jailed long ago.

I shoved my lipstick into my purse when I spotted Cat Trelawney standing behind me in the mirror. God, how long had she been watching me?

"Going somewhere?" she asked.

I looked down at my coat; apparently I would have to admit to something. "I'm tired. Just going back to the barracks."

"But it's still early."

"It's late enough for me," I said, brushing by her. "Good night."

## CHAPTER TWENTY-FOUR

# JUNE 1933

A SIGN ANNOUNCED the town of Agassiz in three miles, so Bill had me turn north to avoid it and we followed some quiet farm roads to Harrison instead. The orderly fields pressed up against the mountains, as though anxiously seeking a toehold for civilization. I thought of the Sasquatch that Lena had mentioned. Surely any strange thing could survive undetected in those steep valleys; they were private and foreboding as bad dreams. We pulled over before we reached the main Harrison road because it was five o'clock and there would be too many people about. Bill determined we should wait until dark before we drove the last mile into town. After we'd concealed the car in the brush near a creek, we sat on some logs to wait. Cruickshank peered longingly at a still pool past the bend and said it looked like a good fishing hole and goddamn if he hadn't had a rod in the Packard, but Bill gave him such a look that he shut up immediately. Then we all sat with our hands in our pockets staring at the sky. After a while Bill brought out some more coke that we accepted to pass the time. I had a momentary worry that we had never been so high before a job. But my thinking was sharper than ever, I thought, so maybe it would actually help me.

The log I sat on was coated with thick green moss and from the end of it a young cedar tree was growing, the roots clutching its host. I thought how a person from the desert would marvel at this country, so full of water and life everywhere; but perhaps they would think it too much, and grow tired of abundance. The rain created monstrous trees that shut out the light, and undergrowth taller than a man crowded you in everywhere. I longed for the freedom of the desert where everything might be seen at once. Was I only capable of wanting things I did not have?

Some kind of trout, very large, leapt from the pool that Cruickshank had pointed out earlier; but he stopped himself from commenting on it, for which I was relieved. No need to rile up Bill. Even though he had said little about Lena leaving, that fact alone showed how hurt he was. Normally he ranted about any setback. If I wasn't so angry for what he had done to Lena, I'd feel sorry for him. There was an important part of him that was missing; the part that allowed people to understand the feelings of others.

The day took forever to fade. Since the only food we had was some tough dried salmon that Bill had got from his Indian friend, it was lucky that none of us felt hungry. Frogs began to croak in the forest and the sound engulfed me. I wandered off to find the source of the noise. It had been so loud I was amazed when I finally discovered one of the frogs, bright green, and it was only two inches long. I tried to scoop it off the maple branch but it leapt away and out of sight. I returned to the boys, strangely dejected. The frogs' chorus continued to amplify until night descended and then they were suddenly silent. This seemed to shake Bill from his own silence, as though they had mysteriously held him in check. He slapped his thighs. "Let's get this show on the road."

The engine turned over and sputtered out before it caught on the second try. We passed no one on the way to Harrison. The view of the lake opened before us, vast and shimmering in the moonlight, a deep gouge filled with glacier water off the mountains. The wind raised the waves into a white chop. We turned left to follow the shore and pulled into the hotel parking lot, which was full of cars, so we were not conspicuous among them. The three-storey brick building looked like a brooding English manor and a mist peculiar to itself rose up, which must be the heat of the underground springs escaping. The air tasted of bitter sulphur. Bill put on his spectacles and my gut wrenched into a knot—this was the signal we were ready to go.

On the way, Bill had explained the plan over and over, but he talked so quickly I did not grasp it as well as usual. But I knew that in Lena's absence I was to be the getaway driver. As the boys went into the hotel through the service entrance, I was content with my lesser part in the scheme. My focus was intense and I would drive with precision and great speed. With my leather gloves I gripped the wheel.

My attention was caught by a motion near the lake. A solitary man was walking along the shore. He turned in front of the hotel and headed toward it, no doubt to enter at the main doors, though I could not see for certain because I was parked partways behind the building. I had not made out his features, but I was struck by the lankiness of his silhouette. Like a scarecrow. With chilling clarity I remembered Moe describing Detective Brooke as such a man.

Surely that could not be. What cause would Detective Brooke have to be in a resort spa in Canada? Did his bones ail him? I told myself there were other thin men. Nonetheless I inwardly urged the boys to hurry themselves. I realized I could not remember the time that Bill had told me to start the car; he usually had these things planned out so exactly. I felt certain that he had not said a time in this instance, but I would still be blamed if I was not ready. Damn it, I was ready, but it would not do to start the engine too soon.

An eagle cried from a great height. I gripped the wheel tighter.

Finally from inside the building there was a deep whump and a tremor communicated in the ground beneath me. I pressed the starter button. A sputter, then nothing. I took a deep breath and prayed. I don't know if God or the Devil aided a man in such a time, but when I pressed the button once more the old Chevy rumbled to life. I flung open the car doors as the boys ran out of the hotel.

They jumped in the car, breathless, and I raced out of the parking lot before their doors were even shut.

A map of where I needed to go shimmered in my mind. Because of the geography, there were some unavoidably public points on the escape route Bill had devised. This worried me. We had to briefly follow the main Harrison road, as the valley formed a narrow funnel. In one section we would have to stay on the Lougheed Highway for a couple of miles before we dipped south to the greater safety of obscure roads through a slough. We'd trace them until we reached the spot on the Fraser River where the Indian was supposed to have the canoe waiting. There I was relieved of the main responsibility of our safety, as Cruickshank would steer the boat. Whatever came afterwards, only Bill knew.

After I'd worked this through and calmed a little as the distance between us and the hotel increased, I realized the boys did not have the same excited air as was usual right after a job.

"Is something wrong?" I asked, not removing my eyes from the road.

"There's hitches," Bill said. "Most immediate—I think we're being followed. Pull over."

"Shouldn't I go faster instead?"

"Damn it, do what I say. They're still a ways back."

Maybe Bill was just being paranoid. I hadn't seen any head-lights. But of course I stopped anyhow, and Bill jumped out and ran back to the wooden bridge we'd just crossed. He fiddled underneath it for a few seconds, and was almost back at the car by the time the explosion went off. The bridge collapsed into the river. If there had been any secrecy to our getaway, that was certainly over.

"That'll hold them up a while," Bill said, slamming the door as I took off again.

"I didn't see nobody," Ramon said.

"Keep looking."

I was too occupied to look back myself, but just before I turned onto the farm roads we had taken this afternoon, Ramon said he saw them. They were stopped where the bridge had been. The threat was undeniable now. The only thing uncertain was whether it was the bumbling local police—though Lord knows how they'd have got on our trail so quickly—or Detective Brooke. I thought I'd better unload my suspicion to the boys, so they knew what we might be dealing with. Then Bill could apply the full extent of his wiles to our escape.

"Fuck a duck," Bill said. "I thought I sensed the bastard, somehow."

"What are we going to do?" said Cruickshank. His voice wavered and I hoped he wouldn't lose his grip.

"I'm thinking on it. Can't you drive any faster, By God?"

I gave the pedal more juice and the car jolted harder. Our silence was punctuated by the gasp of the engine as I shifted up and down, navigating the rises.

"We'll leave the car in the slough," Bill said. "We'll walk through the brush the last mile to the canoe. They'll never track us in there. But just to make sure, we need a diversion like we had on the Nanaimo job. Ramon, that's where you come in."

"Me? What do I have to do?"

"We'll let you off at the railway tracks and you can walk to Deroche. Steal yourself a car. Drive it into Vancouver and ditch it there. I'll give you my spectacles to leave in the glove box. Brooke will take the bait."

"Why do I have to go alone?"

"I need Cruickshank in the canoe."

"What about By God?"

"I have an idea for him later. Anyways, yours is the safest part of the plan. Even if you're pulled over, and you won't be, you won't be in the car that robbed the hotel, and you won't have any of the loot. Nothing to connect you. And you can hide out in the shack at False Creek as long as you want."

"When am I going to get my share?"

"Fuck, wake up Ramon. Does it matter? Your share of nothing is nothing."

"What do you mean, nothing?" I asked.

The three men were silent.

"Somebody tell me."

"There was only five hundred dollars in the safe," Bill said.

"What happened to all the jewels?"

"The fancypants checked out early. The watchman didn't know until he got to work tonight."

"But you still blew up the safe."

"Sure. I'd brought all that dynamite. I like a good blast."

Bill had come unhinged. That was a terrible risk to take for so little gain. But it was done, and there was no choice but to keep running. We were approaching the Lougheed Highway crossing, so I turned off the headlights and stopped the car to stare down the road in each direction.

I heard a noise from the west, sickeningly familiar. Sirens.

"Get the guns ready, boys," Bill said.

At least we'd prepared the car for a shootout beforehand by taking out the rear window—we hadn't entirely lost our senses. Ramon and Cruickshank grabbed the Tommy guns off the floor, and Ramon handed one forward to Bill.

"Drive, By God, drive."

I floored the pedal as we hit the highway and prayed we'd get to the turnoff quickly. The slough was our only chance. We'd have to lose the cops in there somehow.

## CHAPTER TWENTY-FIVE

# CONFLAGRATION

THE PLACE EVERYONE went on the creek was up toward Craigflower Road, away from the barracks and prying eyes. If you saw anybody else they were there for the same reason as you, and would keep your secret in order to keep their own. Of course I wasn't married and had nothing to hide on that front, but affairs of any sort were officially forbidden. When they let women into the Navy they wanted to preserve the moral appearance of the service. Even couples who legalized their relations were punished, because Navy policy was to separate spouses when both were enlisted. I suppose they thought that love dulled our judgement in war.

The path went through a thick conifer forest that shut out most of the moonlight. I tripped on a rock and fell onto my knees, ruining my last silk stockings. My hands stung when I wiped them together to get off the dirt. I was glad it was dark now, or a fine sight I'd make for Link.

Despite the hazards of the trail, I quickened my pace at the thought of meeting him. That he asked me to come was beyond anything I expected. I had spent so many years hardening my heart, I'd forgotten I could have any passions at all. But right now, the signal was clear—I wanted this. There were complications, clearly, what with the wife. But she was a distant object and could be contended with later. I suspected divorce would become more common after the war, which had changed people. Like the young sailors I saw in the mess—they were never the same when they came back from their tours of duty. Some were quieter, some wilder, some harder; but an alteration was sure.

When I arrived at the meadow beside the creek I found Link leaning against a Garry oak, the tree's jagged limbs silhouetted like black lightning.

"I thought you wouldn't come."

"Of course I would. You asked me to."

He took me in his arms, kissing me deeply. The first feeling I had was surprise—I hadn't expected him to move so quickly when he'd only tonight shown interest in me. But it all felt wonderful in a way it hadn't since a long time back—since I was with Bill. Yet Link wasn't crazy or mean or wild, and I wasn't a kid anymore: such qualities no longer attracted me. Link was a good, smart man, the perfect person with whom to share a normal, happy life. Right now, I wanted this more than anything and it felt within my reach.

He caressed my cheek and I looked down, suddenly shy.

With my eyes to the ground I noticed we had trampled some wildflowers that glowed white against the dark meadow. Death camas, I thought with a chill. They grew alongside the purple camas the Salish Indians consumed before the Europeans came. Once the flowers were withered from the plants, and it was time for the harvest, the bulbs of the two species were indistinguishable— one nourishing and one deadly. The Salish had weeded their fields to eliminate the threat, but long neglect allowed the poisonous flowers to return.

Link drew my chin up with his finger and kissed me again. He tasted faintly of liquor. I hoped he wasn't too drunk to remember this—but I would freely accept any recklessness it might bring to his behaviour. His lips were warm and soft. I felt he was giving himself to me entirely and I sank into the moment.

The sky lit with a streak like a shooting star, but strangely low. A rumble followed, then an explosion that jolted my ribs. An orange ball of flame roiled beyond the trees.

The air-raid siren wailed from the base.

Link and I stared at each other and then dropped flat, our hands over our heads as we'd been trained to do. Though we could not get underground we were safest where we were, away from all visible targets. The field's damp soaked through my dress as I lay on my stomach. Two more explosions burst through the siren's moan. Heavy machine-gun fire followed. The dirt was cold against the side of my face. The siren sounded continuously, shattering my thoughts.

The glow against the sky was larger now; something on the base was on fire, I thought. At least the shelling seemed to be over.

"Are you okay?" he asked.

"Yeah. God, I can't believe it. The Japanese? Here?"

"Seems to be."

"Should we go see what happened?" There was a smell in the air now, as of bitter incense and hot metal.

"It's not safe."

"I'm going. Are you coming or not?" I stood up, too quickly it seemed, so I leaned against the oak to settle the spinning in my head.

Link nodded. As we ran, I tossed off my shoes. Even though they were war regulation, the Navy evidently did not picture its women in battle situations—the heel made navigating roots and rocks difficult. In that way the brain has of setting up a safe platform above chaos, I thought to myself that tomorrow, no doubt, my feet would be a mess of bloody cuts, but how marvellous right now that I should not feel anything. Adrenaline surged and I felt capable of facing whatever might come.

When we emerged from the forest we had a full view of the terrible scene. The men's barracks were on fire. There was only a skeleton of the structure left inside the flames: the building was made of cedar, the fastest-burning wood. At least the gymnasium was still standing—everyone had been at the dance. Even though the attack was sudden, there would have been time to get into the air-raid shelter. It must be so; we were the only people about with the exception of a few sailors, who were shirtless in the heat from the fire as they manned the hoses. My eyes stung from the smoke.

I squinted toward the bunker when I remembered that a small crew from the Examination Unit was on shift tonight. With a shock I realized that the old fortifying wall, where it met the ocean, did not look at all the same. There was a jagged break in the top, where one of the antique gun turrets had been; the cement must have cracked and fallen into the sea. But I assured myself that this had nothing to do with the structure of the bunker itself, which was set much deeper into the hillside. But it begged the question: Was the location of the bunker known to the Japanese? A radio unit was an important enemy target.

It must have been a sub, because our patrols would have spotted a ship. Then again, the patrols were awfully thin. It was just the fisherman's volunteer reserve, because the real military was far away in the Pacific. Who knew the battle would come to us? I scanned the group putting out the fire for anyone in authority. Recognizing the Commodore from HQ, I approached him.

"Sir. Is there anything I can do?" I couldn't remember if I saluted when I arrived, so I saluted now just in case. I'd better pull myself together, I thought.

"There's no place for a woman here," he barked. "Will you explain to me," and he stared at my sleeve for my rank insignia, "Third Officer, why you didn't respond to the siren and take shelter?"

"Sir, I was far from the buildings and safest where I was." I had to divert him before he could ask where that might be—or notice my strangely bare feet. What had I been thinking, coming over here? "I request permission to account for my unit," I managed.

"That being?"

"Radio intelligence."

"Report to Captain Bromley-Sinclair, and I'll leave it to him. Go into the shelter under the gymnasium, as that's likely where you'll find him. Let everyone know the all-clear should be sounding soon. The fire's almost under control."

"Thank you, sir."

Even though I'd scarcely finished my salute, I was glad that he turned his back to watch the firemen so I could escape without further scrutiny. Returning to the edge of the forest, I found Link where he'd been hanging back.

"What did the Commodore say?"

"Not much, except he thinks the emergency is over. We can go to the shelter and check on our unit."

"I think it's best we're not seen together. You go ahead."

"All right." I hesitated a moment, wishing he would change his mind. But it was the wisest course, so I left him there, watching the barracks burn.

## CHAPTER TWENTY-SIX

# JUNE 1933

I WAS DOING something that seemed very wrong: I was speeding *toward* the police cars. Bill insisted if we gunned it we'd beat them to the turnoff for the slough. Forward or back, we had no choice but to be on the highway right now, because the mountains and the Fraser River forced a single course between them. The boys had their weapons pointed out the windows, but Bill ordered them not to shoot because we didn't want to set the bastards off before we had to. They weren't in range yet anyhow—thank God. I had a hard time not closing my eyes the way you do on a carnival ride before you throw up.

We reached the turnoff and I wrenched the wheel to the left. The road became much rougher and it slowed us up. The police, still on the highway, drew closer.

"Shoot their tires!" Bill yelled.

The explosion of gunfire hurt my ears. I tore my eyes from the road a moment to glance in the rear-view mirror—the car was stopped dead, steam hissing from the hood.

"What a bunch of fuckwits," Bill said. "It's always so easy." He sounded almost disappointed.

It was not Detective Brooke, then. He was no chump. Must just be the local constables. But that meant our crime was radioed out, and we'd have to be careful wherever we went.

We drove along, silent and watchful, through the desolate brush, scrub the height of a man mixed with patches of swamp, with Bill directing me to turn now and again. Although our route was twisting, I sensed we were heading generally westward. When we crossed a railway track, Bill told me to stop.

"Ramon, this is you. Cross that bridge and keep following the tracks until you hit Deroche. Takes about forty-five minutes."

"All right," he said, getting out the car. He did not complain any more of his mission now that it was at hand. Bill got out also and passed him the spectacles; then he did something I'd never seen him do before. He hugged Ramon.

"Meet you in three months in San Francisco, okay? Miss Lizzy will tell you where to find me."

"I always liked Miss Lizzy," Ramon said. "She has good whores."

As he walked away down the tracks, his silhouette diminishing as the distance between us increased, I wondered if I would ever see him again. What was so sad about that? He was a thug who had much plagued me. This melancholy must be a result of coming off the drugs.

We drove this way and that for another twenty minutes, until Bill pointed down an embankment where we could conceal the car. The road had almost disappeared, and brush scraped against the undercarriage as I came to a stop. Bill pulled a bag out of the trunk and from it he took an axe, before directing us to shove the car down an incline. He walked around the bend to chop off some branches, which he dragged back over the wheel marks to erase them. Then he piled the branches over the hole where the car had gone into the brush. We walked back up to the road to inspect our handiwork. The car was invisible.

As we thrashed through the slough, Bill in the lead, I regretted the dress suit I was wearing, which was meant to blend in at the spa. Mud and water sloshed up my pant legs, and thorns snagged the Italian weave. Cruickshank was similarly equipped; he'd have been better off in his golf tweeds. Bill was in blue coveralls and high boots, lucky man; his scheme for the holdup had been to look like a repairman of some kind. We trudged onward, until by my pocket watch it was one a.m. We arrived at the edge of the Fraser River and its rush was deafening. A horrible creature like a spiny shark, a good twelve feet long, surged to the surface before disappearing again in the dark water. Surely no shark could have made it sixty miles from the sea in fresh water but God knows what it was, so I pushed it out of my mind as a hallucination.

It was not long until Bill found the huge war canoe tied up on a sandy bank. Though I was glad of his sense of direction, I stared at the ancient dugout with misgiving. The interior was scored with deep cracks along the grain and I doubted its seaworthiness. The river was so wide I could scarcely see the other side, and it was running high. While there was no visible whitewater, it swirled with mad boils. Bill waded in, hauling the boat, while Cruickshank and I held the stern. Bill climbed into the front, taking up his paddle.

"You in the middle," Cruickshank said.

As usual I was in the place that did not matter—Bill was the power and Cruickshank the navigator. Resigned, I waded in. The icy water shocked me quickly into the boat, my wet hands slipping on the gunwales. I'd never been in a canoe before. Copying Bill's position, I settled onto my knees, paddle at the ready. Cruickshank leapt in and pushed off from the bank at the same time. The river gripped us instantly, dragging us far downstream. I paddled with all my strength, shouting on each stroke with the effort of fighting the current. Cruickshank angled the nose of the dugout diagonal to the shore, and soon we took a better line; perhaps we would not be sucked to the sea after all. The boat shuddered as we passed over some rough sections. It was slow going and the sweat poured down my face. As we approached an island blocking our route to the shore, the back-eddy helped our boat advance and I could ease up a little.

When we reached the tip of the island, the main current grabbed us again but at least the shore was close now. I leaned heavy into the paddling for the final stretch. Cruickshank redirected the boat's nose one more time and we made it across. Bill was out first, then me. My feet sank into deep river mud. I struggled to hold onto the canoe, which was so heavy the three of us could hardly lift it up the bank. At least it had remained watertight. We managed to drag it up and into some brush.

"The Indian will find it here," Bill said. "And if he can't, that's too bad. I paid him enough he can buy a new one."

My heart was pounding. The emergency passed, I realized how dangerous the crossing had been. The river had an evil force, and if the boat had capsized I'd have surely drowned. My legs were weak under me, but I needed them to function. We were not in safety, not yet. I didn't know where the hell we were, or where we were going. I turned to Bill, and Cruickshank was regarding him also. We were completely in his hands now.

"The river pulled us further down than I expected," Bill said. "We're somewheres above Abbotsford. We'll steal a car to take us east of Chilliwack. That's where we want to cross the border. It's wilder country back there."

## CHAPTER TWENTY-SEVEN

# THE ASHES

THE MAISON DE DANSE had the profound sense of abandonment that came of a panicked leave-taking. Coats were still hanging at the door, and galoshes were scattered beneath them. I paused to slip a pair over my bare feet. A soda bottle had tipped over on a table, leaving a sticky puddle on the floor. The sheet music was still in the metal stands and the instruments lay at crazy angles on the stage. My steps squeaked on the wooden floor. The entrance to the air-raid shelter was at the far end. I opened the door and went downstairs into the deep cement room.

I closed the door behind me and, adjusting to the dim light, I registered a few hundred people lined up on benches along the walls, staring.

"What's happening out there?" asked a sailor sitting near the door.

"The men's barracks were hit, but they're putting out the fire now. The Commodore thinks the all-clear will sound pretty soon."

"So it was the Japs?"

"Looks that way."

"They've finally come to get us."

He sounded shaken, but I had nothing more to say to him. My purpose was to find the Captain, but the room was so crowded I couldn't focus. "Captain Bromley-Sinclair, are you here?" I said, as loudly as I could.

There was no answer. The stale air stifled me.

"The Commodore asked me to account for Examination Unit personnel," I said, blindly, to the crowd. "All of you, please stand now and state your names. Start at my left, near the door, and go counter-clockwise."

As they did so, I counted fifty-one people from my unit. Then there was me and Link. That left twelve on shift in the bunker, including the Captain. But I didn't remember his name being on the duty roster for tonight. I'd read it carefully, to make sure I was not on it myself since I had wanted to go out. A terrible thought struck me—the Captain had never liked going to dances.

No, surely he was in the bunker. I'd go there now.

As I started to open the door, the sailor who spoke to me jumped up and barred my way. "What are you doing, love? The all-clear hasn't sounded yet."

"I've already been up there. It's perfectly safe."

He stood his ground and I assessed the insignia on his sleeve: a single gold chevron.

"Listen to me, Able Seaman. I may be a woman, but I outrank you. Stand aside."

He spit on the floor but he moved his hulking frame. I determined to report him later, though I doubted I'd get any satisfaction from the Commodore. Of course the Captain would take my part and exert whatever influence he could.

The Captain. I had to find him. I ran up the stairs, through the gymnasium, and shoved open the doors to the outside. The men had nearly doused the flames at the barracks but I was drawn to the remaining glow. Embers sizzled at my feet. Men in masks were carrying two stretchers out of the building. I needed to know who was injured, so I rushed up to the first stretcher. The blackened form was scarcely recognizable as a man. I turned away quickly, feeling sick, but still I made myself examine the next stretcher. The men carrying it told me to stay back, but as they could not put down their load, they were helpless to prevent me.

This person was also charred and dead. There was a ruby ring, the one the Captain had always worn on his left pinkie finger, still on the hand. I closed my eyes and turned away, staggering.

The all-clear siren wailed and the grounds were suddenly chaotic with people. The stretchers were out of sight, but soon enough everyone in the unit would know the terrible news. None but me knew the further truth—that I might be in part responsible. I had concealed the piece of paper with the Japanese code. I retreated to the deserted women's barracks, which had been untouched by the shelling. Why couldn't the bomb have landed here instead, where there was no one inside to die? I collapsed into bed, feeling more alone than I'd ever been.

## CHAPTER TWENTY-EIGHT

# JUNE 1933

CRUICKSHANK AND I flipped over the canoe and lay ourselves flat under it to stay out of sight. Being on the wet ground was not a pleasant feeling. I'd rather have been out there with Bill, but he decided a single man walking about in the night would attract less attention than three. Cruickshank and I were stuck there for a couple of hours, and my mind pursued unhappy thoughts in the enforced silence. We'd certainly need new clothes or we'd look the worst sort of vagabonds, the kind that had housewives phoning the police. Also I wondered where Lena had gone and what she was doing. I wished I could have been with her, even if only as her friend, as I used to be. If I hadn't been such a fool as to say I loved her, maybe she'd have accepted me as her saviour from Bill and her companion in escape. I imagined being free of this botched job and the relentless Detective Brooke.

There was a rumble of an approaching engine. Could it be the police? Surely they could not predict such a crazy getaway as this. Like Bill said, they'd be checking the bridges. Maybe also the railway lines—I hoped Ramon had made it to Deroche before they thought of that.

The car stopped. Footsteps approached. My breathing was amplified inside the echo chamber of the upturned canoe, filling me with panic: could it be heard from outside? The canoe flipped off us, leaving us exposed in the dirt like worms. There was Bill standing above us, grinning. Why couldn't he have announced himself? I hated him in that moment.

"Time for you lazy bums to get up. Your ride is here."

"It's a nice one," Cruickshank said, surveying the red Nash coupe. He brushed off his pants, but it was no use; he stared with disgust at the mud that was now on his hands. I didn't bother trying to clean up, but just opened the passenger door and sat down on the white leather seat.

Bill drove along the deserted farm roads, now and again passing a tractor crawling through distant fields with the eternal exhausting industry of the farmer. The light outside was still pale and distorted so that the colour of our vehicle would remain ambiguous to any witnesses, I thought. Didn't red appear black in the dim? Like the blood on Lena's face the last time I saw her. God, I would never forgive what Bill did. It took every ounce of willpower I had to push the memory aside, or I could never sit calmly beside Bill as I needed to do. My fate was bound to his a little longer.

I hoped we would get to wherever we were going before dawn sliced through the sky, but it was overcast so we should have an extra half hour. In my mind I urged Bill on faster, to get ourselves out of sight; and then I worried he should go slower, to be less conspicuous. I didn't know anymore the right thing to do in any situation. I was losing my bearings.

We headed southeast for forty-five minutes before Bill slowed at a ramshackle property, perhaps a farm if one was willing to think in terms of failures—certainly there was no shortage of those in the world. There was a log cabin in a clearing cluttered with huge stumps that had never been pulled, while most of the land was still dominated by the original forest. Instead of livestock there were only a couple of wild deer eating what they pleased from the field. There was an old barn, never painted, and a smaller shack at the edge of the trees.

"This is perfect," Bill said. "We'll hole up here a few days till the heat is off. It's only about three miles to the border. We can make it over the mountains in a night, easy peasy."

"What if somebody's here?" I asked.

"Use your eyes. They ain't. No smoke coming out of the chimney. Look at all the weeds at the front door. The place hasn't been used for years."

"I think we'd better check."

Bill rolled his eyes, but shrugged his assent. We got out of the car, Cruickshank tucking a pistol in the back of his pants.

"Don't be an idiot," Bill said. "A shot would draw attention we don't want."

"Okay. But I got your back, just in case."

Bill put his finger to his lips and he pointed toward the larger cabin. I nodded. Bill took the lead and we picked our way across the rutted field. We got about halfway to the cabin when I spotted a large split rock beside a fresh hole—no doubt the spot where it had lodged until someone moved it recently. I waved my arm frantically toward the hole, but only Cruickshank was in a position to see. He drew out his gun. Bill walked on ahead unknowing and pushed open the cabin door. Cruickshank went around the side of the cabin toward a window, where he could cover us. I followed Bill into the cabin, unsure how I'd be able to help him, or what might befall me.

Inside it smelled awful, like rotten meat, and I pinched my nose shut. My eyes darted everywhere, alert to danger. There was a hand-hewn chair beside a table covered with stained oilcloth that was scattered with mouse shit. A sagging old armchair, coated in dust, sat beside an ancient woodstove. It had rust patches, and a missing leg was propped up with bricks, but the nickel door still shone with the word "Freedom" cast into it. On a raised platform on the other side of the stove there was a heap of rags, which I soon realized was a person sleeping.

I moved quickly but quietly in front of Bill and pointed; his eyebrows raised and that was all. Cool as anything, he walked over and shook the old man awake.

"Hey, mister. We need a place to stay. We inconvenience anybody, your wife or your son or anyone, if we rent that shack out yonder a while? We'll pay you handsome."

The man stared at him, blank and mean. He had thick stubble on his face like boar's bristle. His long johns were stiff and stained, as though he hadn't changed them all winter. He was tough and wiry—a crazy old bugger who'd be something to contend with.

"What?" he said.

"You deaf?"

"Don't need people out here. This is my land. Get out."

The man reached behind his bed. I lunged over him and pulled out a rifle. Bill meanwhile had made his own split-second decision. From a heap of tools leaning against the wall by the door he grabbed a pickaxe. He swung it high and brought it down on the man's chest. The man screamed and blood gushed out of his mouth. Blood spattered on my clothes. Despite my horror I couldn't move away nor stop staring. The man's chest was caved in and he was now limp and utterly silent. Bill raised the pickaxe over his head once more and paused for another swing.

"Jesus Christ," I said. "Stop it. He's dead."

Bill threw the pickaxe clattering on the floor and looked down at himself. "Shit. Got to get some new clothes."

He walked calmly out the door. I grabbed a blanket hanging over a rope near the stove—shuddered—and threw it over the man's body. Cruickshank was waiting outside, silent. He must have seen the whole thing through the window.

"There weren't nobody but the old man," Bill said. "We're all right to stay here."

Despite Bill's assurance, when he disappeared without further explanation of what he planned to do, Cruickshank spoke to me in a low voice.

"We ought to take shifts on watch. Just you and me."

I agreed. While the old man seemed like a lone backwoods type, he hadn't said enough that I was convinced of that fact. What if somebody checked up on him?

Something had changed. We were afraid of Bill now, and not so sure of his reason. That was a vicious thing he'd done.

I took the first watch.

## CHAPTER TWENTY-NINE

# THIRTEEN PLACE SHIFT

THE NEWSPAPER DID not say what time the execution would be. I wish they had so I'd know when it was over. I didn't think it had happened yet, because I still felt Bill's presence: meaning I was still afraid the police would burst into the barracks and arrest me as a thief if Bill found a way to trade my freedom for his life. I had the covers pulled over my head, which was silly, but it gave me comfort. When I was a girl and imagined intruders in the house, I thought if they could not see my face they would leave me be. The feeling of warm safety didn't make any sense then or now.

I sat up and looked around. No one was here except for a couple clerks sleeping after the night shift. All I could hear was the scrabbling of some creature inside the wooden walls. I flung the covers off and put on my uniform. The clock over the door read twelve after nine—I was more than an hour late for my shift but I didn't care. I could not work with such a distracted mind. With the bombing only a few days ago and the new unit commander not yet arrived, everything was in chaos anyhow. I doubted anyone would notice I wasn't there.

In no hurry to get to the bunker yet, I opened the barracks door, stared up at the blue bowl of the sky and walked down to the shore. Did they do the executions outside, I wondered. They did not allow the public to attend anymore, so I was relieved of the idea that I should have been there for him when nobody else was. Now that the end was really here, my image of him had shifted. In life, he was the Bill of the present moment, ruined and cruel. But approaching death, he was overlaid with his previous selves and I felt that his once-grand gestures deserved some memorial. There was a time you could have found hundreds of people to toast him, but they only stuck by in the good times, like when Bill was handing them money.

I approached a weathered green and white dory that was stranded on the rocks. *Island Princess*, someone had painted in a wobbly hand along the side. Funny how even the most humble seacraft were given these aspiring names. I remembered when I was a girl and my father rowed us around Lost Lagoon in Stanley Park, me tossing breadcrumbs to the mallards as they followed in our wake. I had never tried to row myself but it had not looked hard and I yearned for the peaceful feeling of being out on the water. Why shouldn't I go now? I dragged the dory by the frayed rope tied to the bow, and I grit my teeth as the bottom of the boat scraped along the stones. It was heavier than I thought it would be. I pulled it into the surf, my shoes getting soaked before I jumped in and started to row, my back to the horizon where I was headed. I could not cry for Bill, though my chest was tight around one hollow place as though it had been gouged out with a knife, like paring the rotten part from an apple.

I wasn't sure how long I planned to row or how I would even know how far I'd gone, since there were no reference points on the open ocean. But the Esquimalt peninsula had grown small, and the radio tower was the only landmark on the base I could make out from this distance. I wasn't tired yet but it struck me I should stop before some strong current dragged me out further. My soul felt an emptiness that was both freeing yet terribly sad, and I believed Bill was now dead. I looked at my watch and it was 10:04 a.m. I bobbed on the waves. Could you miss a hurricane? Not really; yet the world required a sense of awe or even fear so one could appreciate the quiet daily decency of being alive.

So that was it. The police had not come for me and I felt sure now that they never would. As much as my panicked mind had wanted to blame Bill for letting slip my notorious history to Miss Maggie's flunkies, I should have known better. A silent betrayal was not in Bill's nature; he did things grandly. If he'd betrayed me he'd have let me know what he'd done so he could wallow in his dirty triumph.

He must have known from the start that getting a pardon was hopeless. He was the most notorious criminal within a thousand miles. He had forced me into an impossible situation, and the failure with Constantine was not my fault. The wind was picking up and as the boat rocked I grabbed the sides. Bill had been an imperturbable sailor and would have gone on to his endpoint no matter the risks. As the hangman put on the noose, he would have stared into this sky and not seen God. He would face death squarely, and perhaps he even told the hangman a joke. I could see that. I rubbed my eyes and they were wet with tears after all.

I rowed and rowed back toward the shore, my biceps hurting from the strain. I had gone out too far. I stopped to rest, letting the oars hang in the water. Was it possible I had become something like Bill without meaning to? At first, I'd seen him as a leader of men and looked up to him. For him, knowledge was power. He memorized the floor plan of every bank, the design of every vault, and every side road on our getaway routes. He led us through difficulties no one else could manage and emerged, if not exactly a hero, at the top of his game. Everyone deferred to him. Ever since then, I had wanted to be regarded as a superior person too. So now that I was a codebreaker, I needed everyone in the unit to see I was the best at our esoteric craft. But in the case of the pigeon code, hoarding information on the chance of a heroic breakthrough might have made me responsible for the Captain's death. This was as horrible as anything Bill had ever done. I should have shared the message with the entire unit as protocol demanded. We would have applied our joint abilities to crack the code, and the Japanese attack could have been discovered in time. I had confided in Link, it's true, but that was not enough. Sharing the code with him was a self-interested act—a secret known by one is lonely, while a secret known by two is intimate.

It was possible the pigeon code did not refer to the attack on the bunker, but to something else. I could pretend I just found it and hand it over for decryption. I'd need to get the code back from Link—I wished I hadn't dragged him into this. Guided by the radio tower, I continued rowing back to shore, struggling against the wind.

THE NEXT MORNING I composed myself carefully before going to the bunker. I splashed my face with cold water and applied makeup to conceal the circles under my eyes. As I slid into my chair, no one gave me a second glance or commented on my missed shift, just as I'd hoped. Everyone was preoccupied with the Captain's funeral the following day. Even Link did not meet my eye; I had not expected that and it made me feel abandoned somehow. I reminded myself that he needed to be discreet, because of his wife, and things would be different when we were alone. I tried to focus on the cable from Admiral Yamamoto that I was piecing together, but I made little headway. It was amazing how being ignored took up so much space in my mind, since it was by definition nothing.

I sighed and looked at the clock on the wall, but less than an hour had passed. Across the room, Cat Trelawney stretched her arms and looked at the clock also. Her face flushed, and she stood up and left. Her eyes were darting everywhere—if she was up to no good, she had a thing or two to learn about not looking suspicious. Planning to follow her, I gathered some files off my desk as though I was going to the clerks' office. I paused: this longing to do her harm, to control her through information, came from the part of me that I now wanted to leave behind. As Cat left the room, I put my files down and settled back to my work.

Despite my resolution, I couldn't help but watch for her return. She was gone more than twenty minutes, and she sat down with disheveled hair and glowing cheeks. So that was her game: she'd been with a man. I supposed it was Bouvette, though for a moment I wished I had followed her to know for certain. Fraternizing between the sexes was forbidden and if caught she would be punished. I tapped my pencil on the oak surface of my desk, but stopped myself as Cat looked at me, startled by the noise. I couldn't help but give her a smile, which she would take as a knowing smile if her guilty conscience saw it that way. She stared down at her papers, frowning as though hard at work.

I was drawn from my conjectures when Link stood up from his desk, locked the drawers and grabbed his jacket from the hook by the door. I waited a moment before I got up myself, climbing up the stairs and into the light. Soon enough I spotted Link ahead of me on the way to the mess and I hurried to catch up with him. When I said hello, he kept his eyes to the ground and said it was best we were not seen together. I was angry—he was carrying discretion too far. We had always spoken in public, as friends, before the night of the attack. Did he think I would go crazy and throw myself at him in front of everyone? Keeping my tone cold and even, I insisted it was not a personal matter but one of grave importance to our work. With obvious reluctance, he agreed to meet in half an hour.

"Where?" I asked.

"At the creek."

He turned from me and left, so I gathered no hint of his intentions. Could he mean to continue our liaison where we left off? If not, the location was ill chosen. But I could not guess anything yet; objectively, the creek was the only private place on the base.

In my impatience I went there immediately. Waiting, I pulled newly furled leaves from the maple branches that hung low to the ground and tore them into little pieces. When I saw Link approach at last, I tossed the damp leaves from my palm and they fluttered to the ground. He stopped well away from me, his hands in his pockets. I gave him a smile that I feared was a little wobbly. So this was how things were.

"About that code I gave you. I think I should turn it in to the Unit, pretending I just found it. Maybe we could prevent another disaster . . . " As soon as the words were out, I wasn't sure I could do it. I'd waited too long, and Miss Maggie had enough suspicions about me already. The hope flared that he would suggest turning it in himself; that he would want to protect me. Instead, he laughed.

"Don't worry about that. It wasn't a Japanese code. It's from the local fishermen's militia—amateurs playing around. They used a Caesar cipher, thirteen place shift." He pulled the slip from the pocket inside his jacket.

"Jesus, I feel like such an idiot. I was only focused on Japanese letter patterns. "

He studied the code for a few more moments. "It's just garbage, really. 'No fish off Point Flattery. Meet at Port Renfrew bar tonight.' No use reporting it."

"I'm so relieved. I was sick with thinking I had a part in what happened." I put my hand on his arm, but he drew away.

He muttered something about having to get back, and he left me in the forest alone. My eyes burned but I did not cry. After waiting until I was sure I wouldn't catch up with him, I followed the path back to the barracks, kicking my feet in the dirt. I passed the chaos of carpenters building a new dormitory for the men, this one made of sheet metal. They would re-do the women's next. Flammable cedar had been a terrible choice in a time of war. But they were acting too late; the disaster had already happened.

At least I did not have any fault in the Captain's death. God, a substitution cipher. The Caesar! Nothing could be simpler. I stuffed my hand into my jacket pocket to retrieve the slip, but it wasn't there. That's right, Link hadn't given it back; but it did not matter now.

## CHAPTER THIRTY

# JUNE 1933

CRUICKSHANK WAS GONE. I couldn't exactly blame him, but it was a shock that he should sneak off like a dog, after we'd been together nearly two years. During the first watch, standing at the edge of the forest behind a large cedar that afforded a view of the road, I had seen nothing for two hours until a single automobile puttered down the road. I caught a glimpse of the occupant, and then ducked behind the tree. I was certain it was Detective Brooke. Once the car was out of sight, I ran to the shack to tell the boys.

"He'll never get me alive," Bill had said, with an unholy glint in his eyes.

Cruickshank had not looked up from the stick he was whittling.

When Cruickshank took his turn on watch, I fell into a doze as the afternoon sun warmed the shack. My sleep was fitful, punctuated by dreams of the horrible thing Bill had done to the old man. I awoke again and found my limbs had gone cold, so I checked my pocket watch. Six o'clock, and Cruickshank was not back. I went to look for him outside.

"Can't find Cruickshank anywhere," I told Bill, who was stacking firewood at the door. "You seen him?"

"He's scarpered," he said. "But we don't need him. I've fixed everything. I hid the car in the barn, and I found us some new clothes. Don't know how they'll fit though." Bill dropped a pillow-case he'd used as a sack on the ground near my feet. He must have taken the stuff off a clothesline down the road, and I hoped he hadn't been seen.

"That's no matter." I cleared my throat, nervous to broach it but my conscience would not rest. There was one decent thing we could do. "Shouldn't we bury the old man?"

"Why? The Devil will find a man wherever he lies. We don't need to break our backs."

"What if someone comes around? They'll see his body on the bed and sound the alarm."

"That is a point, By God, I will consider." He stuffed his hands in his pockets and stared musing out the window. "This is wild country. If we leave the door of his cabin open, wolves or bears will tear him up by morning. It'll seem he died of natural causes."

This had a cold laziness I did not like, but I could not think how to dissuade him. He started off to enact his plan, such as it was; but he paused and turned back, tossing a newspaper onto the table before he left. I supposed he must have stolen it from someone's mailbox—I hoped even Bill would not have had the gall to go into a store and buy it. As I read the headlines my stomach churned.

### HARRISON HEIST LINKED TO SEATTLE GANG
### 4 FUGITIVES DODGE POLICE DRAGNET
### "LOOK FOR THE WOMAN," TIP IN CASE

I grabbed the table to steady myself. The article seemed to know everything about our movements. It even stated that we had camped at an Indian village near Lake Errock the day before the robbery. Who had squealed on us?

I ruled out Cruickshank because he had not been away long enough to speak to a newsman for the afternoon paper. So there were four possibilities, I calculated. Perhaps Ramon had been caught, and gave us away; but despite his many flaws, he had an iron will that I did not believe the police could bend. Second, there was the night watchman the boys had left tied up. Even though he'd been paid off, he could well have cracked under questioning. But it would not make sense to reveal too much about us, like where we camped, because the police would grow suspicious of his involvement. Third, there was mention of our escape in the canoe: the cops could have traced it back to the Indian, who, to save his bacon, would claim we stole it after he innocently allowed us to camp near his village, not knowing we were criminals.

There was a final possibility, and the thought of it made me sweat all over: Detective Brooke had been shadowing us even before the robbery, and knew all our doings. I had a habitual fear of the man; he'd been a spectre over us for so long. But why had he not closed in by now? Maybe, I thought, he had overreached himself. After waiting for us to commit our crime at the hotel, he had not been able to catch us in the act like he intended.

"Look for the woman," the newspaper said. That meant Lena was in danger. If Brooke was stymied in finding us, he'd go after her. I could not bear to think of him catching and interrogating her. I knew she would not turn us in, because Lena was unbreakable. But they would put her on trial, and she would have to bear scorn, infamy and punishment. It was not right.

Bill came back to the shack, whistling. He scarcely glanced at the newspaper in my hands, though of course he must have read it. Once more I marvelled at his incredible cool, though now I wondered if it was a sign of insanity.

"We'll head over the border tonight," he said. "I don't want to be here when the wolves tear up the old man. The noise would bother my sleep."

I was not certain that creeping through the mountains at night, where the wolves lived, would put us in a better situation. But right then, I hardly cared if they killed us: it would be an ending. My life seemed like a dark room, the last window bricked up when Lena left. The only person left in that room with me was Bill, yet as I looked at him I knew that I hated him.

It came to me what to do.

I waited until Bill nodded off before the fire and slipped the newspaper off the table before leaving quietly for the other cabin, where the old man's body lay. Feeling nauseous, I regarded the blanket I'd covered him with, blood now soaking through in stains like a map of the world. I scrawled the words "Maple Falls" on the article about our gang. I lifted the blanket, trying not to look too close at the mutilations, and left the newspaper near the old man's feet. Bill deserved to be caught and punished for this. As for me, I did not care what happened. I was done.

Certain that Detective Brooke would find my message, I returned to the shack to wait for nightfall. Sitting down I stared at Bill as he slept, feeling a sense of calm I had not felt in a long while. I wrote out the story of this heist, which I know to be our last, in a rush on some loose papers that I'm keeping in my pocket. I have no more fear of Bill finding it out, because hopelessness has a surprising strength. In any case, he hardly knows what's real anymore and pays no mind to what I do.

## CHAPTER THIRTY-ONE

# THE RECORD SHOP

I SAT SILENT and alone on the tramcar as I went downtown to buy some flowers for the Captain's funeral. It was a sad mission but I was relieved to be going to a place where no one knew me and I could walk down the streets unobserved and unremarked on. Perhaps it would be possible to forget myself in such a circumstance. I stared out the window at the houses along Esquimalt Road, so ordinary. Today I wished for the comfort, the blamelessness, of an ordinary life. I wondered if it was too late to change and do something merciful and good—I could be a nurse. I rubbed my eyes but made myself stop because I knew them to be red. I had been sleeping terribly, unable to shake my visions of the Captain's charred body. Even worse was imagining Bill's hanging. I saw his face bulging and blackened above the noose, and his eyes were wide and glassy. Then a hand would cut the rope so his body thudded to the ground in a grotesque pile, the arms bent underneath him.

Link seemed to be avoiding me, which made everything harder to bear. I had hoped for consolation from some quarter. It was true that everyone in the bunker was subdued, so I should not be surprised that Link was also. People sorely missed the Captain. I yanked the bell when I realized the tram had already crossed the blue bridge, and I got off on Government Street. I paused in front of the tobacconist's shop where I had often bought gifts for Constantine. Despite the association, I was fond of the place, with its wood panelling and old-fashioned glass cabinets. A kind grey-haired man presided behind the counter, and he had joked with me while he helped choose the best Cuban cigars. But there was no point in going inside today because there would be little on the shelves. The war had strangled the supply of all fine things from abroad. Standing still among the flow of pedestrians, I was amazed how the housewives bustled along the street, cheerfully buying what they could with their ration cards—the war's only inconvenience to them. It was merely another facet of life, like a spate of bad weather. The base was removed enough from the city that the authorities could suppress news of the shelling. Some had heard the explosions and seen the orange flames light up the night sky, but the official story held that some faulty wiring started a fire near the munitions dump from the Great War. When the local air-raid wardens were given authority to enforce blackout measures the next day, it was presented as a simple precaution in line with what they had done recently in Los Angeles.

I walked past Searby's Chemist, and then the Bank of Montreal in the château-style building on the corner. I stared at the ground and picked up my step. It had been at the Bank of Montreal in Vancouver that I had met Bill. I thought of what Byron had written, and how it confirmed I'd done the right thing in leaving Bill. Was that why Bill had got hold of the journal and hoarded it all these years—was it possible he always wished I'd come back to him? I would never know.

I approached the Dagleish Record Shop, which was one of the few modernized buildings on the street. I remembered how Link mentioned the Bach record he wanted me to hear. Not long ago I'd believed there was a chance that a good man could care for me, and that this time I would not undervalue goodness the way I had with Byron. In my mind I lingered in that alternate universe where

Link would take me by the arm and we'd crowd into a booth, and he'd share his favourite album with me. I paused at the plate-glass window and looked inside. There was Link, flipping through the racks of records. A man approached him and stopped beside him, blocking the line of sight between Link and me. As they flipped through records in the classical section, the man did not look at Link, but his lips were moving in speech. They clearly knew one another. The man's hair was streaked with grey at the temples, but he was trim and handsome. He seemed familiar, and then I remembered him from a party I went to at the Lieutenant Governor's mansion when I was with Constantine.

I backed away from the window and hurried down the block. I didn't want Link to come outside and see me here, as though tailing him like a jealous girlfriend. Passing a group of teenage girls, I wondered if I had ever been giddy like that. They were probably whispering about a boy. Grow up, I wanted to shout at them.

I entered the florists' shop, the bell on the door jangling, and I was dispirited by how empty it was. Of course there were no more imported flowers with the war; but no one could stop the relentless effort of local gardeners in June, and there were bouquets of roses against the far wall. I chose a large yellow bunch for the Captain.

WHEN I GOT back to the barracks, there was a parcel on my bedside table. It was from Ottawa. I tore open the brown paper and found a new uniform inside—the jacket had two stripes with a loop on the sleeve. I fingered the smooth silk braid. I was a Second Officer now, the highest-ranking woman on the base. Miss Maggie had exerted her influence, proving the value of being her ally. Of course my stripes were only blue while the men's equivalent insignia for Lieutenant—like Link wore—were gold. But I was not in a mood for quibbling, because I was very low. I started ironing my uniform so it would be ready for the funeral this afternoon. The steam hissed on the board as I pressed each seam open until it was perfect.

Fastening the gold buttons, I kept my hands steady. I had to bear up against displaying myself in public. Holding my back straight,

I walked to God's Acre, the veterans' cemetery beside the base. In the chapel, a severe box with hard oak pews, I kept my composure even when Link stared at my new uniform but did not come over to speak to me. So he would stay true to his wife. But why then had he made the first move? It was cruel. I grabbed the blue hymnal from the rack in front of me and blindly flipped through the pages. The board indicated the organist was playing song 142, but it took me forever to find it. The "Dead March" of *Saul*.

I tried to listen to the Commodore's speech extolling the Captain, but his words failed to capture the man I knew. All the things that were wonderful about him were outside military protocols. He was the sweetest rogue that ever lived, and now he was gone. I took a shuddering breath. The psychology of a crowd was difficult to overcome; many among the hundreds seemed close to weeping. Everyone had loved the Captain.

What would my own funeral be like, when the time came? I would only have a crowd like this if I died in the service, because attendance would be compulsory. Otherwise, I feared, it would be as lonely as my father's. Besides myself at the graveside, there was only my aunt, who'd taken the train from Calgary, and one man my father had known from the post office. How could someone so good and kind have such a small circle to mourn him? I dimly remembered some friends of his coming to our house when I was little, but they had disappeared over the years. His gloom over the death of my mother had closed him off. Perhaps it was the very smallness of his life and death that drove me to do the big, crazy things I had done. But had there been any point? Despite the years I had spent with the Clockwork Gang, those who were left would not convene in public for my funeral, because of the danger to their own necks. Not even Byron, who had once been devoted to me, would come; he'd never bothered to see me again after he got away from Bill.

I made myself listen again to the Commodore. The name of the second victim turned out to be Soini, a young Petty Officer whom the Captain had mentioned to me occasionally. They went downtown for drinks on their leave days. I'd seen them once together on the base, the man handsome and blond, intent on their conversation. I wondered how much there had been between them. Whatever it was, they were united in death. The Commodore announced they were both awarded the Pacific Star, and I stood with the others to salute. Sailors heaved the two coffins onto their shoulders to take them outside and lay them in the cold, hard earth.

## CHAPTER THIRTY-TWO

# JUNE 1933

WE CROSSED THE Skagit Range by following the Chilliwack River, then turning south at Liumchen Creek. There were stars to guide us, cold and distant, but only a new moon for light, so it was tough finding our way through the brush. Bill of course was always in the lead, but around two a.m. by my watch he became confused. As I had done the night Lena left, he chose a path that gradually disappeared until we were crawling on our hands and knees through thickets of devil's club that tore my clothes and raked my skin. Of course this mistake could have happened to anyone, it being such a wilderness, but it had never happened to Bill before. The gang had always believed he had a map of every square inch of the Pacific Northwest burned into his brain. Now his internal compass had wavered, a sign that he was losing his grip at last. He was shaking something fierce. It was a cold night, but as I considered his waxen pallor I wondered if it was not something more. Perhaps he was sick. I was left only to speculate because Bill would admit to no trouble, just cursed under his breath and said that the trail must have grown over since the last time he'd crossed this range, back in the Twenties, and that we should turn around to get our bearings at the creek again.

Just before dawn we emerged from the mountains into a wider valley that Bill said was America. We had managed to cross the border undetected, though the damage to our appearance was severe. We had mud up to our knees, and I had a three-inch rip in my left sleeve where the skin showed underneath. Bill had a bloody slash across his cheek. As we approached the edge of Maple Falls, Bill announced that we would stop at a diner to get some grub and coffee. I thought this plan unwise but said nothing. I had distanced myself from my own life, and it was quite freeing. Anything could happen and I did not care.

When we entered the diner it was empty except for two old men, each at his own booth and sullenly minding his own business. The people in these parts were poor and not friendly with outsiders. Bill nodded at the waitress, who looked startled a moment by the wraith who had acknowledged her.

"It's been a while, Bill," she said, putting two coffees in front of us. We were at our own booth, as far from the other men as could be managed.

"I'd like to talk to Ned."

The waitress jerked her head to the back. She had likely been pretty once but now she was blowsy, heavyset, a false blonde with dark roots showing. Bill walked through the doorway to the kitchen. He and the man exchanged something and Bill disappeared a minute before returning to the table.

"What did that guy give you?"

"Nothing," he said, his eyes darting.

It struck me he must have bought some coke and was concealing it from me. That was the only thing I could imagine right now to improve my frame of mind and it seemed I'd have none of it.

"He a friend of yours?"

"No," Bill said, lively now, thrumming his fingers on the table. "But he's somebody that can be bought. It's his cabin we're using. We should get going."

My legs were stiff as I stood up from the booth and I couldn't help moaning as I hobbled outside. Stopping had been a bad idea.

With every step I took, searing pain shot through my right foot. I remembered tripping on a rock going down a slope hours ago, but it hadn't hurt then; the adrenaline must have covered it up. Though a straight-shot route would not have been far, we had probably walked twenty miles during the night because of the squirrely mountain trails that Bill had led us on. My clothes were rags and exhaustion was in my very marrow. I was tired of running from Detective Brooke. More than that, I was tired of being shackled to Bill.

Yet being caught would not be the end of it. In jail, would we not be together also? Looking at his goddamn face every day for the rest of my natural life. Because we'd be put away that long, if we did not hang. We had stolen more money than any gang in the history of the Pacific Northwest. We'd shot at cops, and they were known to dislike that and take a special vengeance. Whatever came, I did not think I would wait too long in suspense, because the cook or the waitress would likely betray us once Detective Brooke arrived in Maple Falls.

## CHAPTER THIRTY-THREE

# OTHER LOYALTIES

I PLANNED TO do something I had not done since I was with Bill: get pie-eyed drunk. I wanted to shake the hopeless sensation that refused to leave me, day or night, since Link started avoiding me. He had even switched to a desk against the far wall, where his eyes—should he lift them from his papers—would only see straight down the hall, away from me.

When I entered the canteen, wearing my Clear Red lipstick to remind myself I hadn't gone entirely to the dogs, I caught Bouvette's eye. It would be good to learn more about him, but Cat Trelawney was wedged against him in a large booth that did not require such coziness, so I walked up to the bar instead. Lucky for me, Sub-Lieutenant McCormick was there by himself, and I sat down beside him.

"What are you drinking?" I asked.

"Crown Royal. What do the ladies drink these days?"

"A nice Hawaii cocktail with pineapple. But I'd prefer what you're having."

He gestured for the bartender, who poured another tumbler of the sweet tannic whiskey I sometimes used to have at Mahone's speakeasy. It was better than I remembered—no doubt Mahone watered it down. I studied McCormick while his profile was turned. I guessed him to be in his early forties, and both his name and accent announced his Scottish heritage; he had the ruddy cheeks, prominent ears and sharp nose that often went with that lineage. I imagined if he grew a beard it would be red, like a Viking's. His arms looked powerful under the navy serge.

"I don't suppose you are a rower?" I asked.

"How'd you guess?" I squeezed his bicep and he laughed. "My father wanted me to do everything they did in the Old Country, since we never lived there until I went to Cambridge."

"You went to Cambridge," I said, admiringly, and he promptly gave me his whole life story. His father had worked in the Japanese consulate in Tokyo, which explained his placement in the language division—I had consulted him sometimes on my translations. He went on to praise Japanese culture to the high heavens. Evidently he had not picked up any diplomatic caution from his father.

"I studied swordmaking, same as how the samurai did it. Such a history of honour they have. And the craft is incredible. I learned to make a signature on the molten blade from sand. There are so many symbols to it—impermanence of mortal existence and all that. I loved it, but my father was upset about it being so foreign. He tried to make me quit, but I promised that every hour I spent with my *sensei*, I would spend an equal time training on the water. Guess it was a lot. I got a scholarship for rowing despite myself. But I've always wanted to get back to Japan again. Shame about the war, really."

Miss Maggie would find this interesting. His sympathies for an enemy nation were quite pronounced—I was amazed he made it through the screening process for the Examination Unit. But they desperately needed Japanese linguists and would have accepted him as a diplomat's son. Even at the beginning, they did not trust the Japanese population living on the West Coast for this work; and these last few months, the government had started sending them to prison camps inland. The newspapers had all supported this harsh policy as protecting Canadians from treachery in a time of war. I smiled at McCormick and touched his arm. His unashamed humanity made him more likeable to me.

"The Japanese are just people like any others," I said, and I meant it. I had heard the young men screaming as their planes crashed, and imagined their mothers' faces when they got the news. It seemed the sides one took in a war were little more than a coin toss in the backrooms of power. Even when it came to the Nazis. While they were committing grave crimes, this was not the reason they were declared the enemy; it was their overlarge territorial ambitions that moved the Allies to action. "We could use more people like you, who really understand their way of thinking," I said, and he returned my smile. I felt a pang for baiting him, but I continued. "What I've made of my latest message so far has me frightened. I was meaning to consult with you, to finish it." I leaned in closer. "Admiral Yamamoto's still talking about invading Australia, it seems. I think they could do it. What if they win the war? Are we just bashing our heads against the wall?"

"Could be," he said. "They're damn fine strategists. More bold than the British by a mile. The Brits just sat around trying to avoid the war for years. The Japanese went out and made it happen. Unfortunately for us."

"Do you have friends in Japan, from school?"

"I mostly mixed with the other expats. But there were a few wealthy Japanese whose parents sent them to study in English at our academy. Good chaps. But we lost touch long ago. I imagine they're serving somewhere or another. The whole country's been mobilized. Strange to think of them as the enemy."

"Your father must have made friends there also."

"He did. But that's all over now. These diplomats, they know how to change sides in a flash. Not sure I really mastered that. But war is war, and I'll do my bit."

Certainly McCormick wasn't afraid to have his own opinions, and that was a rare thing. "I'm enjoying this whiskey," I said, taking a sip. There was just the right amount of ice: two cubes. Chilled but not watered down too much. "I used to drink Crown Royal back in the day."

He laughed. "You can't be more than twenty-five."

"That's sweet. You keep on thinking that."

McCormick turned when someone tapped him on the shoulder, and I followed his gaze: it was Link. Heat burned through me, which I took for rage, and I stared down at the bar.

"Captain Somerville wants to speak with you," Link said. "ASAP."

McCormick made his apologies and left. Somerville was the new head of the Examination Unit, and we were still getting a feel for him. So far he was cold and correct, and I thought we would not become friends as I had been with the Captain. He did not have his equal anywhere. I did not have time to sink into my private gloom, though, as Link unsettled me by sitting down at the bar in the spot where McCormick had been.

"There are plenty of other seats free," I said.

"But this is the best seat in the house." His words were slurred—so he was drunk. I raised my hand for the bill.

"Can't we talk?" Link said, leaning closer. "This hasn't been easy for me."

"Me neither."

I had no desire to be hurt by him again. I wished he would go away so I could finish getting over him. It was far more difficult when he was right beside me. Oh, he was handsome.

"But you can stay for a minute, at least," he said.

I nodded curtly. I was angry with myself for wavering, and angry with him for sensing it. Link put up two fingers and wagged them at the bartender, who, without commenting on my sudden change in plans, brought over two more Crown Royals. The man departed to the far end of the bar where some sailors were having a loud conversation, which would hopefully drown us out.

"What were you talking to McCormick about?" he asked.

"Nothing much."

"What've you been doing lately?"

"Nothing much."

"Please, help me out here. I've been working through a lot of things."

Was he was thinking of leaving his wife? I tamped down the hope and took a drink. "I was thinking of that Bach you mentioned when I passed by the record store the other day and saw you in the window. I would have popped in and said hello, but you were busy speaking with someone."

"Was I?" Link asked, tapping the bartop with his fingers in a staccato rhythm.

"I met him at a party once. Sharp dresser."

"Oh, him."

Given that Link was the one to approach me, he wasn't being very chatty. I tried to recall who the man was. He'd stood out at the party because he was outfitted with Parisian flair—in pale grey pinstripes and a yellow cravat—that marked him as an outsider. In Victoria the well-to-do ordered quiet suits from London. But the man wasn't French—that was right, he was the Spanish Consul. I had only talked to him a moment, until Constantine tugged on my arm to socialize elsewhere. He had been nervous of me talking to eligible men.

"The Spanish Consul," I added, hoping to spur the conversation.

Link finished his whiskey in a gulp. "I hardly know him. We met at a lecture on classical music. Tchaikovsky, I think it was. I just bumped into him at the shop."

Link's face was pale and I wondered at the change; he'd been so bold when he first sat down. He spoke closer to me and low. "There can't be anything between us. I have a wife. I have other loyalties."

I wanted to scream and stomp and overturn glasses and chairs, but instead I matched his quiet tone. "I never asked you to do anything."

"I'm sorry. I was weak. Just forget about me."

"I will. Gladly."

I rose and left him alone at the bar. For all I cared he could drink till he fell on the floor and puked up his insides.

As soon as I was out the door and had closed it carefully behind me, I bolted to the bunker. I had to stop thinking about Link as though he was somebody special. I turned on my desk lamp and unlocked the drawer, pulling out some blank sheets of paper. I wrote out a report for Miss Maggie, feverishly over hours, wording and rewording. Putting Link on paper beside the other two men made me feel he was no more or less important than McCormick or Bouvette. It was as though they were part of a substitution cipher, one person interchangeable with the other. All strangers. This was how it had to be.

I did not have much to say about any of them, officially, since I hadn't learned anything conclusive. But Miss Maggie said to put everything in, and she would weigh the importance of it. For now, there was this. Charles Bouvette's father worked for Foreign Affairs, which might give him access to state secrets, but he had not spoken indiscreetly. He was intimate with Cat Trelawney, I wrote, not minding if she got dragged in for questioning since she'd squealed on me about the map room. Robert McCormick was a blabbing sort of person with an unusual love of Japanese culture, which could confuse his loyalties. And Link Hughes had a wife to whom he was very attached, which could lead one to question what he might do if captured, in order to protect her. I was annoyed to see my pen had pressed harder into the page when I wrote that. I shook out my hand before continuing. He liked classical music, and spoke with the Spanish Consul about this mutual interest.

I paused, wondering if I should include this after all. The Spanish were officially neutral in the war, and the Consul had even been invited to a party at Government House. But that was more than a year ago. Since then, the Spanish government had allowed thousands of volunteers to go fight with the Germans against Russia while only a few hundred, mostly the anarchists who had opposed Franco, had joined the Allied battles. But really, a record shop in Victoria could not be further removed from all that. What harm to talk about music with a man who was here by sanction of our own government? I myself had spoken with the Spanish Consul.

Link would just have to answer a few questions about him, that was all. My pen still hovered over the page. I did not know who Miss Maggie had assigned to watch me—but what if they saw what I saw on my leave day? If I did not include this information, she would know I was holding back.

At around one a.m. I finished the final draft, and without ever putting my name anywhere, nor Miss Maggie's, I addressed it to the post office box in Washington, DC, where I had been told to mail it. I licked the envelope and pressed it shut firmly, hoping to enclose my feelings within it when I sent it away.

## CHAPTER THIRTY-FOUR

# JUNE 9, 1933

WE SKULKED ALONG the railroad for a while, until Bill pointed up a trail and I followed him through the forest. I was sick at heart when I saw the rundown cabin we would hole up in until the end came. In the dawn, crows were circling and cawing and one swooped so low that its claws scratched my scalp. It was a horrible feeling, but I didn't believe in otherworldly messages. We must have been too close to its nest.

Bill kicked open the door and it nearly came off its old hinges. "Papa's home," he called out, and laughed.

Gritting my teeth, I set the door back in place behind us and the dusty room blackened. I found an old tea crate to use for a chair, and after sitting down I had nothing to do but think. I was struck by the contrast with how I'd been living the year before, in the mansion on Capitol Hill. We'd sunk to this for the sake of five hundred dollars and Bill's expanding mania for havoc.

"Don't look so glum, chum," Bill said. "Want a little snow?"

I nodded and he tapped a small pile from an envelope into my palm. As I stared at the dome of white powder, it reminded me of Mount Baker, which had been shimmering on the southern horizon since we started this ill-fated job. After sniffing up the powder I went to the door and looked outside, to seek out that singular and lonely peak. But there were only green folded hills before me, so that I supposed we were on the flanks of the mountain itself. Mount Baker was an old volcano, but it was covered now in ice, and I wondered when the last time was that it blew. Though it was sleeping and quiet, its potential for disaster lay ever within it.

The day passed in the tense boredom of alternate watches, and when night fell the only place to lie down was the plank floor. It was uncomfortable and I stayed awake for much of the night. At the palest dawn, before the birds sang, I heard a noise outside the cabin.

My body froze. There was a sound of breathing, though I hadn't heard a single twig snap to mark the approach of anyone. Could it be Detective Brooke at last? The breathing circled the cabin, heavy. I lay absolutely still.

A face stared in the window. My brain could not assemble the meaning of it. Through the dirty cracked glass, it was crazy as a Picasso picture.

A bear, huge and shaggy: that's what it was.

It placed a paw on the windowpane, as though claiming us. It would not be such a bad way to die, I thought. This creature bore us no hatred—it was just acting as it must.

Bill leapt off the floor and grabbed a shovel on his way out the door, screaming and yelling. The bear lowered itself from the window with no apparent concern. I could see no more but I heard it huff once as Bill continued screaming like a madman. Maybe Bill was beating it to death, or maybe he was getting torn to pieces.

I waited.

"What the fuck," Bill said, suddenly back inside the cabin and throwing the shovel on the floor where it clattered so loudly it felt like it was inside my very head. In the dim I couldn't see if the shovel was bloody. "I thought we was being followed. Wonder how long that bear was on our trail?"

"Probably since the last place. He might have got a taste for human blood from the old man you left. Maybe we still smell of him."

"Shut up about that. We changed our clothes. Anyhow, I've saved our necks thirty times since you knowed me. That was some crazy motherfucking bear. But I ran it off, easy peasy."

We settled back to our spots on the floor, and I covered my face with the crook of my arm to block out the expanding morning—and the sight of the smear left on the window from the bear's paw. I was wrong about the bear: he had marked us. Lena had told me the Indians in these parts had many stories about bears, and would never eat them because they were humans in a transformed state. But whatever that bear might be, I'd proved myself lacking in courage.

I WOKE LONG ago, but Bill is still lying on the floor, sleeping innocently. I believe now that he is impaired in some crucial way but it seems to be how he was made, and how can you blame someone for that? It's like conscience was a limb he was born without.

I remember too late I have that limb, and it feels heavy now.

I hear the sirens in the far distance. They will close in soon. I regret putting Detective Brooke on our trail. No matter how vicious Bill became, this act of betrayal made me the coward and the worthless one. I will redeem myself in the showdown that's sure to come.

I would like my ashes to be scattered in the Strait of Juan de Fuca, in memory of crossing it to do our first job together. I have read that Juan de Fuca was either a hesitant discoverer or a great liar, because he claimed to find a great inland sea but did not affix it on his map. But a later mariner decided to trust in him and gave the place de Fuca's name—a generous act that left himself unheralded by history. In any case, we were all happy that day on the water, and Lena was so lovely as she sat on the boat with the wind blowing her hair. That was when my love started, and it has never ended.

I wish you could have loved me, Lena, but I hope you remember me fondly as someone who would have done anything for you. Know above all that you did the right thing in leaving Bill.

Goodbye.

## CHAPTER THIRTY-FIVE

# THE BARREN ROCK

I TUGGED DOWN my jacket and adjusted my cap to regulation angle as I stood in the hall by the conference room door. Miss Maggie was up from Washington and had summoned me. I kept my eyes to the floor as some co-workers passed in the hall, and they did not speak to me. Sometimes I felt that no one at all talked to me anymore, since Link had stopped doing so last month. Or perhaps they simply knew that Miss Maggie was nearby and did not want to disturb the dragon in her lair. As soon as they had disappeared around the corner, the door flung open as though by its own power.

"Stillman!"

I walked inside and closed the door behind me. Miss Maggie was perched on the front of her desk, watchful and too close. I stood awkwardly before her a moment and then saluted, even though officially she had no rank. She was more important than anyone in our unit. She gestured at a chair, and I sat down though it was not comfortable with her looming over me.

"So we have discovered our spy," she said.

I was floored, but simply raised an eyebrow and attempted to look noncommittal.

"Lieutenant Hughes had us all fooled."

"Lieutenant Link Hughes?"

She nodded, smiling a tight little half-smile.

"You don't think there might be some mistake?" I asked, clearing my throat as my voice cracked.

"Oh no. It was all in your report, how he met with the Spanish Consul. The Spanish Consul is the contact for the Japanese here. Acting on your tip, we confirmed it was Hughes who was feeding him information. He was the leak we'd been looking for."

His words from the final night we spoke came back—"I have other loyalties." I remembered Link's pale face.

"Were you attached to him?" Miss Maggie asked.

"No."

"That's good. It's best to operate on facts, not emotions."

"What will happen to him?"

"The official story is he's being transferred to one of the listening stations in the South Pacific. He could prove useful to us—we have ways of convincing people to change sides."

"What if he won't change?" Whatever reasons Link had for what he did, I knew they must be firmly held. His loyalties were misplaced, but loyalty was simply a form of love. Who knew what caused it?

"He will."

Would they torture him? Did our people do that?

I had done something horrible. I had been angry enough at the thought of him rejecting me, that I was willing to risk him being questioned. But I had not imagined it going this far. I thought that he could turn around any interview with a simple explanation. Why didn't he leave the base after he knew I saw him with the Consul? "Scarpered." Bill's word came into my mind. Yes, Bill would have scarpered. But Link hadn't known I was reporting to Miss Maggie.

I had been the cause of his capture.

"I know there was something between you," Miss Maggie said.

I did not deny it again. Whoever Miss Maggie had put on Link had found me out too. What was I thinking? She probably didn't even need a spy. My feelings must have been quite obvious to anyone in the Examination Unit.

Had there actually been something between us, mutual and real, or had he just used me? I could not see any benefit to his advances, since we worked in the same department and were privy to the same information. Then I remembered the coded slip of paper that he had never returned to me. Was it really just an innocent message between fishermen in the volunteer reserve, as Link said? What had I handed over to him? I had been a fool.

"It could happen to anyone," she said. I stared at her in surprise. "I am reminded of that every day when I look in the mirror." She turned the mutilated side of her face to me and laid her hand on her cheek. "A man did this to me. It was no car accident, and religion did not prevent me from correcting it. All bunk. I encouraged those rumours because I didn't want anyone to know my weakness. How I stayed with a man longer than sense would dictate, until he beat me one time too many. I wanted to remember never to love, never to trust again. That was why I never had the surgery."

She was sitting on her hands now, staring straight ahead, a contained bundle of will. "But my troubles are over, while yours may be just beginning. You consorted with a traitor. Did you not?"

"I didn't know." I swallowed, my throat dry. "Are you pressing charges?"

"I told you my story because I thought it would help you make a decision that's useful to me. You are fluent in Russian?"

I was baffled at the turn her conversation had taken, but I nodded.

"The war is going in another direction. We are confident now that we will beat the Japanese—we essentially have, since Midway. But it will take a while to finish the job. In the meantime we have to get ready for what comes next. We're setting up an important listening station in Alaska, on one of the Aleutian islands. To be close to the Soviets. It's a dreadful place, I assure you. But even if you are not in prison, think of what a woman of your calibre will face when the war ends. With all the soldiers returning to work, the men will take precedence. And you, with the rank of First Officer, one of only a handful of women in your country—"

"I'm a Second Officer."

"You'll get another promotion. But if you return to civilian life, it won't do you any good. If you stay with intelligence, you'll be important in our new activities. You are an experienced codebreaker who speaks Russian. Later, when the war ends, it would suit us if you continued your academic studies and went to the Soviet Union."

"To research the Tlinkit language with Dr. Phipps?"

"Exactly. The perfect cover. But for now, all I can promise is a lonely posting on a very cold island. At the rank of First Officer. You will be second in command there."

"But the Japanese are still occupying the Aleutians."

"Only two islands in the far west, and they'll be pushed out soon. Don't worry, there's plenty of space in Alaska. You'll be well away from the front lines until the island we want is clear. I understand this is very sudden, but you must let me know by tonight, before I leave. The offer will not stand after that. We need our organization in place."

I stared at the floor. There was nothing for me here except the possibility of jail, though I thought Miss Maggie would have applied this threat more forcefully if she was sure of convicting me. If I left the service after the war, what Miss Maggie said was true enough. I might never get a professorship at the university with all the men back. She was trying to make me believe that the Alaska post was a reward for handing Link to her so that my gratitude would become loyalty. But really, it was more of a punishment than anything. As she said, the Aleutians were a dreadful place. An Arctic island would be the same as a prison, with nowhere to go outside the barracks, and her minions would have me under perpetual watch. Yet it was the safest place for me, and where I belonged. I would be isolated from people and the possibility of being harmed, or doing harm. This was my only real choice.

"I'll do it." I would have to learn to be colder, and the land I was heading to would be my instructor.

"Good. You'll leave tomorrow, then. At 0700 on the *Edmunston.*"

Trying not to shake, I stood up from the chair to leave. Walking out the door of the bunker, I put my hand to my cheek, echoing Miss Maggie's gesture; I remembered that night years ago when Bill struck me and cut my face. I had left him in time and had no lasting scar. Though perhaps I was equally deformed inside as Miss Maggie was, with the best parts of me ruined forever.

I hurried to the barracks to pack my bag. Now that my decision was made, I could not be gone too soon. No one would miss me. Today was a day that presaged Alaska, I thought, grey and cold. The grim waters of the North Pacific connected the shores I knew to that strange land. It was ironic that while I had always dreamed of going to Alaska to see the Tlinkit totem poles, the ship would pass them without stopping on its way to my distant outpost. The sky hung low with swollen clouds, oppressing the ground. There was scarcely a space to exist between them. But it would be worse up north; instead of rain there would be ice and snow. There would be no lush forests, but only barren rock.

The barracks were quite empty, it being mid-morning, so there was no risk of talking to anyone. As I folded up my clothes, I realized how much my life was stripped down: all I had was a second uniform, for formal occasions, and a couple of dresses for my leave days. Crumpled in the bottom of my trunk were the silk stockings I had worn the night Link asked me to the dance. They were ruined from when I fell down. I should really send them to the scrap drive, but I shoved them in my pocket instead. I would burn them so I could see, with my own eyes, this remnant of my foolishness destroyed.

I returned to my house in Rockland that afternoon for the last time. The white plaster glowed with a golden afternoon sunshine and its beauty made me ache a little. It was hard to believe I would be heading for perpetual winter, but the weathervane glinted on the roof and veered sharp west. There was a gale warning for tonight, and storms would be frequent on my trip north. My route to Alaska would take me through the Strait of Juan de Fuca. It was sad that Byron dreamed of that inhospitable place on what he believed was his last day on earth. I was surprised when his journal revealed he was with Bill until the shootout, because the news story never mentioned anything about him.

I could never forget the headline announcing the end of the Clockwork Gang:

## NOTORIOUS BAGLEY CAPTURED!

When I read it, the air went out of my lungs. I had just arrived in Calgary and was walking down busy 8th Avenue when I bought the day's paper at a newsstand. I staggered into the nearby Palace Café and collapsed in a booth with high walls to conceal myself as I laid the paper flat on the table. Everything felt surreal. I remember there was a strange painting of a camel on the wall; it stood alone in the desert and stared with a gimlet eye. Empty fedoras hung on hooks like the remnants of men. The waitresses wore white uniforms like nurses, and their ghostly blurs reflected on the pressed-tin ceiling. Bill was captured and the gang was history. There was disbelief and then anguish, and I admit now there was relief. I had left in time— Bill was no longer invincible.

I went inside my house, walking with a quiet tread. I put up the ladder and slid open the trap door to the attic. Unlocking the trunk, the tumblers undisturbed as always, I removed the diary that Byron had dedicated to me, "For Lena," written in his hand. I smoothed the crumpled and stained end pages that he had penned in those final days after I left. The rest of the pages were pristine, smelling faintly like the ink on dollar bills when new minted. A nostalgic smell for me. It had been risky to keep the ledger this long, but my belief in my ability to hide it had not been misguided. If Miss Maggie had found it, she would have used it against me from the first. But I was ready to let go now.

Laying the journal over the andirons, I lit a match and watched it burn, the edges curling. It was only a moment until my past had vanished. But in a way it didn't matter that the journal was gone, because the most important things were never recorded.

Love was supposed to be a noble thing, but it had done Byron no good at all. I had been the cause of his coming to hate Bill, and I was the reason that he left the note for Detective Brooke. I did not wish to blame Byron for that one betrayal of Bill. Byron had planned to make amends before fate gave him a chance to slip away. I knew he had to be alive. If not, the newspaper would have chronicled the police's takedown of another member of the Clockwork Gang. He had every right to save himself. The detective had been circling our gang as far back as Seattle, and could well have captured Bill without that final clue. The chaos Bill left in his wake would be a beacon to any pursuer.

There must have been something wrong with me to have loved Bill so—he was a menace. The flaw in my makeup was not resolved, since I had next settled my heart on a traitor. Link had turned out to be just as dangerous as Bill. How had I deluded myself that I had finally chosen a good man, like Byron had been? There were few of his kind. It seemed the world itself lacked a moral compass, or at least not one I was capable of reading. I couldn't believe I was ordered to spy on the Russians when they were not even nominally our enemy. But maybe it was best that I didn't have to make the decision of friend or foe since I had made so many errors. I would learn to flow with the tide.

The next morning I boarded HMCS *Edmunston*, an escort corvette that had been sent here for repairs after being damaged at Midway. It was now on the way to Alaska to join the American fleet against the Japanese. It was not the safest form of transport, even though my journey north would be within "friendly" waters. I knew better than anyone how the Japanese subs were sneaking under our lines. Despite Miss Maggie's assurances, my assignment was uncomfortably close to the front. I wondered if she planned for my demise there; it would be very easy to account for it. My step faltered a moment but then I thought I would know soon enough, and held up my chin. If I made it through I would have to be hard like Miss Maggie. I could become important in intelligence, and perhaps make some great discoveries about the origins of the Tlinkit language in my work with Dr. Phipps.

As I stepped up the gangway, a sailor tried to relieve me of my bag, but I held on to it and refused to take the hand he proffered me. I could make my own way.

# NOVEMBER 12, 1945

IT IS HARD to know where to live when you have little interest in that pastime. Nonetheless, I had to settle somewhere when I found myself suddenly free after the shootout, and the Olympic Peninsula of Washington was as remote as anyplace I could hope to find in the Lower 48. But my first stop of Port Angeles was too rough and chaotic with the sawmill there, so I carried on. Sequim means "still waters" in the Klallam Indian tongue, so I'm told. I didn't know that yet when I passed through and the bus stopped at the county line. The driver yelled "Skwim!" I liked how the way you say it is not like it's spelled, as though there is a part of it hidden that you will never know. I stared out the window and all I saw was some old fellows sitting around smoking at the depot. This is a place where nothing happens, I thought, so why not get out here and stay? I took a deep breath and stood up to grab my duffle from the rack above my head, wincing at the pain in my arm. It was bandaged up pretty good and I hoped I wouldn't need to see a doctor again. I had got it treated when I got off the boat in Port Angeles, where they were used to the loggers getting in fights every Saturday night, and bullet wounds were not worth a second glance.

I was right about my first opinion of Sequim, about the nothing. The big to-do is the annual irrigation festival. It doesn't sound glamorous but there is a princess each year. I smile at her from afar as she is anointed on her big day because everyone deserves to shine once in their life. I have a white scar the size of a quarter as a souvenir of my dramatic past, but no one asks about it when summer heat drives me to wear short sleeves. They are blessedly uninquisitive folk here; it must come from being farmers and clam diggers, always staring into the black earth with a single purpose.

Sometimes I even think I found here the peaceful savannah I craved during the madness of my bank robber days. I like to walk the plains toward the mountains, away from the irrigated fields of the single-minded farmers and into the wild lands, where rare lilies are sprinkled in the grass that turns nearly white from drought; Sequim is sheltered from storms by the Olympic Mountains and receives less rain than Los Angeles. I am quite near Mount Baker as the crow flies but cannot see it because other peaks block the view. I find I need to be near enough to my past landmark to feel it wasn't all a dream, but I do not want to be reminded of it every moment.

I thought I would never write again after I scrawled my final farewell to Lena. Even when I found myself not dead at the end of it all, I didn't pick up a pen. The kind of craziness only Bill could invent is the only thing in my life worth putting on paper.

As soon as we heard the crunch on gravel of police approaching, Bill shot at them out the cabin window while I crouched in the corner because I did not have a weapon. The shooting went on for what seemed a long time, Bill pulling magazines from a pack stashed at the cabin to reload the Colt. I felt disembodied, not a part of anything, thinking that Bill did not trust me anymore since he did not give me a gun, but I was a terrible shot anyhow. When would I have a chance to show courage? My mind was drifting like that until there was a physical shock as though somebody had smashed my arm with a sledgehammer. I stared around to see who did it but there was no one. When a warm sensation ran down my arm I looked there and saw blood. I believe I then collapsed, in shock but still conscious.

Bill stayed at the window shooting at the cops until there was a click, click. He rummaged in the pack but came up empty. He shook out the Colt's spent magazine and stared at it, disbelieving. "Fuck a duck," he said under his breath.

There were a few more shots from the cops and then a silence.

"Throw your gun outside," a policeman yelled.

Bill gave me a strange look that, given my pain, I did not have the presence of mind to interpret. Was it a grin? I remembered how angry he got when he always won at poker, how sometimes he even cheated to lose. He nudged open the door and tossed out the pistol.

"Come out with your hands up."

First Bill put his hands out the door so the cops could see them, slowly working his way outside and raising his arms. His silhouette vanished as the door closed behind him. "Guess you got me, boys," he said.

I was meanwhile lying on the dirt floor, clutching my arm and writhing with agony, while I heard the police move in with excited shouts to nab him. Would they kill us both? Suddenly I felt fear and realized I was part of this world after all. I roused myself to run out the back door while the police were occupied with Bill. I dashed to the edge of a grim hemlock wood and turned to look back through a screen of branches. No one was trying to chase me—I was peripheral as usual.

I thrashed through the forest until I was well clear, and then I clambered down to a creek to deal with the wound in my right forearm. I ripped off my good sleeve and tied it as a tourniquet. Feeling faint, I dunked my arm in the icy water to clean it and examined my injury, and saw at least there was an exit on the other side. The bullet was not in me.

I followed the waterway until I made it to Fairhaven on the coast, where I knew there were opium painkillers and silent Chinamen to be found. I hired a boat to take me to the Olympics because mountains always make the best refuge. Sitting on the open skiff, I finally thought to check my pockets for my papers, but they were not there. I must have lost them in the brambles.

That was the end of my writing, until today. My bound journal I know is secure in its safety deposit box in Seattle, where I had taken the precautions of a miser in keeping it locked and concealed. I still send money to my lawyer every year so that he can make the payments for it under his name. Working for criminals made him a most silent and confidential sort of lawyer. I liked to think of my past contained like a tumour, now benign, which cannot spread. I've never felt any urge to revisit it.

It's been twelve years since I got off the bus at the county line—that's what I'd been thinking idly to myself as I rubbed my arm before walking into the Ponderosa. The fall air was cold and clammy, which always made my old wound ache. The saloon doors swung open-shut-open-shut behind me as Frank looked up from his mopping. Pride swelled in me as he greeted me.

"Howdy, boss."

I am the manager here and I've made a success of the Ponderosa with my financial know-how, if I do say so myself. I've had a fondness for rough drinking establishments since the speakeasy days. This place had been shuttered during Prohibition but that ended after I'd been in Sequim a few months. I saw my opportunity and found out who the owner was and bought the dusty old place for a song.

"Who's your pal?" Frank asked. Puzzled, I turned around and saw a grizzled old sailor standing behind me. This was a strange sight. While we were only a couple of miles from the sea, the old harbour was not busy, and the only uniforms I got in here were local boys trickling home from the war, most of whom had chosen the land service of the army, being more comfortable with dirt than water.

"I don't know him," I said.

"But he knows you," the sailor said in his turn. His rasping voice made me shudder a little; it sounded painful. "Name's Shively. I have a telegram that you might want to see private like."

"Please come to my office."

He followed after me with an unsettling drag at every other step, making a shuffling sound on the floorboards. At least this odd fellow could not sneak up on anyone, I thought. I closed the door of my office, which was undecorated except for a carved India shelf stacked with leather-bound ledgers, one for each year, each one fuller than the last as my business prospered. Drink was a perpetual motion economy. Men drank away the sorrows of the Depression and came out even when they shouldn't, to escape their wives' harping; then the war years were good to the farmers in these parts and they rewarded themselves with the company of each other at my saloon. I sat at my oak desk and gestured the man to take the comfortable club chair in front of it, but he shook his head. He handed me an envelope, which I unsealed.

CHICKENS TO BE PLUCKED IN BANGKOK. I NEED A GOOD NUMBERS MAN. I WILL WAIT FOR YOU AT THE RAILWAY TERMINUS AT NOON ON THE 1ST OF EVERY MONTH UNTIL YOU ARE FOUND BY GOD.

While the block type of the telegram was anonymous, the voice of the sender never could be. I was glad to be already sitting. "You know the man that sent this?"

Shively just shrugged and grinned. "I knowed I got to find you if I had to go to the ends of the earth. Which I nearly did do."

My first thought was: How did Bill manage it? I had read the notice of his execution at New Westminster in the paper. He was some kind of Lazarus. I felt both horrified and exhilarated at the thought of him not being dead.

Shively settled on the edge of my desk and looked down at me like my own personal gargoyle. His nose was hawkish and his eyes deep set, his face attracting more shadow than light. He seemed sinister now. "There's a ship leaving for the Far East every day. I won't leave till I see you aboard."

"Do you know the mood of the man that sent this?" I could not bring myself to say his name. The guilt I felt for putting the cops on our trail with my note was something terrible, and I wished it could have flowed out of me with the blood from my bullet wound that day. The regret had stayed with me always. Bill, if not dead, had to be hiding from the law deeper than any man ever had.

Shively stared at me with a silence that I took to indicate he did not get my meaning. I had to know if he'd gone off the drugs.

"Do you believe him to be in his right mind?" I asked.

"Never been a sounder."

Despite myself, I was interested by what chickens Bill might mean. And I liked the thought of Bill waiting in the terminus each month, for me, and me not showing, and imagining that he felt a little disappointment when my face did not appear among the strangers in a strange land. Bangkok.

I had to admit I was tired of still waters.

J. B. MacKinnon

**Alisa Smith** is the bestselling coauthor of *Plenty: One Man, One Woman, and a Raucous Year of Eating Locally* (Crown). Her freelance writing has been published in *Outside, Reader's Digest, Utne Reader, Ms. Magazine, Canadian Geographic, Elle Canada,* the *National Post,* and many others, winning two National Magazine Awards. She served as a judge for various literary awards and has lectured widely on writing. She is based in Vancouver, where she is now hard at work on the sequel to *Speakeasy.*